THE GARDENE

Andrey Kurkov was born in St Petersburg in 1961. Having graduated from the Kiev Foreign Languages Institute, he worked for some time as a journalist, did his military service as a prison warden in Odessa, then became a film cameraman, writer of screenplays and author of critically acclaimed and popular novels, including the cult bestseller *Death and the Penguin*.

Amanda Love Darragh studied French and Russian at Manchester University, then spent the following decade working in Moscow and at BBC Worldwide in London. Amanda won the 2009 Rossica Translation Prize for her translation of *Iramifications* by Maria Galina, and she has translated works by Ilya Boyasho, Igor Savelyev and Anna Lavrinenko, among others.

ALSO BY ANDREY KURKOV

Death and the Penguin
The Case of the General's Thumb
Penguin Lost
A Matter of Death and Life
The President's Last Love
The Good Angel of Death
The Milkman in the Night

ANDREY KURKOV

The Gardener from Ochakov

TRANSLATED FROM THE RUSSIAN BY
Amanda Love Darragh

VINTAGE BOOKS
London

Published by Vintage 2014

2 4 6 8 10 9 7 5 3 1

First published with the title *Sadovnik iz Ochakova* in 2009 by Folio Publishers, Kharkov

First published in Great Britain in 2013 by Harvill Secker

Vintage
Random House, 20 Vauxhall Bridge Road,
London SW1V 2SA

www.vintage-books.co.uk

Addresses for companies within The Random House Group Limited can be found at: www.randomhouse.co.uk/offices.htm

The Random House Group Limited Reg. No. 954009

A CIP catalogue record for this book is available from the British Library

ISBN 9780099571872

The publication was effected under the auspices of the Mikhail Prokhorov Foundation TRANSCRIPT Programme to Support Translations of Russian Literature

The Random House Group Limited supports the Forest Stewardship Council® (FSC®), the leading international forest-certification organisation. Our books carrying the FSC label are printed on FSC®-certified paper. FSC is the only forest-certification scheme supported by the leading environmental organisations, including Greenpeace. Our paper procurement policy can be found at: www.randomhouse.co.uk/environment

Typeset in Quadraat by Palimpsest Book Production Limited, Falkirk, Stirlingshire

Printed and bound by Clays Ltd, St Ives plc

The Gardener from Ochakov

1

'Ma, your friend's at the gate, and she's got another dodgy man with her!' Igor shouted cheerfully.

'Keep your voice down, will you?' said his mother, coming out into the hallway. 'She'll hear you!'

Elena Andreevna shook her head as she looked reproachfully at her thirty-year-old son, who had never learned to lower his voice when necessary.

It was true that their next-door neighbour, Olga, did seem to be taking rather too much of an interest in her personal life. As soon as Elena Andreevna and her son had moved from Kiev to Irpen, Olga – who was also fifty-five years old and single – had taken her under her wing. Elena Andreevna had divorced her husband before she'd retired, largely because he had started to remind her of a piece of furniture, being inert, silent, perpetually morose and apparently incapable of helping out around the house. Olga had been smart enough not to get married in the first place, but she spoke about it casually, without regret. 'I don't need to keep a husband on a leash,' she had once said. 'Put them on a leash and they start to behave like dogs, always barking and biting!'

Elena Andreevna went out to the gate and saw her neighbour. Next to her stood a wiry, clean-shaven man of around sixty-five with an expressive face and a determined chin, closely cropped grey hair and a faded canvas rucksack on his back.

'Lenochka, I've brought someone to meet you! This is Stepan. He fixed my cowshed.'

Elena Andreevna looked sceptically at Stepan. She didn't have a cowshed, and nothing else needed fixing. Everything was in perfect working order, for the time being, and she wasn't in the habit of inviting unfamiliar men into the house for no reason.

Although the look of amused indifference in Elena Andreevna's eyes had not escaped his attention, Stepan politely inclined his head.

'Do you by any chance need a gardener?' he wheezed, his voice full of hope.

Stepan was dressed smartly in black trousers, heavy boots and a striped sailor's undershirt.

'People usually hire gardeners at the beginning of spring,' remarked Elena Andreevna, unable to hide her surprise.

'I prefer to start now and finish in late winter. I can prune the trees and tidy everything up, and then I'll be on my way. Trees need looking after all year round. My rates are quite reasonable, too – I'll be happy with a hundred hryvnas a month, plus board and lodging. Mind you, I'm quite fond of cooking myself.'

A hundred hryvnas a month? Elena Andreevna thought with astonishment. Why so little? He looks perfectly strong and capable.

She glanced over her shoulder, hoping to consult her son, but Igor wasn't in the yard. Which was probably just as well. He might have accused his mother of losing her marbles in her old age.

Elena Andreevna sighed. 'We don't really have any room in the house,' she said, reluctant to make a decision without her son's input.

'I don't need to sleep in the house. I'll be fine in an outbuilding, as long as I have something to put over myself when it gets cold. I never touch alcohol, and I'm completely trustworthy.'

Elena Andreevna looked at her neighbour. Olga nodded, as though she had known Stepan for years.

'Well, I suppose you might as well stay for now,' conceded Elena Andreevna. 'We've got a shed, and it's empty at the moment. We don't keep any animals. There's a bed with a mattress, and an electric socket. I just need to speak with my son . . .'

The shed was just visible behind the house. Stepan nodded and began walking towards it.

'How long have you known him?' Elena Andreevna asked her neighbour.

'He was here before, about two years ago. He didn't steal anything, he fixed everything I asked him to and he did a bit of gardening. I wouldn't think twice, if I were you! He's a useful chap to have around.'

Elena Andreevna shrugged and went into the house to look for Igor. He was greedily smoking a cigarette when his mother told him the news. The gardener's arrival didn't seem to interest him much.

'He can dig up the potatoes,' said Igor. 'It's more work than the two of us can manage.'

Stepan dug the potatoes up, single-handedly, in no time at all. Then he laid them out in the yard to dry. Seeing this, Elena

Andreevna was quietly glad of his help and gave him a hundred hryvnas straight away – a month's salary in advance. She cooked some of the potatoes for supper that evening and served them with braised beef.

In the morning Igor was woken by an exuberant spluttering and snorting outside his window. He looked out and saw Stepan standing there in nothing but a pair of black underpants, pouring cold water from the well over himself. What piqued Igor's curiosity was the top of Stepan's left upper arm. It bore a number of blurred dark blue marks, as though someone had tried to cover up or remove an old tattoo. Igor went out into the yard and asked Stepan to pour a bucket of water from the well over him too.

The water burned Igor, in a good way. He too gave a loud and exuberant snort. Then he asked Stepan about the marks on his shoulder.

Stepan contemplated his landlady's pale, skinny son, wondering whether or not to give him the time of day. Igor's piercing, light green eyes seemed to invite honesty.

'You know,' Stepan said quietly, 'I wish I knew. I was about five years old at the time. It hurt, I know that much. I can remember crying. Apparently my old man included some kind of secret code in the tattoo. Either for me, or for himself. My uncle never really explained it. He just said that my father sent me to him on the train, and then he went off somewhere and disappeared. I never saw him again. I was brought up by my Uncle Lev and Aunt Marusya in Odessa. They told me that my mother left my father when I was about three. I was forever asking my uncle to tell me more, but he took the full story to the grave.

'All I learned was that there was more to my father than met the eye. He was sent to the labour camps in Siberia three times. What for? No one knows. Maybe there's some important information contained in the tattoo, but as I grew my skin stretched so that the ink blurred, and it's impossible to make any sense of it all!'

Stepan glanced at the marks on his shoulder. Igor moved closer and inspected the blurred tattoo. It was made up of a number of dark blue blotches, which didn't appear to form either letters or a recognisable image.

'Where's your old man?' Stepan asked suddenly.

Igor looked into the gardener's eyes and shook his head.

'Somewhere in Kiev. My mother left him a long time ago. She did the right thing,' said Igor. 'He wasn't interested in either of us.'

'Don't you ever see him?' Stepan asked with a hint of disbelief.

Igor thought about it. Then he shook his head again.

'Why would I want to? We're all right, just the two of us. I've got a couple of scars to remember him by.'

Stepan's face flushed with anger. 'Did he beat you?'

'No. My mother used to send me off with him to the park or the fairground rides. He would always let me go off by myself, so he could go and drink beer with his friends. Once a cyclist knocked me over and broke my arm. The second time was even worse.'

The gardener frowned. 'All right,' he said, waving his hand dismissively, 'that's enough about him!'

Igor was amused by Stepan's desire to change the subject. He grinned and his eyes returned to the tattoo.

'It might be worth trying to decipher it, you know,' said Igor, after a few moments' reflection.

'And how do you suggest we go about that?'

'We need to take a photo first. Then we can play around with it on-screen. It might work, you never know! It's worth a try. I've got a friend who's great with computers – he might be able to help us.'

'Well, there's a bottle in it for you if you manage to figure it out,' grinned Stepan.

Igor fetched his camera and took several photos of Stepan's shoulder.

2

Igor drank a mug of coffee, then sat down at the computer and merged the photos together. He zoomed in on the composite image, zoomed out again, rotated it this way and that, but the blurred tattoo remained incomprehensible.

'All right,' Igor murmured to himself, 'I'll go and see Kolyan in Kiev. If he can't do anything with it either, then I'll have to admit defeat. And I guess I can forget about that bottle from the gardener!'

He downloaded the photos onto a memory stick and put it in his jacket pocket.

'Ma, I'm going into town,' he said to Elena Andreevna. 'I'll be back some time late afternoon. Do you want me to pick anything up?'

Elena Andreevna looked up from her ironing. She thought about it.

'Some black bread, if they've got any fresh,' she said eventually.

The sun was climbing into the sky. The pleasant, warm smell of summer lingered in the air. It didn't feel at all like autumn – it was as though the seasons were deliberately disregarding the calendar. The grass was still green, and even the leaves still clung to the trees.

The minibus taxi to Kiev picked Igor up about five minutes after he reached the stop. It set off again as though it were being piloted by a Formula One racing driver, rather than an unshaven old man wearing a cap who happened to be the husband of the local pharmacist.

The driver turned on the radio, which was tuned to his favourite station, and looked in the mirror to see whether any of his passengers would object. It did happen. The former head teacher at the school, for example, couldn't bear Radio Chanson. But she obviously had no business in Kiev today, so he could listen to whatever he liked.

Igor started thinking about Stepan's tattoo, and he was seized by a sudden moment of doubt: maybe Stepan was lying? Maybe the tattoo was some kind of prison 'badge' and he'd tried to get rid of it himself to cover up his shady past? Igor should have asked Stepan whether he'd been inside himself. Didn't he say that his father had been imprisoned three times? Well, the apple never falls far from the tree, or so they say . . . Although come to think of it, what did Igor know about his own apple tree? Enough to hope that he wouldn't turn out the same way.

Coincidentally, and rather appropriately, the song that came on Radio Chanson at that moment was a prison ballad about a mother waiting for her son to come back from a labour camp. It distracted Igor from his thoughts, and he continued his journey in a blank reverie, just staring out of the minibus window and not thinking about anything. He arrived in Kiev half an hour later and took the metro to Contract Square.

His childhood friend Nikolai, otherwise known as Kolyan, worked as a computer programmer in a bank. Well, maybe not a programmer but an IT specialist of some sort – he was responsible for troubleshooting, or monitoring the programs, something like that. Like many computer experts he was distinguished by certain idiosyncrasies, as though he himself had been infected at some point by a computer virus. He had a tendency to change the subject at the drop of a hat, and instead of answering a specific question he would often start rambling on about something completely irrelevant.

He'd been the same ten years ago, and he'd been the same twenty years ago. The two of them had grown up together and attended the same school. Even the army hadn't separated them – they had ended up in the same military unit just outside Odessa. Military service had been like a holiday for Kolyan. The unit commander had just had a computer installed in his office, and Kolyan taught him how to play games on it. From then on the colonel would send Kolyan to Odessa once a week to fetch new games. Kolyan wasn't stupid – he never brought back more than one game at a time.

Igor often went to see him when he was in Kiev, just to catch up over a beer. Kolyan's working hours were pretty flexible. Only once had he been summoned back to the office, when one of the programs had frozen.

Kolyan emerged from the depths of the bank holding an umbrella.

'It's not raining,' said Igor, looking in surprise at the umbrella.

'You're right,' agreed Kolyan, unperturbed. 'But in half an hour's time, who knows? The weather's like the dollar exchange rate at the moment. It can change several times a day.'

They walked to Khorevaya Street and sat down at a table in a small, cosy cafe.

'What are you having, then?' asked Kolyan. 'I'm funding the refreshments today.'

'You're a banker – funding things is your job! Let's have a beer.'

'I'm not a banker, I just work in a bank. So don't get any ideas about a side order of caviar.'

After taking a sip of draught lager from his old-fashioned pint glass, Igor took the memory stick out of his pocket and put it on the table. He told Kolyan about the tattoo, and about Stepan.

'Can you do anything with it?'

'I'll try,' nodded Kolyan. 'The computers are all behaving themselves today, so I haven't got much on. Why don't you hang out in Podil for a while? Stay local, and I'll call you on your mobile if I have any joy. If not, well, I'll call you anyway!'

As they left the cafe, it began to drizzle. Kolyan shot a triumphant look at his friend. He opened his umbrella, waved goodbye and walked off in the direction of his bank.

Igor didn't feel like wandering about aimlessly without an umbrella, even though it wasn't raining very hard. He headed for the Zhovten cinema and got there just in time to see *Shrek the Third*. The film made him laugh out loud. Part way through the film, he noticed that there wasn't a single child in the cinema – only old people.

When Igor came out into the foyer after the film had finished, he saw a notice on the wall that explained the strange audience demographic: 'Free admission for pensioners and disabled individuals of all three categories on Tuesdays at 11 a.m.'

It had stopped raining, but the sky was still full of heavy clouds. Igor started walking towards Kolyan's work. As soon as the bank sign came into view, his mobile rang.

'Right, you can come and meet me at the bank,' Kolyan said cheerfully.

'I'm already here.'

'What do you mean?'

'I'm standing outside,' explained Igor.

Kolyan came out a couple of minutes later. Igor noticed that he was holding a piece of paper rolled up into a tube.

'Come on then, show me,' he said, burning with curiosity.

'Ha! As if I'm going to show you straight away!' retorted Kolyan. 'No, you'll have to be patient – you owe me now. And it just so happens that I'm hungry. And hunger makes me mean – well, at least, not very cooperative.'

Kolyan dragged Igor towards a cafe. On the way, they passed the Petrovich nightclub.

'Oh, look! "RETRO PARTY here every third Friday",' he read from a poster. '"Come in retro fancy dress for a chance to win a guided trip to North Korea, a holiday to Cuba or an excursion to Moscow, including a night visit to the mausoleum." Cool!' Kolyan turned to his friend, his eyes ablaze with excitement. 'Can you imagine? A night in the mausoleum! You, alone in the dark . . . with Lenin! Eh?'

Igor shrugged. His mind was elsewhere.

'Can't you just show me?'

'No, I'm not going to show you anything on an empty stomach,' insisted Kolyan. With a final glance at the poster, he started walking again. Five minutes later they arrived at Cafe Borshch.

'So, what are you having?' asked Igor, knowing that Kolyan was going to take pleasure in keeping him in suspense, watching his growing irritation and milking the excitement and impatient curiosity that were written all over his face.

'Let's see now . . . I'll have a Russian salad, *okroshka* soup and some fruit cordial,' said Kolyan.

Igor relayed this information to the waitress and sat down opposite Kolyan, without ordering anything for himself.

'Aren't you having anything?' asked Kolyan, surprised.

'I'm already full with curiosity. Anyway, your appetite's enough for both of us.' Igor gave a forced smile. 'So, are you going to show me or not?'

'All right, here you go.' Kolyan held the tube of paper out to him.

Igor opened it up. The printout was black and white – or rather, grey and white – but perfectly comprehensible. Stepan's shoulder was no longer visible, but there were words and an image. The letters looked unsteady, shaky, ready to dissolve again at any moment into a random agglomeration of dots.

'"Ochakov, 1957, Efim Chagin's House",' read Igor. There was an image of an anchor beneath the words. 'Where's Ochakov?' asked Igor.

'Don't you know?' asked Kolyan, surprised. 'On the Black Sea, somewhere between Odessa and the Crimea. Berezan Island is just off the coast . . . You know, where Lieutenant Schmidt was shot. Or haven't you ever heard of *Battleship Potemkin* either?'

Igor nodded, picturing the approximate location of the little town on a map of Ukraine.

'Did he seriously not know what the tattoo said?' asked Kolyan.

Igor smiled. Now his friend was the one itching to know more.

'He had no idea,' said Igor, shaking his head.

Half an hour later, they went their separate ways.

'Hey, don't forget it's my birthday in two weeks! I'm expecting a present!' Kolyan called after his friend.

'I'll be there,' promised Igor, turning round for a moment. 'As long as you remind me nearer the time!'

Igor bought a loaf of Darnitsky rye bread before getting the minibus back to Irpen. On the way home, he kept looking at the printout of the reconstructed tattoo. His imagination was on fire, and even Radio Chanson could not tear his thoughts away from the words and the anchor. He had gone to Kiev with one mystery, and he was coming home with another. Well, it was essentially the same mystery, but knowing more about it only made it more fascinating.

Igor went through the gate and straight round to the back

of the house, to the shed. Stepan was inside, sitting on a little stool up against the wall. He was reading a book.

'What are you reading?' asked Igor.

'Just something about the war,' answered Stepan, getting up.

He closed the book and put it on the stool with the cover facing down, as though he didn't want Igor to see the title or the name of the author.

'Well, I've managed to decipher your tattoo!' declared Igor, with childish pride.

'Have you now?' the gardener asked in surprise. 'What does it say, then?'

Igor held out the piece of paper.

'"Ochakov, 1957, Efim Chagin's house",' Stepan read aloud slowly. Then he froze, his eyes fixed on the words.

Igor stood waiting for the gardener's reaction.

'Go on now,' said Stepan, his voice suddenly cold. 'I need to be alone for a while, to think about everything.'

'Such a thinker,' Igor muttered scornfully, as he turned away. He went into the house. As he left the bag containing the loaf of bread in the kitchen, he glanced at the old set of scales that stood on the windowsill. One pan of the scales held the weights, which ranged from 20g to 2kg. In the other, elevated pan lay the electricity pay book, which was held down with a weight as if to stop it flying away. Not only did his mother use them to weigh out ingredients when she was cooking, even though she was probably more than capable of cutting 100g of butter or scooping out 200g of flour by instinct alone, but she also kept all her paperwork and important documents in the pans. The scales were like her office desk.

Igor poured himself a glass of milk and went into the living room to watch television. There was a detective film on the New Channel. Under normal circumstances Igor would have sat happily and watched it to the end, but today nothing seemed to hold his attention. Nothing, that is, except the enigmatic printout. After sitting in front of the screen for about quarter of an hour, Igor put his shoes on again and went out into the yard. He walked over to the shed and glanced inside, but Stepan wasn't there. He wasn't in the garden either, or the vegetable patch.

Igor went into the shed to see if the gardener's things had disappeared. They hadn't – his rucksack was hanging on a nail above the bed, and his clothes, folded as though they'd just been ironed, lay neatly next to the woodworking tools on the old wooden shelf unit.

3

That night Igor went back to the shed, hoping that Stepan would have returned. He still wasn't there.

Puzzled by the gardener's disappearance, Igor went to bed. He lay there for a long time, closing his eyes and turning from side to side, but he just couldn't get to sleep. Something – either excitement after his trip to Kiev, or some vague, niggling anxiety – was keeping his body alert. A couple of times he thought he heard footsteps in he yard. He got up and went to the door to investigate, only to be greeted by silence – the kind of silence that was full of nocturnal noises. Somewhere out there, an aeroplane was flying high up in the dark sky. Somewhere out there, a drunken tramp was bewailing his loneliness. Somewhere out there, a foreign car was racing through Irpen at top speed.

To eliminate all distractions Igor shut the little top window, and eventually sleep overcame him.

In the morning, his lack of sleep was further exacerbated by a mild but persistent headache. He'd always had headaches like this, ever since he was a child. He was used to the pain. Sometimes he barely even noticed it.

'Are you up yet?' called his mother from the kitchen. 'Come and have breakfast.'

Igor ate a fried egg, drank a glass of milk and then made himself a mug of strong tea. While he was drinking it, he noticed the telephone bill in the raised pan of the scales, held down by a weight. With a smile, he took a second weight from the other pan and put it on top of the bill.

'Can you make Stepan a cup of tea too? And take him some bread and salami,' said Elena Andreevna.

Igor nodded automatically, then remembered the previous evening.

Maybe he's back already, he thought. If he is, then he's bound to appreciate a mug of tea and a sandwich. Hopefully it'll put him in the mood to talk.

The Darnitsky bread was still perfectly fresh – Elena Andreevna always kept it sealed in a plastic carrier bag. Igor cut two thick slices, spread them thickly with butter and placed a slice of salami on each.

The door to the shed was ajar. Igor couldn't remember whether or not he'd shut it the night before. He knocked anyway. There was no answer.

Leaving the mug of tea on the doorstep, Igor went inside. Everything was exactly as he'd left it. Stepan clearly hadn't been back.

Igor picked up the mug again and shut himself inside the shed. His eyes came to rest on the gardener's rucksack. The only source of natural light in the shed was a small window to the right of the door, and the strange, unnatural gloom created a rather mysterious atmosphere. Of course, there was nothing to stop Igor flicking the switch and revelling in the brightness of the 100W light bulb that hung from the ceiling. He could have brought the reading lamp over too, as the shed had been fully adapted for the use of power tools and boasted three electrical sockets. The tools themselves lay on the shelves and in two wooden boxes.

But Igor preferred the mysterious atmosphere, perhaps because Stepan himself had disappeared so mysteriously after reading what had been tattooed on his shoulder . . . Or perhaps because, in spite of the gardener's disappearance, part of the mystery was still here, waiting to be discovered. But where? Could it be in the rucksack?

Igor had been brought up to respect other people's property, whether it was fixed or movable or even jumped and barked, like their neighbour's dog Barsik. But he was in the grip of an urgent, insistent curiosity, which would not allow him to take his eyes off the half-empty canvas rucksack. Moreover the rucksack had been left open, its buckles undone.

Eventually Igor lifted the flap and cautiously looked inside, but he couldn't see anything at all. He switched the light on and looked into the rucksack again. At the bottom of the rucksack lay a box with a picture of an electric razor on it, along with various items of clothing, some socks and a pair of canvas shoes.

Igor paused for a moment to listen to the outside world, then took the cardboard box out of the rucksack and carefully opened it. It did actually contain an old-fashioned razor, complete with instructions and a spare set of rotating blades. Igor turned the razor over in his hands. It seemed odd that Stepan should choose to use such an antique. Then again, Stepan himself was something of an antique, at least in comparison to Igor. Not in any way rare or valuable, but still a relic of the twentieth century. People like him were always hoarders, hanging on to things that were familiar from their childhood.

As he went to put the razor back, Igor noticed something sticking out of the instruction booklet in the bottom of the box. He lifted the instructions up with one finger and took out an envelope, which was also from the previous century. The postmark was clearly visible: 19.12.99.

Suddenly he heard a noise outside in the yard. Panicking at the thought of being caught in the act, Igor thrust the box containing the razor back into the rucksack. Only then did he realise that he was still holding the letter. He hurriedly stuffed it into his trouser pocket, switched the light off and left the shed.

But Igor had no need to worry as Stepan was nowhere to be seen. Igor heard the noise again and realised that it was coming from the yard next door, where their neighbour was attacking an old cherry tree with a chainsaw. He was evidently stocking up on firewood ahead of the winter – for the sauna, not the house. His house, like the one Igor and his mother lived in, was heated by a gas boiler.

Holding the chainsaw away from the trunk of the tree, which was already lying on the ground, the neighbour called out to Igor, 'How's it going?'

'Not bad,' answered Igor, his voice unusually loud. 'Everything's fine!'

'For now, maybe, but it's going to start getting colder next week.' After sharing this piece of information, the neighbour turned his attention back to the job at hand. The chainsaw resumed its high-pitched whining. Igor nodded and hurried into the house.

'How's Stepan? He's not too cold out there, is he?' asked Elena Andreevna.

'He's not there. I don't know where he is, but I think he's been gone since yesterday.'

To Igor's surprise, his mother did not react at all to the news of the gardener's disappearance. Well, he thought, I suppose he's left all his things here so he can't have gone for good. Noticing with relief that his headache had passed, Igor decided to stop worrying about it and made himself another mug of tea.

Elena Andreevna looked into the kitchen a few minutes later, dressed in a smart outfit. 'When he gets back, ask him to sort through the potatoes again,' she said. 'And he can start taking them down to the cellar.'

'Where are you going?' asked Igor.

'To the post office, to pick up my pension, and then to the cobbler's – it's time to fix my winter boots.'

The front gate was visible from the kitchen window. Igor watched his mother leave, then took the envelope out of his pocket. Inside was a New Year's greetings card, which read: 'Dear Papa, I hope the new millennium brings you happiness and joy! I wish you good health, your Alyona.'

Igor looked in surprise from the card to the envelope. It had been sent by Alyona Sadovnikova, 271 Zelenaya Street, Lviv, and was addressed to Stepan Iosipovich Sadovnikov, 14 Matrosov Street, Brovary, Kiev Region.

Sadovnikov, that means 'gardener', he thought, smiling. So, he's followed his destiny!

Igor sipped his tea and looked out of the window again, at the young apple trees that had been planted in front of the house three years previously. He noticed, possibly for the first time, their yellowing leaves. They were a late-cropping variety, and the rosy-cheeked apples that still hung from their branches would keep well in storage until April.

Torn scraps of wispy cloud were racing across the sky. Rays of sunlight, their warmth and brightness already fading, fell through them and among them to the autumn ground.

Igor felt like going for a walk, but first he copied both addresses from the envelope into a notebook. Then he went to the shed and put the card and the envelope back where he'd found them.

A cool breeze blew into Igor's face. He walked as far as the bus station, where he brought himself an instant coffee from a kiosk for one hryvna. He moved to the side of the kiosk and stood there, enjoying the way the thin disposable cup burned his fingers. He would have to wait three or four minutes before he could drink it. Igor looked around, watching the cars as they drove past.

A minibus from Kiev pulled up at the station. As the passengers began to get out, Igor suddenly spotted Stepan among them. Stepping down from the minibus, he stopped to light a cigarette. He looked preoccupied, maybe even depressed. When he finished his cigarette, he threw the stub to the ground and crushed it with the toe of his boot, then set off down the street towards their house.

Igor took his time finishing his coffee, then followed the gardener home. On the way he remembered that he had left the bread and salami and the mug of tea in the shed. The tea would be stone cold by now, of course. The bread and salami would be fine, though – unless the mice had eaten it.

About twenty minutes later, holding a fresh mug of tea, Igor knocked on the door of the shed.

'What are you knocking for?' Stepan asked in surprise as he opened the door. 'It's your house, not mine.'

Nevertheless he was glad of the tea and seemed to enjoy the sandwiches too, smacking his lips with pleasure as he ate.

'I went to visit an old friend of mine,' said Stepan. 'I was going to ask him for money for the trip. I saved his life once, so he owed me one. But he never got the chance to repay me – turns out he's dead. He moved in with a good woman in Boyarka about ten years ago and she kept him off the drink, which always used to be his weakness, but he died anyway. It was his heart, apparently. I have to get the money somehow . . . I have to go back there.'

'Go back where?' asked Igor.

'To Ochakov, of course! To Chagin's house. My father was definitely there at some point. Maybe I've still got some relatives there, and I can finally found out the full story. I don't suppose you could lend me a bit of money, could you?'

Igor thought about it. He did have some money, since he'd been saving up for a motorbike. But there was no point buying a motorbike until the spring.

'Can I come with you?' he asked.

'If you like. I'd be glad of the company. What if we find treasure there?' asked Stepan, smiling. 'We can split it between us. No, that wouldn't be fair . . . You're half my age, so I'll give you a third of the treasure!'

A cunning smile played on Stepan's unshaven face, with its prominent cheekbones.

'We won't need much cash,' he continued. 'Just the cost of the minibus to Kiev, train tickets to Nikolaev, the minibus to Ochakov, and food and accommodation when we get there.'

'All right,' Igor nodded. 'When are we going?'

'As soon as possible . . . Tomorrow!'

Igor shook his head. 'My mother wants you to sort through the potatoes and take them down to the cellar. And you'd better tidy the garden and the vegetable plot up a bit too, otherwise it'll start to bother her.'

'That'll only take a couple of days,' promised Stepan. 'And I'll come back here afterwards, for as long as you'll have me! At least until the spring.'

'All right,' said Igor, looking closely at Stepan. 'I'll phone and book the train tickets. But I'll need to give both our surnames . . .'

'My surname is Sadovnikov,' said Stepan.

Igor couldn't help smiling. He felt childishly triumphant, as though he'd managed to catch someone out. He already knew Stepan's surname!

'What's so funny?' Stepan asked mildly. 'Everyone should try and live in accordance with their name. If your surname means cobbler, you should become a shoemaker, and if it's Sadovnikov, you should become a gardener. That's all there is to it. What's your surname?'

'Vozny.'

'"Carter", but you haven't got a horse or a cart!' Now it was Stepan's turn to smile.

'I'm buying a motorbike in the spring,' Igor declared earnestly. 'Or maybe earlier, if we find treasure in Ochakov.'

'A motorbike? Good for you,' nodded Stepan. He had suddenly grown serious too, only more genuinely so than Igor.

4

Igor told his mother about the trip to Ochakov three days later, on Friday. Elena Andreevna was in good spirits, either purely by chance or because the house and garden were both looking tidy. She was only mildly surprised to learn of her son's planned trip to Ochakov with Stepan.

'What are you going to do there at this time of year?' she asked. 'The sea's too cold for bathing.'

'Stepan used to have family in Ochakov,' replied Igor. 'He wants to find their house, to see if anyone's still living there.'

'When's the train?'

'Tomorrow night, at seven.'

'Well, tell Stepan that he can join us for dinner this evening. I bought a whole chicken.'

Stepan's face had a bluish tinge from shaving just before dinner, and his shoes were freshly polished. He looked quite smart, in spite of his creased trousers and his baggy black sweater.

Elena Andreevna straightened the yellow tablecloth that covered the round table and set out plates and glasses. She took from the dresser an opened bottle of vodka and a small bottle of home-made wine that their neighbour had given them. Then she went to the kitchen and came back carrying a deep earthenware dish, which contained a roast chicken and braised potatoes. She carved the chicken herself and served it out.

'Please, help yourself,' she said to Stepan, indicating the vodka with a nod of her head.

'Thanks, but I don't drink,' he said quietly.

'Would you prefer wine?' she asked, looking at him kindly.

'I'm better off not drinking at all,' said Stepan, a little more loudly this time. 'I've already drunk more than my fair share, as they say. I prefer to keep my mind, body and soul in balance these days.'

Igor shook his head in astonishment. He sounded just like the Baptist they knew, who lived three houses down.

Elena Andreevna fetched a large jar full of home-made cherry juice.

'There you go,' she said, passing it to Stepan.

Stepan calmly poured some for himself and then turned

to Igor. Igor held out his glass. Elena Andreevna decided to treat herself to a glass of home-made wine.

She wished them an enjoyable meal and began eating, with an occasional surreptitious glance at the men to check that they were indeed enjoying the food.

'Will you be gone for long?' she asked, after a pause.

'A couple of days,' Igor shrugged. 'We'll call you.'

Her gaze came to rest on Stepan, who suddenly seemed uncomfortable. He ran his hand awkwardly over his freshly shaven cheeks.

'I'll make up for it when I get back,' he said. 'I mean, if I end up staying a bit longer.'

'Don't be silly!' Elena Andreeva waved her hand. 'I didn't mean that. I just get a bit bored here on my own.'

After lunch the following day, Stepan and Igor took the minibus taxi to Kiev. The gardener's half-empty rucksack lay at his feet. Igor's bag contained a sweater and a parcel of food that Elena Andreevna had prepared for the journey. Radio Chanson was blaring out of the minibus speakers.

Igor glanced at Stepan, who was sitting next to the window.

'Where are we going to stay?' he asked.

The gardener flinched.

'We'll find somewhere . . . It won't be a problem finding a bed for the night. Let's just concentrate on getting there, for the time being.'

After drinking a cup of tea in the glass-fronted cafe at the station, they sat for about two hours on a hard bench in the waiting room. Finally there was an announcement to say they could board their train. Stepan threw his rucksack over his shoulder and glanced back at Igor.

They were the first ones in their compartment.

I hope we'll have it to ourselves, thought Igor, shoving his bag under the little table by the window.

Sadly, Igor's hopes were dashed just a few minutes later when two business travellers stumbled into their compartment, both of them around forty years old. They asked Igor to stand up and stowed two identical suitcases into the space beneath the bottom bunk. They also had a large carrier bag full of clinking bottles, which they left standing in the middle of the floor.

'Are you guys going all the way to Nikolaev?' one of them asked.

Stepan nodded.

'In that case we'll have no problem passing the time,' promised the business traveller. 'We've got enough beer to go round, and if it runs out we can get hold of something stronger from the carriage attendant. We're on first-name terms!'

Igor noticed Stepan frown and turn to look out of the window. Meanwhile, the business travellers wasted no time emptying the bag of its contents: five bottles of beer, half a litre of Nemirov vodka, a whole salami, a loaf of bread and a small plastic bag full of salted cucumbers. The compartment immediately began to smell like a drinking den.

'Hey, why don't you go and get some glasses from the carriage attendant's compartment?' the second business traveller suggested to Igor.

'He's not there. He's checking everyone's tickets.'

The second business traveller narrowed his eyes knowingly.

'Don't worry, he's still on the platform – he won't start checking the tickets until the train leaves.'

Igor reluctantly went to the staff compartment. The door was open, and there was no one inside. He took four glasses from the shelf.

'There you go, see? And you said he was checking tickets!' the second business traveller exclaimed happily.

It suddenly occurred to Igor that the two passengers might be brothers, so alike were they in their ordinariness and lack of distinguishing facial features. Each of them had a moustache, two eyes and ears, a nose and a mouth. And that was it! Their faces were completely generic, as though they had undergone some kind of surgical procedure to remove anything that might be considered worthy of note. Or was it simply the result of back-to-back business trips, chronic sleep deprivation and too much to drink?

One of the business travellers had already opened a bottle of beer and was pouring it out into the glasses. The movements of his hands were smooth and practised, and his face was frozen in an expression of anticipation.

'Not for me,' Stepan said curtly, looking up.

'Why, are you ill?'

'Worse.'

'It's only a glass of beer!' The business traveller waved his objection away and looked at Igor. 'What about you?'

'Just a little,' said Igor. 'We've got to work tomorrow.'

'Really? We're going dancing!' The man burst out laughing. 'This isn't a holiday for us either, you know. Two days of underwater welding, half a litre each to warm us up, and then back again!'

Igor was impressed by the phrase 'underwater welding'. The one with the bottle held his hand out to Igor.

'Vanya,' he introduced himself. 'And this is Zhenya,' he indicated his colleague.

'I'm going for a cigarette,' said Stepan. He stood up and left the compartment.

The train began to move. Zhenya poured a shot of vodka into his colleague's beer and his own, then indicated that Igor should do likewise. Igor declined.

The carriage attendant looked into their compartment and asked for their tickets, greeting the business travellers as though they were old friends.

'Just do me a favour, OK? No singing tonight,' he remarked amiably on his way out.

When Igor finished his glass of beer, he decided to go and look for Stepan. He found him standing in the covered section between their carriage and the next one.

'Surely it wouldn't have hurt you to wet your lips, just to be polite,' he said.

'If I were to so much as wet my lips, as you put it, then no one in the carriage would get any sleep,' smiled Stepan. 'No, I'm happy sticking with tea.'

'What's going to happen if we find some of your relatives in Ochakov?' asked Igor. 'Do you think you might move there and live with them? Or will you stay with us?' He immediately felt embarrassed by the question.

'Who knows?' Stepan shrugged. 'Well, let's say I do find someone . . . But why would they want anything to do with me? I haven't got any money, and I'm not legally registered anywhere. I'm not looking for help or friendship, or anything really. I learned to stand on my own two feet a long time ago. We can just introduce ourselves, and that'll be it. At least I'll know that my daughter and I aren't alone in the world. But I doubt I'll discover any relatives there . . . You don't need a tattoo to help you find your family. No, it must be to do with something else.'

To their surprise, when they returned to the compartment all the bottles on the table were empty and the business travellers were already lying on the top bunks.

'Help yourselves to pickles! There are still a few left,' one of them said.

A row of minibuses stood on the square in front of the train station in Nikolaev, with the names of their final destinations displayed inside their windscreens. Igor immediately noticed that one of them said 'Ochakov'.

'What time are you leaving?' Igor asked the driver, who was noisily cracking sunflower seeds with his teeth.

'When we're full,' he answered.

When they arrived in Ochakov, the sun was shining with all its might over the town. The grey Khrushchev apartment blocks near the unremarkable two-storey, glass-panelled bus station were illuminated in its rays, along with three kiosks and several old women selling apples on the pavement.

Stepan looked around then made straight for the old women. Igor hurried after him.

'How much for your apples?' Stepan asked one of them.

'Two hryvnas a kilo,' she answered. 'But I'll let you have them for one and a half.'

'Would you happen to know where we could find a place

to stay for a couple of nights? Somewhere with reasonable rates . . .'

Stepan's abrupt change of subject didn't seem to surprise the old woman.

'Why have you come so late in the season?' she asked, spreading her hands in a gesture of commiseration. 'The only people in the sea these days are drunks and children.'

'We're ice swimmers.' The gardener smiled. 'No, we haven't come to swim – we're here to see the town.'

'There's nothing here to see!' remarked the old woman. 'Mind you, the church isn't bad . . . and there's an art museum somewhere in the centre. That's worth a visit, so I'm told . . .'

'We'll certainly add it to our itinerary,' nodded Stepan. 'But first, we need to find a place to stay.'

The old woman looked them up and down.

'I've got a room . . . But I won't let it out for less than ten hryvnas a day. And that's without food, of course.'

'Fine, we'll take it,' said the gardener, giving the impression that he was agreeing reluctantly to her terms.

'Masha, can you sell mine for me?' she asked, turning to her neighbour in the makeshift roadside market. 'I'll be right back.'

Her neighbour nodded.

Leaving the bus station and the Khrushchev blocks, they followed the old woman past a succession of detached houses.

'Where are you from?' she asked as they walked.

'The capital,' replied Stepan.

They soon turned into the yard of an old brick house. Igor headed straight for the steps leading to the front door.

'Hey, not that way!' the old woman called from behind

them. She led her guests round to the back of the house, where they saw two brick outbuildings. She removed the padlock from the door of one of the buildings and gave it to Stepan, along with the key; then she opened the door and showed them inside. The room contained two iron beds, which had been made up neatly. A little table and two chairs stood by the small window, and there was a wooden shelf unit against the wall, which was identical to the one in the shed behind Igor's house.

'Well, make yourselves at home,' she said. 'I'm going back to finish selling the rest of my apples.'

She looked at them on her way out.

'Would you mind paying me in advance?'

Igor held out twenty hryvnas.

'That's for two nights. If we stay longer, we'll pay you more.'

After Stepan had smoked a cigarette, he and Igor went out to have a look round the town. The road they were walking along seemed to go on for ever.

'I thought Ochakov was smaller than Irpen,' Igor sighed.

'It doesn't matter which is bigger or smaller – they're both the kind of town where everyone knows everyone else,' Stepan declared confidently. 'Which is not necessarily a good thing. People can immediately spot an outsider.'

Their landlady's name was Anastasia Ivanovna. That evening she knocked on the window of their room and invited them into the house for dinner.

Anastasia Ivanovna's house smelt of old clothes. It was a smell that Igor recognised from his childhood. His grand-mother in the country had kept an old trunk full of dresses, coats and scarves, and whenever Igor looked inside he had been hit by the same peculiar, musty smell. It wasn't an unbearable smell, or even particularly unpleasant – it was almost sweet, and something about it reminded him of fallen autumn leaves.

Anastasia Ivanovna fed her guests braised cabbage with mushrooms. She didn't offer them anything stronger to drink than tea, which she poured straight away from a large glazed teapot.

'Have you lived here long?' Stepan asked her.

'Born and bred here, I was,' said their landlady.

Stepan's eyes lit up.

'You haven't by any chance heard of Efim Chagin, have you?' he asked in a clear, dry voice.

'Fima Chagin?' she exclaimed. 'Of course I've heard of him! Half the town used to know Fima Chagin!'

A dreamy smile appeared on her face.

'Fima was handsome, he was, and smart. All the girls had an eye for him. Such a shame he was killed . . .'

'How was he killed? When?' asked Igor, unable to contain himself.

Their landlady thought about it for a moment.

'It must have been during Khrushchev's time . . . Yes, that's right. Just after Khrushchev sent Gagarin up into space. Or was it before that? After the satellite he sent up . . . I remember, everyone was whispering about space at the funeral.'

'And the house he used to live in . . .' Stepan began cautiously. 'Is it still there?'

'Of course,' nodded Anastasia Ivanovna. 'Why wouldn't it be?'

Stepan looked at Igor. His eyes burned with excitement, and his lips spread in a barely perceptible smile.

5

Igor didn't sleep very well that night. The iron bedstead creaked every time he turned over and kept waking him up. Fortunately it didn't disturb Stepan, who lay fast asleep and snoring in the other bed.

Eventually Igor opened his eyes, rolled over onto his back and lay there staring up at the low ceiling, which was barely visible in the darkness. He thought about the evening they'd spent with their landlady. He remembered the way she'd broken into an almost girlish smile when she'd been talking about Fima Chagin. It had looked so strange on her wrinkled old face. Later on she'd let slip that she herself had been in love with Fima, as had many of the other girls in Ochakov. Apparently Fima Chagin had been a striking individual – tall and thin, with a prominent Adam's apple and a sharp nose. He had just turned up in Ochakov one day, after the war. His grandmother lived in a big house, and when she was suddenly taken ill his parents had sent him from Kakhovka to live with her, so that when she died the house would stay in the family. According to their landlady, the grandmother recovered and shared her house with her grandson for the next ten years. They got on well, and their life together was certainly never dull. When Fima first arrived he had sought out the local troublemakers and picked fights, in an attempt to prove himself. He soon earned their respect and they began to consider him one of their own, as though he'd lived in Ochakov all his life. He went fishing with the other lads or down to the port to steal things, taking anchors from boats that belonged to outsiders and selling them at the market. Every now and then he was caught, but he would simply break free and run away. And he kept on running until the divisional inspector got him locked up for two years.

When Fima came out he seemed much older, more aloof. He had stopped running. From that point on he walked slowly, with authority. People came to visit him from all kinds of far-flung places – from Taganrog, from Rostov, from Odessa. Sometimes they would stay at his house for several weeks and then simply disappear, but others came in their place, all of them thin and wiry. He grew rich. The divisional inspector would greet him in the street, turning a blind eye to it all. This went on for five or six years, maybe even longer, until one day he was found stabbed in his own home.

Igor thought of the flame that had burned in the old woman's eyes when she told them about Fima Chagin's murder. Fima had been found, she said, lying on his back in the middle of his living-room floor, a knife sticking out of his chest. Near his body they'd found two bundles of roubles and a note that read: 'For a proper send-off'.

The old woman had promised to show them the house the following day.

Igor eventually dozed off just before morning, but in no time at all the birds began chirping and squawking right in his ear, or so it seemed, and his eyes snapped open. Stepan had opened the window, letting in the sounds of the clamorous autumn morning that was coming to life in the warmth of the rising sun.

Greeting him with a nod, Stepan went out into the yard wearing just his underwear. From the yard came the sounds of a bucket being lifted and water being poured from the well. Then the gardener made a loud spluttering sound and ran straight back inside, wet to the waist.

After shaving, Stepan went out into the yard again. He returned immediately holding two large apples, one of which he threw to Igor.

'Breakfast!' he announced, taking a bite out of his own apple.

About quarter of an hour later the familiar voice of their landlady called to them from the yard. She hadn't asked for their passports the previous day, or even their names. So when she knocked on the window, she just called, 'Gentlemen!'

The 'gentlemen' left their room. Stepan secured the padlock and checked it twice.

'It's on Kostya Khetagurov Street,' said Anastasia Ivanovna, once they'd set off. 'Not far from here. It's an office of some kind now, for a pension fund, or something similar.'

They turned left past a small shop and saw a number of two-storey brick buildings, but kept walking until they came to a patch of wasteland and a burnt-out wooden hut. Beyond this vacant plot, behind a low metal fence, stood an unsightly single-storey building with a high socle around its base. Double wooden doors served to emphasise the building's unwelcoming bureaucratic nature. There were two signs, one on either side of the doors: 'Organisation of Ochakov Labour

Veterans' and 'Public Office of A. G. Volochkov, Deputy of the Nikolaev Regional Council'.

The old woman stopped. 'There it is,' she said. 'It looks exactly the same!' Her voice sounded tearful. 'In Fima's day the house used to be divided into just four big rooms with old stoves, but there must be at least ten rooms in there now. I came here once, to the veterans department. I thought they might be able to help me get some extra money on top of my pension.' She waved her hand sadly. 'And about five years ago, it must have been, I saw Egorov here, the divisional inspector who got Fima locked up. He must be dead by now.'

Stepan stared at Anastasia Ivanovna with interest.

'Divisional inspectors usually live to a ripe old age,' he said pensively. 'Maybe we ought to check . . . Where did he used to live?'

'I don't know the address, but I know which house it is. It's down there.' She waved her hand along the street. 'Towards the sea. It used to have a red fence.'

'Maybe we could call on him now?' suggested Stepan. 'We really do need to speak to him, if he's still alive.'

It took about five minutes of gentle persuasion before Anastasia Ivanovna agreed to take them to Egorov's house.

They arrived at a small stucco house with a red fence around it. The door was opened by a young girl with freckles, who must have been about six years old.

'Is your grandfather at home?' the old woman asked her.

'Grandad!' the girl shouted back into the house. 'It's for you!'

A wizened old man looked out into the hallway. He was wearing a dark blue woollen tracksuit emblazoned with the

Dinamo football club logo. At the sight of two strange men on his doorstep he froze. Then he noticed the diminutive figure of Anastasia Ivanovna beside them, stooping beneath the burden of her years, and his expression softened.

'Nastya, is that you?' he asked, unable to take his eyes off the old woman.

'Yes, and these two lodgers of mine twisted my arm until I brought them to see you,' she said, indicating Stepan and Igor. 'Can we come in?'

The old man nodded.

He led them into the living room, trying on the way to capture a moth that had flown into the hallway. He invited them to sit down at a table covered with a velour cloth.

'So, what can I do for you?' he asked, sitting down opposite them.

'Well,' began Stepan, 'I think Fima Chagin was either a relative, or a friend, of my father's . . . I just want to find out for sure. That's why I've come to Ochakov.'

'And what does this have to do with me?'

'Well, you were the one who put him away, so you must know something about him,' said Stepan. 'What about his friends, for example? He must have had friends. Who were they?'

'Friends?' repeated the old man. 'Maybe he did have friends. I don't know. As for what he got up to . . . how can I put it? Let's just say he had his fingers in a number of pies. He sold stolen goods, he had suspicious visitors . . . His house was like a kind of "poste restante" service. People used to leave things with him to look after for a year or so, sometimes longer. They would pay him for this, of course.

People reported him, and the police came with search warrants, but they never found anything. So he just carried on like that, right up until he was killed. Would you like some tea?'

Anastasia Ivanovna brightened and nodded on behalf of herself and her lodgers. While they were drinking their tea Stepan tried his best to find out more, but the old man had nothing further to tell.

'My father must have been one of his visitors,' Stepan reflected that evening, when they were sitting on the beds in their little room. 'And I bet he left him something to look after as well . . . So he was a thief, after all.'

The following day they went to a hardware shop near the market, where Stepan bought a crowbar and two torches. Igor paid, albeit reluctantly.

His apprehensions proved to be well founded. That evening, the gardener grabbed the torches and crowbar and led him out onto the street.

'We're just going to scope out Chagin's house for a bit first . . . Get a feel for the place,' he said in a low voice. 'Then we'll take a look inside.'

The dark southern sky hung low above them, and the smell of the sea tickled their noses. Somewhere nearby, a radio was blaring out Turkish music.

After walking past Chagin's house several times, they went into the yard and hid behind a tree to the right of the doorstep.

'We could get locked up for this!' Igor panicked. He knew what was coming next.

'For what? For trying to understand my childhood? It's not like we're robbing a bank,' Stepan reassured him.

They stood there for about twenty minutes, just listening. The silence was broken only by a single car going past. The town was obviously early to bed as well as early to rise.

Stepan deftly forced open the padlock with the crowbar, then levered the door up until the built-in lock disengaged from its mortice. The door opened.

Stepan slipped through the gap with Igor close behind him. They shut the door and immediately found themselves in pitch darkness. Stepan switched on his torch, and Igor did the same.

'The police aren't stupid,' whispered Stepan. 'If they came here with search warrants they would have checked under the floorboards, and in the attic. They must have searched the old stoves too . . . I bet they've all been ripped out, though.'

They were in a kind of hallway, with various doors leading off it. Stepan shone his torch along the walls and over the cast-iron radiators, which had been painted white. He approached the closest set of double doors, which were marked 'Public Office'. Before Igor even noticed the doors opening, Stepan was inside, illuminating the walls and floor with his torch.

'Right,' he said. 'We need a system, otherwise we'll be here all night. You stay here while I go back and open all the other doors, then we can start working our way round clockwise.'

Igor switched off his torch and stood motionless in the darkness, listening to the hushed whispering of the doors as they opened one by one, yielding to pressure from the crowbar.

It wasn't long before Stepan returned. He touched Igor on the shoulder and motioned for him to follow. Together they went back into the hallway and then walked around each of the rooms in turn, shining their torches over the floors, the walls and the unprepossessing Soviet-style furniture. They ended up back in Deputy Volochkov's office.

'Right, here's what we're going to do,' said Stepan, voicing his thoughts aloud. 'We can rule out the attic and the floors. There are no stoves. That just leaves the walls. Do you know how to sound out walls?'

'What do you mean?' asked Igor.

'Like a doctor. Rap on them with your knuckles, and if they sound solid keep going. But if they sound hollow, then stay where you are and call for me. We'll do it together. I'll start to the right of the doors, and you can start to the left.'

In the pitch-black silence, they started knocking on the walls: right up to the ceiling, and right down to where they met the floorboards. In the third room, to the right of an enormous, brooding safe, Igor thought the wall sounded different.

'Stepan!' he whispered urgently. 'I think I've found something.'

Stepan went over to check.

'Yes, it does sound empty just here,' he said, although he sounded unconvinced. 'I'll go and check from the other side.'

He came back pleasantly puzzled.

'The wall sticks out strangely on that side,' he said, grasping the crowbar in his right hand. 'Right then, here goes!'

The exertion was reflected on his face as he smashed the crowbar into the wall. After a certain amount of resistance the crowbar plunged deep inside.

'Now, that's interesting,' whispered Stepan, shining his torch onto the wall.

He widened the hole he had made. Igor noticed pieces of dark plywood sticking out of the plaster. It took the two of them them about ten minutes to open up a section of the wall big enough to shine their torches inside.

'Well, fancy that!' exclaimed Stepan. The light from their torches fell on three old-fashioned leather suitcases, covered in dust and building rubble. 'All that time they spent searching for left luggage, and we've finally found it!'

Stepan dragged the suitcases out one at a time. He blew the dust and debris from them, then brushed his clothes down and switched off his torch. They left the building carefully, trying to make as little noise as possible. Stepan even managed to close the front door silently behind them.

The streets were equally deserted on the way back to Anastasia Ivanovna's house. What a lovely little town! thought Igor.

They put the suitcases on the floor in their room. Stepan wiped them with the cloth rag that served as a doormat.

'We'll have to leave early, before the market opens,' Stepan said firmly.

'Aren't we going to see what's inside?' asked Igor.

'We'll open them up back at your place, when we can take our time over it. Let's just concentrate on getting them there, for the time being.'

Igor was not inclined to argue. They had two hours left before sunrise. Stepan was already packing his rucksack. He paused and looked at his young companion.

'Put twenty hryvnas on the table,' he said. 'It wouldn't hurt to leave a good impression.'

6

Kiev welcomed the returning travellers with pouring rain. The sky hung dark and low over the train station. Wearing his rucksack on his back and carrying one of the old leather suitcases, Stepan walked briskly towards their suburban commuter train. Igor was carrying the other two suitcases as well as his own bag, and he struggled to keep up. At least the suitcases weren't heavy. Though this did call into question the value of their contents.

The puddles in the streets of Irpen reflected the autumn sun. It had obviously rained there earlier in the day.

'Let's take a taxi,' suggested Stepan, looking around. They were not exactly inconspicuous with their three large, old-fashioned suitcases. Igor also noticed a few passers-by looking at them in surprise.

There were five or six cars waiting for passengers in front of the little station. Stepan and Igor chose an old brown Mercedes. The journey to Igor's house took less than five minutes. The driver, who had a moustache and was wearing camouflage hunting overalls, helped them to unload their luggage from the car. They took the suitcases straight into Stepan's shed.

'Why don't you go and have a little rest?' said the gardener solicitously. 'Come back in half an hour. Then we'll open them up and see what's inside.'

Igor looked at Stepan then glanced cautiously at the suitcases, which were standing on the concrete floor next to the old wooden shelf unit. Then he turned and left.

'So, how did you get on?' asked his mother, as soon as she saw him. 'Did you see much of the town? Did you find anything? I bet you're hungry!'

'Put the kettle on,' said Igor, ignoring his mother's questions. Not that she seemed to be expecting any answers.

Igor went into the bathroom and washed his hands and face. His face was pale and swollen from the rough train pillow. He ran his hand over his prickly, unshaven cheeks, and his eyes fell on the little shelf beneath the mirror, where toothbrushes and disposable razors bristled out of a plastic cup.

Igor had a shave and brushed his teeth. Now he felt a little more alert, but at the same time he couldn't help wondering what Stepan might be up to in the shed.

'Tea's ready, son,' his mother called from the kitchen.

Igor poured a second mug of tea and put a spoonful of sugar into his own, and two into Stepan's.

'Oh, thanks!' the gardener exclaimed in surprise, when he saw Igor at the door of the shed.

Igor noticed that Stepan was holding the crowbar from Ochakov. Before taking his mug from Igor he put the implement down on the concrete floor. They drank their tea in silence, sitting on stools with the door half shut. The light hanging from the ceiling seemed unusually bright. Igor kept glancing nervously at the suitcases. He was dying of curiosity.

Eventually Stepan picked up the crowbar again and bent over one of the suitcases, although it wouldn't have taken more than a screwdriver to prise open the two weak locks.

The first suitcase opened without a sound. Inside were two packages wrapped in thick brown paper and tied up with string. They were about the same size as those boxes that women's winter boots came in – the kind his mother kept in her wardrobe, full of photographs and balls of wool with knitting needles sticking out of them.

Stepan picked up one of the packages and gauged its weight, biting his lip in concentration. He turned it over and stared at the three large letters that were written on the back in indelible pencil: I.S.S. Stepan gave a heavy sigh, although it was not tiredness that showed on his face but a kind of reflective contentment, as though he'd found what he'd been searching for his entire life.

'Iosip Stepanovich Sadovnikov,' he said after a pause, stroking the initials with the forefinger of his right hand.

Squatting down, he placed the package on the floor and began to unwrap it. Inside was a large bookkeeping ledger. Stepan grinned self-consciously, as though he didn't quite know what to do next. There was an inscription on the front, handwritten neatly in fountain pen. Stepan read it out: *The Book of Food*.

He put the book on the floor and took the second package out of the suitcase. The look of calm contentment had left his face, as though he knew the pleasant surprises were over. The second package was marked with the same initials and contained about a dozen small paper packets. Stepan opened one of them and caught his breath. He tilted the packet, and Igor watched in astonishment as a number of transparent faceted crystals fell into his palm.

'Are they diamonds?' whispered Igor.

Stepan tore his eyes away from his hand and looked up at Igor.

'No idea,' he said, tipping the little stones back into the paper packet. He opened another of the little packets and looked inside. 'We'll have to ask an expert.'

Igor thought about the money he'd spent on the trip to Ochakov. The money he'd been saving towards the cost of a motorbike. He hadn't spent that much, as it turned out, but without his money they wouldn't have been able to go at all. Meanwhile, Stepan put all the contents back into the suitcase and put it in the corner of the room. Then he turned his attention to the remaining suitcases.

The second, which yielded as easily as the first, contained several little parcels wrapped in white cloth. They were also signed with indelible pencil. Each parcel was marked with different initials, but the handwriting was the same.

'Those aren't your father's,' Igor said warily.

'So what?' answered Stepan, forcing a smile. 'My father had a son, maybe this lot didn't.'

Ripping one of the parcels open along the seam, Stepan pulled out a cardboard box. He shook it, but it didn't make any noise. He opened it to find five antique gold pocket watches, carefully wrapped in handkerchiefs.

'Choose one,' Stepan said to Igor. He still had a furtive, scheming look about him, but he was noticeably more relaxed.

Igor froze. He didn't know whether the gardener was genuinely offering him one of the watches or whether he was joking.

'Go on, take that one,' urged Stepan, prodding the largest watch.

Igor picked it up and opened the protective cover. The watch really was quite beautiful. He turned the little dial on the side and lifted the watch to his ear, but it was silent.

'It's not working,' he said despondently.

'So take it to a jeweller and get it fixed. Let's see what else is in here . . .' Stepan picked up the second parcel.

Igor was closely observing Stepan's every move. He watched as the gardener opened the parcels one by one, taking out gold coins, signet rings set with precious stones and gold bracelets studded with emeralds. Once Stepan had familiarised himself with the contents of the second suitcase, he put everything back again.

Sensing that Stepan was sneaking sideways glances at him, Igor suddenly felt quite depressed. It was obvious that the treasure they'd found in Ochakov was really worth something. The contents of the suitcases were valuable enough for men to fight over, valuable enough to cost lives. Being in possession of, or even in proximity to, so much gold was potentially fatal in any era.

But when Stepan opened the final suitcase, his expression changed to one of bewilderment. Inside the suitcase lay a neatly folded old-fashioned police uniform, together with a pair of leather boots, a leather belt and a peaked cap. Stepan stuck his hand underneath the uniform and rummaged about in the depths of the suitcase. Suddenly he paused, his hands still hidden, a triumphant smile hovering about his lips – the smile of a child catching crayfish from the riverbank with his hands.

When Stepan finally took his hand out of the suitcase, he was holding a gun in a holster. Then he pulled out two bundles of Soviet banknotes, which looked enormous in comparison to the contemporary currency.

'That's it, then,' he declared, with a sigh of disappointment. He threw both bundles of money back into the suitcase, on top of the uniform, and placed the gun and its holster down carefully alongside them. 'You might as well have this lot. A little souvenir of our trip to Ochakov!'

Igor stared at the gardener. Does he really think he can buy me off with a moth-eaten old uniform and a broken watch? he thought. To be fair, the watch was probably worth more than he'd spent on their trip . . . But what about everything else they'd found? The contents of the first two suitcases must have been worth a fortune! And even if they split the bounty as Stepan had jokingly suggested, if Igor received only a third of what they'd found, that would still be a huge amount of money. Igor smiled and felt a rush of adrenalin.

But the gardener's thin smile, which could easily have been mistaken for a grimace of pain, seemed to exude bitterness.

'I'm going to go and lie down for a bit,' whispered Igor.

'Take it, take the suitcase. Don't worry about the locks, I'll fix those later.'

Igor took the suitcase containing the police uniform and the gun and went out into the yard without another word.

When his mother saw the suitcase, she clasped her hands together in surprise. 'We used to have two like that at home, about fifty years ago. Did you buy it at a flea market?'

'No, someone gave it to me,' Igor answered curtly and slipped past her into his room.

The autumn evening fell early and surprisingly quickly, catching Igor unawares. They'd only got back that morning, and they didn't seem to have spent that long examining the contents of the suitcases, but it was already getting dark. His arms were aching and he felt like yawning.

Without bothering to wait for the supper that his mother was already preparing, Igor made himself a sandwich. Then he went into his room and lay down on his bed. He was assaulted by exhaustion and thrown into a realm beyond normal sleep, a realm beyond dreams of any kind.

When the beef and vegetable casserole was ready and the potatoes were boiled Elena Andreevna looked into her son's bedroom, but she couldn't bring herself to wake him up. Noticing the gold pocket watch lying on a handkerchief on Igor's bedside table, she picked it up and examined it with a mixture of curiosity and apprehension. She gave a deep sigh.

Elena Andreevna didn't want to sit and eat dinner by herself, so she decided to ask Stepan to join her. She put her shoes on and went out into the yard. She knocked a couple of times on the door to the shed and then opened it, coming face to face with a startled Stepan, who had clearly just got up from his bed.

'I've made dinner, but Igor's fallen asleep . . . Would you like to keep me company instead?' she asked, looking directly into the gardener's eyes.

'Me?' he asked, momentarily disconcerted, as though he'd been deep in thought and the invitation had been an unwelcome interruption. 'Of course, it would be a pleasure. Thank you. I just need to lock up.' He glanced around the room and his eyes fell on the shelf unit where he kept his things, and where all the tools were stored. He took a padlock from one of the shelves and put his jacket on.

Elena Andreevna watched, intrigued, as he closed the door carefully and padlocked it. She'd never seen him lock it before.

'So, did you find any family in Ochakov?' she asked, putting a plate of casserole and boiled potatoes on the table in front of Stepan.

'Not quite,' he said, shaking his head. 'But we found some people who remember them, which is something. And we found a few bits and pieces . . . things that used to belong to my father.'

'You don't say!' exclaimed Elena Andreevna. 'Someone kept them all that time?'

'Indeed,' nodded Stepan, wondering how best to change the subject. 'So how are things here? What's the latest?'

'You've only been away for a couple of days.' His landlady shrugged. 'Nothing's changed. Well, the kiosk near the station was robbed one night, and there was a fight near the Customs and Excise training academy, but that's it really. Igor's asleep . . . Should I wake him?'

'No.' Stepan waved his hand. 'Let him sleep it off. Has he been out of work long?'

'Yes,' nodded Elena Andreevna.

'Why? Can't he find a job?'

'He's not even looking,' sighed Elena Andreevna. 'He had an accident when he was little. Five years old, he was. I told my husband to take him to the playground, but he met someone he knew and started chatting and Igor ran off towards the carousel. It was just slowing down, and one of the metal seats caught him on the head. He suffered what they call a closed head injury. He was in hospital for two months, and I never left his side. The doctor warned us to expect brain damage so we were prepared for the worst, but he ended up making a complete recovery . . . He just gets headaches every now and then. He was lucky. I spent years watching over him like a blade of grass, trying to protect him.

'Then when he finished school I sent him out to find a job. One day he came home and said that he'd found one in a furniture factory, here in Irpen. He started leaving the house every morning, and he told me all about the job itself, what his friends were like, that kind of thing. He even brought some stools home once, said he'd been given them because they were slightly damaged. We're sitting on them right now, in fact.' Elena Andreevna paused and looked down at her stool. 'About three months later, I needed to find him urgently during the day so I went to the address he'd mentioned, but there was no furniture factory there. Well, at first I wanted to challenge him about it, and then I decided I ought to take him to see a doctor, to a psychiatrist . . . In the end I just told him I hadn't managed to find the factory, and he immediately stopped going. So, here we are. Things aren't so bad – I get my pension money, and we manage to make ends meet . . .' Elena Andreevna trailed off, lowering her eyes.

Now Stepan felt awkward too because the change in his landlady's mood had been caused directly by his curiosity. But Elena Andreevna's sadness didn't last for long. She licked her dry lips, and when she looked up at the gardener her eyes were alive again.

'Is the town pretty?' she asked.

'Ochakov? Not particularly. It was quite grey. It's probably nice in the summer, but not now.'

Elena Andreevna offered Stepan a shot of vodka, but he politely declined.

'Elena Andreevna, I'm going away this evening for a couple of days,' he said after a pause. 'It's nothing to worry about – I'm just going to see some friends who live not far from here, on the way to Kiev. I'll sort everything out in the garden and the vegetable patch as soon as I get back. We've got plenty of time to prepare for winter.'

'Yes, there's plenty of time,' agreed Elena Andreevna.

She had the impression that something was bothering Stepan. He'd seemed tense over dinner. Elena Andreevna was pleased with her casserole – the meat and vegetables were particularly tender – but the gardener hadn't said a word. On the other hand, he'd eaten everything on his plate and even scooped up the last of the gravy with his bread . . . Maybe he was the kind of man whose actions spoke louder than his words.

7

Igor woke up at about 3 a.m. He switched his light on and sat on the bed for a while, just thinking. Then he decided to go out into the yard.

As he approached the shed, he was astonished to see the padlock on the door. It occurred to him that Stepan might have gone for good, taking his treasure with him. He very much hoped that wasn't the case. Igor couldn't for the life of him remember where they kept the spare keys.

His mood ruined, Igor went back to the house and tiptoed into the living room. The house was surprisingly quiet. His mother was asleep, and the mice hadn't started rustling about under the floorboards yet. They only came into the house in the winter, when it got really cold, and the first frosts wouldn't arrive for at least another two months.

As Igor opened the top cupboard of the dresser he remembered that a bottle of walnut liqueur had been lurking in there for some time. He extracted the bottle carefully, selected a small shot glass and walked over to the table. He sat on one of the chairs, which had a knitted rag cushion tied to the back with a couple of ribbons, poured himself a shot and started thinking. He thought about the trip to Ochakov and the nocturnal 'treasure hunt'. Whichever way you looked at it, they had definitely broken the law. But then again, wasn't everyone breaking the law these days in one way or another? With the possible exception of his mother. Actually, he'd never done anything illegal before the trip to Ochakov. It had simply never occurred to him. Something had been holding him back in Ochakov too, whereas Stepan didn't show even a moment's hesitation. He'd known exactly what he was doing when he took Igor to the hardware shop to buy a crowbar. And he'd known exactly how to use it too, to open doors and smash padlocks. He'd said that his father had been in prison three times . . . Maybe Stepan had too? Yes, that was it. He must have been in prison, and when he came out he hadn't been allowed home! That would certainly explain the vagabond lifestyle.

Igor sipped his liqueur. It was strong and viscous, bitter but sweet. The pleasant assault on his senses distracted him from his thoughts. He stopped thinking altogether and simply sat there, without moving. Suddenly he ran his hand over his naked thighs, realising for the first time how cold he was. He wondered whether he ought to get dressed. Yet he finished his drink slowly, returned the bottle to the dresser and tiptoed back to his bedroom.

In the morning he was woken by his mother's quiet, reproachful voice. 'So, drinking vodka in the middle of the night now, are you?' she asked, glancing into his room. 'You should take a leaf out of Stepan's book – he doesn't drink at all!'

'That's right, he's already drunk his fair share!' answered Igor, still half asleep. He opened his eyes and looked at his watch. It was 7.30 a.m. 'Is Stepan back then?'

'I haven't seen him. Get up, if you want some breakfast. Look, people are already on their way to work,' she said, glancing pointedly out of the window.

Igor sighed. Now she's going to start on about me getting a job.

'We manage all right, don't we?' asked Igor, getting out of bed.

'What if we didn't have my pension?' His mother's voice sounded louder than usual.

'What difference does your pension make? It's only one thousand five hundred hryvnas! I get the equivalent of two hundred dollars from the bank every month in interest. 'Isn't that enough?'

'But you're not earning it, are you? You're a parasite,' his mother continued, lowering her voice. She was worried that any disagreement about the importance of work would lead, as it usually did, to a full-blown argument and two days of sulking. 'You'd have been arrested for it in Soviet times!'

'It's no wonder the Soviet Union collapsed then, is it?' countered Igor, although his tone of voice had also changed. 'Seriously, it's not like we're struggling financially, is it? If something interesting comes up, of course I'll apply for it.'

It was true – after they'd sold their apartment in Kiev and bought the house in Irpen, they'd put the rest of the money into a savings account and were now living off the interest. Igor went to the bank once a month to withdraw it. He would bring it home and put it on the kitchen table; then he would take half for himself, leaving the rest for his mother. He'd already grown so accustomed to this way of life that he'd come to think of the trips to the bank in Kiev as his job.

Elena Andreevna soon calmed down. She ladled hot buckwheat into a bowl for her son, placing a knob of butter on top. The butter immediately began to melt, seeping down through the grains. Igor picked up a large spoon and ate his buckwheat slowly, looking out of the window.

'I'll ask around,' he promised suddenly, glancing apologetically at his mother. 'Maybe something'll turn up here in Irpen . . . I'm bored too, you know, just sitting around all day.'

Elena Andreevna nodded.

'Prices keep going up,' she said. 'Cheese is already sixty hryvnas a kilo, for example . . . But they never increase my pension, and our interest rate hasn't gone up either.'

Igor had no desire to prolong this depressing conversation. After finishing his buckwheat he poured himself a mug of tea and started thinking about what sort of job he could get, but his thoughts soon turned to Stepan – or, rather, to his absence. He thought about the antique suitcase containing the police uniform and the Soviet roubles. He thought about the gun. Stepan's 'generous' gifts. To be fair, some tourist would pay good money for a vintage Soviet uniform at the flea market in Kiev. Maybe he should take it into town and try his luck.

Igor sighed and went into his bedroom. He opened the suitcase, took the uniform out and checked the pockets. In one of them he discovered an ID pass belonging to a certain Lieutenant I.I. Zotov.

'Maybe his name was Igor too.' Igor smiled, looking at the small black-and-white photo. The young man in the photo was no more than twenty-five years old.

Igor picked up the two bundles of Soviet hundred-rouble notes. They felt heavy. What did he really know about the era when this money, which was no longer of any practical use, had circulated around a country that no longer existed? Almost nothing, despite the fact that he'd been born in that era himself – during the last Soviet five-year plan, as his mother liked to say.

Igor didn't understand what the big deal was about five-year plans. What was the point of them? He pulled a face. School had been a ten-year plan, one he'd had to endure personally! But why were five years significant? He shrugged and threw the useless currency back into the suitcase.

'Are you going to the shops today?' called his mother from the kitchen.

'Yes, I was just on my way out,' replied Igor.

He put the police uniform neatly back into the suitcase,

placing I.I. Zotov's identification on top. Then he closed the suitcase and pushed it under the bed.

It was drizzling outside, so Igor took an umbrella. For some reason he had a song from an old Christmas film going round and round inside his head.

When he reached the first kiosk, Igor bought a packet of cigarettes and lit one straight away. Just at that moment a young lad appeared at his elbow. He didn't have an umbrella, and his wet hair was plastered to his forehead. He was wearing a canvas jacket and heavy army boots.

'Hey man, can you spare a cigarette?'

Igor held the open packet out to him, looking at the lad with amusement.

'Cover it up with your hand, at least, or the rain will put it out.'

'I'll smoke it here, under the roof,' the boy replied calmly. He lit his cigarette using the tip of Igor's, then sheltered under the roof of the kiosk to the left of the window.

'Where on earth did you get those boots?' asked Igor. 'They don't make them like that any more.'

'I found them in my dad's shed. They're army boots,' the boy replied earnestly, not noticing the irony in Igor's voice.

'Lucky you! They knew how to make boots in the old days. Not like now.' Igor looked down at his cheap Romanian boots, which he'd already had fixed twice.

'They don't really fit me,' grumbled the boy. 'My dad's feet were bigger than mine . . . Could you spare another one?'

Igor took a cigarette out of the packet and held it out to the boy. Then he walked off, without saying goodbye. When he reached the bus station he stopped and took a moment to look around. He walked over to the noticeboard and scanned the handwritten and photocopied adverts stuck to the wall. They were all 'For Sale' or 'Wanted'.

Maybe I should join the police, thought Igor. I've already got a gun! He smiled. Then he thought about the uniform and sighed.

He felt like a coffee, but after a cigarette you need a real coffee and instant was the only option anywhere near the station. Deciding that it would be better than nothing, Igor went into a little shop, ordered one and drank it right there, next to a glass counter that was showcasing several varieties of sliced sausage and smoked chicken. Igor suddenly remembered the shopping his mother had asked him to get. He checked his pockets then asked for a fresh loaf of bread, half a kilo of sliced sausage, some butter and a tin of sprats. Poverty was certainly not an issue. Unable to control this burst of purchasing zeal, Igor looked directly at the young sales assistant and declared in a firm, confident voice, 'And a bottle of Koktebel brandy. No, not that one – the one with five stars!'

He was feeling happier now. It was nearly lunchtime, and hunger was gently tickling his insides. On the way home, he reflected on something that had only just occurred to him: he drank more brandy, or felt like doing so, when it was raining.

Igor and his mother had lunch sitting opposite one another in the kitchen, next to the rain-streaked window. Elena Andreevna was happy to partake of the brandy, although Igor was on his third glass before she had even finished her first.

'I wonder where Stepan's got to,' mused Igor.

'He's a grown man,' his mother replied with a shrug. 'And

besides, he's not officially registered here. So what if he's decided to move on? He's got no one to answer to but himself.'

'Mmm, not officially registered anywhere,' nodded Igor. 'People like that are usually wanted by the police.'

'Hold your tongue!' exclaimed Elena Andreevna. 'You never know what life is going to throw at you. It's only by the grace of God that you're not in his situation. He's clearly an honest and reliable man. And he thinks before he speaks. Unlike you!'

Igor said nothing. He glanced at the scales on the window-sill. He poured himself a fourth glass of brandy, still thinking about the gardener.

Later that afternoon, his mobile phone rang. It was Kolyan, brimming with his usual enthusiasm.

'Hi! What are you up to?'

'Nothing much. I'm at home.'

'Aren't you coming to my birthday party?'

'Oh, is it today?'

'Yes, that's why I'm calling. Come to the Petrovich club in a few hours' time. You know, the Retro Party place. Just make sure you wear a Young Pioneers' neck scarf or something like that, in keeping with the theme. They love all that Soviet stuff. The owner's probably a former Komsomol activist.'

Igor glanced at the wet window. He didn't feel like setting foot out of the house, let alone travelling to Kiev, but he couldn't exactly say that to his best friend without offending him. It was already too late to try and get out of it by pleading a cold or an upset stomach. If he'd wanted it to sound plausible, he should have said it right at the start of the conversation.

'OK, I'll think of something. I'm drinking a brandy in your

honour as we speak,' said Igor. 'Any specific requests, as far as presents are concerned?'

'Presents? Oh, you know me – I'll be happy with anything. Apart from flowers. I can't stand cut flowers. It's like watching your money wilt. No, I'd prefer hard cash!'

'Do you take roubles?'

'Roubles, dollars, it's all the same to me!'

Igor smiled, thinking about the Soviet roubles in the suitcase.

'Fine, roubles it is then! See you later!'

8

Igor's head was buzzing slightly from the brandy. He stood looking at the police uniform, which he'd laid out on his bed. The leather boots stood on the floor, shiny and proud. Nearby, on the bedside table, lay the bundles of Soviet hundred-rouble notes. They were held together with bands of paper.

I could take it with me and get changed there, thought Igor. He gave a sigh, then waved his doubts away. Oh, what the hell! I can put my anorak over the top. It's dark outside anyway, no one will be able to see.

Igor pulled on the boots, realising immediately that they were at least a size too big. He found some thick woollen socks, put them on over the thin pair he was already wearing and tried the boots on again. Now they seemed to fit.

'OK,' he nodded decisively. 'I'm a retro police officer for the evening. And I'll pay for everything with retro money!'

Igor put on the tight-fitting breeches and the tunic. He tightened the belt around his waist and went over to the mirror, leaving the gun and its holster on the bed. A smile crept over his face. He liked what he saw.

'Nice one,' he murmured. 'The girls are going to love it!'

Taking the gun out of the holster, he turned it over in his hands as he contemplated taking it with him. Common sense penetrated the brandy fog.

He stuck the gun under his mattress and closed the empty holster, then picked up the gold watch and put it in the left-hand pocket of the breeches. He would show it off in front of the birthday boy, if he got the chance. He looked out of the window. It was no longer raining. He went out into the hallway, trying to make as little noise as possible. His mother was watching television in the living room.

Looking down at his feet in order to avoid the puddles, Igor walked out of the gate and headed towards the bus station. As he walked he ran his hands over the pockets of the breeches, enjoying the way they bulged with the bundles of roubles. If only they were full of hryvnas, or – even better – dollars! The evening seemed darker than usual. Igor looked up at the heavy sky. Never mind, he thought, the party at the Petrovich club should be fun. He just had to make sure he didn't miss the last train home, as the shared minibuses could be pretty unreliable late at night.

The darkness seemed to wrap itself around Igor for a few seconds. It seemed strangely impenetrable. Either that or something was wrong with his eyes. In this 'dark' moment

Igor suddenly remembered that his uncle had died from drinking fake brandy. First he went blind and started crying out, 'I can't see anything!' Then he stopped speaking altogether, lay down on the sofa and died. Or so Igor had been told – he hadn't witnessed it first hand, of course. But ever since then he'd checked the smell of opened bottles of brandy before drinking from them.

Igor was still able to feel the hard surface of the road with every step, so he brushed off his alarm and kept walking. Suddenly the darkness released him, and he saw lights in the distance. He looked around, trying to work out whether his eyes were playing tricks on him or whether the street lamps had simply gone out. It happened sometimes. You could be sitting watching television at home, when suddenly – snap! Complete darkness. Sometimes it lasted for five minutes, sometimes several hours.

Behind him was a solid wall of darkness. Nothing was visible except the lights up ahead. Must be a power cut, thought Igor. He nodded decisively and carried on walking.

Igor suddenly felt a little wave of pleasure as he thought about the boots. They were so comfortable! They'd been at least a size too big when he'd first tried them on, but now they felt as though they'd been made to measure by a master cobbler. His delight abruptly changed to suspicion. He stopped and looked down at the boots but found that he could hardly even see them. He cleared his throat and quickened his pace, hoping to reach the lights more quickly.

I should have reached the bus station by now, and that's always brightly lit, thought Igor. It's surrounded by kiosks too, and what about that little bar? He peered into the distance, feeling increasingly anxious. The lights weren't where he expected them to be.

Igor started to feel hot, either from anxiety or from the strange feeling of disorientation, and he broke into a nervous sweat. He took his anorak off and threw it over his shoulder, hooking his finger into the loop inside the collar.

'Hey, lieutenant! What's the hurry?' a woman's voice suddenly called from behind him. 'Have you got the right time?'

Igor stopped and glanced over his shoulder. He couldn't see anything.

'No,' he said warily, peering into the darkness. 'I've got a watch, but it's not working.'

'Lucky you!' The woman's voice contained the hint of a threat.

'Manka, you idiot! Are you blind? He's a policeman, not a soldier!' Her male companion's voice was an urgent whisper. 'Come on, let's go! Hurry up!'

Igor heard footsteps hurriedly receding. Now he was scared. He started walking towards the lights again, as fast as he could. He reached them eventually and came to a halt in front of some well-lit gates, behind which he could see grey factory buildings.

'"Ochakov Wine Factory",' Igor read aloud and looked around.

Something stirred in his pocket, and the sensation unnerved him. He put his hand in and felt the golden watch. Its heart had started beating. Surprised, Igor took the watch out, and when he brought it to his ear he heard a loud ticking sound.

What the hell's going on? he thought. How can a watch

suddenly start working, just like that? And what's this Ochakov Wine Factory doing here in Irpen? Maybe they've just built it, I guess. That's what it's like these days . . . new buildings are going up as fast as old ones are coming down.

He suddenly heard a familiar tune from behind the fence, followed by a man's voice. 'The time is midnight in Moscow.'

Igor shook his head and frowned. He opened the watch's protective gold cover. Both hands were pointing straight to twelve.

Suddenly he heard a door slam, followed by the sound of footsteps behind the gates. Igor quickly darted to one side, just as a small lorry with a covered wagon drove out of the gates. It was an old model, the kind Igor had only ever seen in films set in the past. The lorry drove out onto the square, turned right and slowly drove away, its headlights illuminating the road ahead. The gates closed after it, and then everything was silent once again.

Igor looked around. The lorry had disappeared into the night. Igor's eyes were drawn back to the factory entrance, now the only source of light, and beyond them to the roof of the security guard's booth and the grey factory walls.

Igor contemplated knocking and asking the security guard where he was, but before he had the chance one of the gates swung ajar. Igor heard an urgent whisper, and then a head poked out of the gap between the gates. It paused, apparently listening.

'Go on, get a move on!' urged a man's voice from behind the gates. It was loud enough to reach Igor, who had retreated back into the darkness.

A young lad emerged, with a strange bulky sack thrown

over his shoulder. He looked around, waved back at the security guard and took several awkward steps away from the gates. Then he stopped and adjusted the sack. The gates closed again behind him, and there was a heavy metallic sound as the guard drew the bolt.

Igor emerged from the darkness and walked briskly towards the lad, intending to ask for directions to the bus station.

Seeing a policeman striding purposefully towards him, the lad threw the sack to the ground and froze. The sack barely made a sound as it hit the ground but lay there shuddering, as though it were alive. It seemed to be made of leather.

'I . . . uh, it's the first time I . . .' began the lad, stammering in fright. 'Please don't . . . It'll kill my mother if she finds out! She's got a weak heart . . . My father fought in the war, came back a cripple . . . died a year later . . .'

'What on earth are you talking about?' asked Igor, astonished. The lad's incomprehensible fear had immediately put him in control of the situation.

'The wine,' the lad whimpered hopelessly. He looked down at the leather wineskin.

'How far is it to the bus station?'

The lad stopped snivelling and looked up at the man in the police uniform, not quite understanding the question.

'About twenty minutes' walk,' he said, his voice a little steadier.

'What's in there?' Igor prodded the leather sack with the toe of his boot. It yielded easily to the pressure and then quickly regained its strange form the moment he removed his foot.

'I told you, it's wine . . . It's the first time . . . It's Rkatsiteli . . . I've never done it before . . . Don't arrest me!'

Igor suddenly understood the reason for the lad's alarm, and the reason he was acting so guilty. He smiled.

Noticing the smirk on Igor's face, the lad grew nervous.

'I'll take it straight back!' he said, looking pointedly at the sack.

'Hang on, let's not be too hasty,' replied Igor, trying to imitate the wine thief's peculiar intonation. The lad didn't sound like a local. 'Where are you from?'

'From Ochakov. I grew up here. My mother works at the market and I work here, at the wine factory.'

'From here? From Ochakov?' repeated Igor, puzzled. 'Hmm, there's something funny about all this.'

'What do you mean?' the lad asked cautiously.

'It's just that . . .' said Igor, looking around. 'It's a bit dark, isn't it? How old are you?'

'Twenty-one. My name's Ivan Samokhin. My patronymic is Vasilievich.'

'When were you born, Ivan Vasilievich Samokhin?' Igor began to speak more slowly, carefully enunciating every word. He noticed that his own intonation sounded a bit different too.

'The eighth of May . . . 1936. It's a pity I wasn't born a day later, then my birthday would have been on Victory Day.'

Igor thought about it. But it couldn't be 1957 – that was ridiculous! Igor looked at the wine thief, then at the sack of wine.

'How come you drink so much?' he asked.

'It's not for me! I used to be really good at sport . . . I even represented our region in cross-country running. No, it's to sell at the market,' said the lad. Then he stopped abruptly, beating his right temple with his fist in frustration at his own indiscretion.

'I see,' said Igor, beginning to nod.

'How long will I get?' whispered the lad. 'Ten years in prison? Or more?'

'What date is it today?' asked Igor, ignoring the wine thief's question.

'The third of October.'

'Come on then,' said Igor, as though he'd had an idea. He pointed to the wineskin. 'Pick that up, and let's go.'

Vanya Samokhin picked up the leather sack and threw it over his shoulder. He looked back at the policeman. 'Where are we going?' he asked, apparently resigned to his fate.

'To the bus station!' Igor motioned with his hand to indicate that the lad should walk in front, as though he really had been arrested.

Vanya Samokhin walked slowly. His burden was heavy and awkward. It would have been different if the wine had been his, but it wasn't any more. He wanted to stop and look back at the policeman, to appeal once more for mercy, and to offer him the sack of wine for his kindness. Unfortunately this particular lieutenant was clearly a man of integrity. Neither his eyes nor his voice gave any indication that it would be worth even trying to negotiate with him.

They walked along in the darkness for about five minutes. The silence was broken only by the soles of their boots against the cobbles. Suddenly Vanya Samokhin stopped.

'What's the matter?' The policeman's voice struck him in the back.

'I'm worn out.'

'Is it much further?'

'About ten minutes.'

'All right, have a little rest,' said Igor, his voice somehow softer, more human. Vanya Samokhin immediately felt a spark of hope. This was the first time the policeman had spoken as though he weren't wearing a uniform.

Vanya Samokhin carefully lowered the sack of wine to the ground, then straightened up and took a few deep breaths.

'Is it all right if I smoke?' he asked.

'Go ahead,' replied Igor.

'Er, I haven't got any cigarettes,' admitted Vanya Samokhin.

Igor took out a packet of cigarettes, opened it and offered him one.

'I don't recognise these,' said Vanya Samokhin, unable to hide his surprise. 'You're not from round here, are you?'

'No.' Igor shook his head.

'So where are you from?'

'Kiev.'

'The capital!' exclaimed the lad, fear returning to his voice. 'Did they send you here to investigate the wine factory?'

'Why, are things really that bad?' Igor's lips curled into a half-smile. 'Have you and your friends cleaned the place out?'

'No! Well, sort of . . . But the management aren't involved!'

'No, I'm not here to investigate the wine factory,' said Igor, deciding to play along with the conversation. 'I'm here for a completely different reason.'

'A completely different reason?' repeated Vanya Samokhin, inhaling the smoke from his cigarette. 'Because of the gangs?'

'Exactly,' nodded Igor, looking straight into the lad's eyes.

'Yeah, they're everywhere these days. Are you after Chagin?'

Igor flinched involuntarily at the sound of the familiar surname. This made Vanya flinch too, as though the policeman's reaction had alarmed him: had Fima Chagin's reputation grown to such an extent that even policemen from the capital were afraid of him?

'Why, do you know him?' asked Igor.

'Everyone knows him! Well, I've seen him around, but I don't actually know him. Why would I? I'm an upstanding citizen!'

Igor started laughing, quietly but with genuine amusement. His shoulders shook as he pointed at the sack of wine.

'But I'm not a real thief . . . I'd never kill anyone,' whined Samokhin. 'This is the first time I've ever taken something that doesn't belong to me!'

'I somehow doubt that.' Igor's voice sounded colder now. It had put the police uniform back on again, and even Igor could hear the difference. 'Your mother works at the market . . . I catch you taking wine from the wine factory . . . Tell me, what does your mother sell?'

Vanya Samokhin seemed to choke on his answer and started hiccuping. The cigarette fell from his mouth and hit the ground, sending a shower of sparks across the road. Vanya bent down and picked it up. Still hiccuping, he wiped the end with his fingers and put it back in his mouth.

'Let me see . . . Does she, by any chance, sell wine?' Igor asked with a smile.

'Yes,' nodded the lad. 'We make our own. Our whole yard is covered in vines.'

'You make some, and you take some,' Igor remarked laconically. He noticed that Vanya Samokhin's eyes were darting from side to side, as though he'd decided to make a run for it and was trying to decide on his escape route.

'Pick up the wine!' ordered Igor.

Vanya Samokhin's eyes immediately stopped darting about. With a heavy sigh he picked up the sack of wine and heaved it onto his shoulder. He looked back at Igor.

'Don't worry,' said Igor. 'I'm not going to arrest you.'

The lad's mouth fell open, and the unfinished cigarette fell out of his mouth again. This time Vanya made no move to pick it up. He just stared at Igor.

'You'll have to write a declaration, though, and I'll expect you to help me with some information. Shall we shake on it?'

Vanya bit his dry lips and paused before answering.

'You're an upstanding citizen, aren't you? You just said so! Well, upstanding citizens help the police with their inquiries.'

Vanya nodded.

'Like I said, I'm here for a specific reason,' continued Igor, entering into the spirit of his performance. 'I'm not interested in your petty crime,' he said, nodding at the sack. 'Take it home and give it to your mother.'

'So what are you interested in, comrade lieutenant?' Vanya Samokhin asked, warily but at the same time rather obsequiously.

'Chagin and his gang . . . Actually, mainly his gang.'

Vanya nodded again. 'I'll do whatever I can to help.'

'Good. Can I spend the night at your place?'

'I thought you were going to the bus station.'

'There aren't any buses at this time of night, are there?' asked Igor, with a barely perceptible smile.

'No,' answered Vanya, flustered.

'So what would be the point of going to the bus station? Can I spend the night at your place?'

'Of course! In that case . . .'

Vanya set off again, leaving his sentence unfinished. He walked with renewed vigour and seemed to carry his stolen burden with greater ease. Igor fell into step a few paces behind him, as though subconsciously keeping a safe distance. They entered the sleeping town unnoticed and unobserved. Fences appeared along the sides of the road, and behind them detached houses made dark silhouettes against the grey sky. Ochakov was fast asleep. Lights flashed somewhere in the distance, but the windows of the houses were dark. About fifteen minutes later they turned into a courtyard that was overgrown with vines. Vanya took the sack of wine into the shed, then cautiously opened the door to the house and let Igor in.

They went into what must have been the living room. 'You can sleep here,' said Vanya, gesturing in the half-darkness towards an old-fashioned sofa with a high wooden back that extended up the wall, incorporating a mirror and shelves for displaying ornaments. 'I'm afraid I don't know where the sheets are.'

'Don't worry about it, I'll be fine with a blanket,' whispered Igor. 'Where do your parents sleep?'

Vanya silently pointed at some folding wooden doors.

'Mother sleeps in there, on the left, and my room's at the end of the hall.'

He went off and came back carrying a quilted blanket.

'Can I go to bed now?' he whispered. 'Is it all right if I write the declaration tomorrow?'

'Go ahead! You can write it tomorrow,' nodded Igor.

Vanya left the room but returned almost immediately.

'Here, comrade lieutenant, drink this. It'll help you sleep.' He handed Igor a large glass of white wine. It smelt sharp and sour.

Barely suppressing the desire to wrinkle his nose, Igor carefully took the glass and sipped the wine. He looked at Vanya and nodded. Satisfied, Vanya nodded in response but didn't move.

'Is it from the wine factory?' asked Igor.

'Yes,' said Vanya. 'Our home-made wine's not ready yet . . . You have to drink it all, otherwise you won't be able to appreciate the taste!'

The last thing Igor felt like doing was getting into an argument with Vanya Samokhin about wine-tasting techniques, so he downed the wine in three mouthfuls and handed the glass back to his host. Only then did Vanya leave the room.

Igor removed his boots, unbuckled his belt and undressed. He folded the uniform and placed it neatly on a nearby chair, then quickly lay down and pulled the blanket over himself. He was immediately sucked into a strange kind of weightlessness. As his sense of spatial orientation ebbed away, he twitched and fell into the abyss.

9

Igor woke up with a headache. His head wasn't actually aching so much as buzzing, as though several bees had flown into it and were unsuccessfully trying to find their way out, bumping repeatedly into his temples, the back of his head and his forehead.

He opened his eyes and wiped a hand over his sweaty brow. He forced himself into an upright position and sat on the edge of his bed. Everything outside his window was grey, and he could hear the monotonous murmur of television voices from the living room.

'Ma!' called Igor, and immediately the sound of his own voice intensified the painful buzzing in his head.

Elena Andreevna looked into her son's bedroom.

'What's up, son?'

'Have we got any aspirin? I've got a splitting headache.'

'Did you have too much to drink yesterday, or is it the old pains?' asked his mother, with a mixture of disapproval and sympathy.

'Too much to drink,' Igor nodded.

She went into the kitchen, where they kept all their medicines in an old shoebox in the cupboard.

Igor stood up and walked over to the window, then turned and looked back into the room. His eyes fell on the police uniform, neatly folded in a pile, and the old-fashioned peaked cap.

That was a pretty strange dream! Or did it really happen? thought Igor.

He sighed and took a tracksuit out of his chest of drawers. As soon as he was dressed, he called Kolyan.

'Hello there!' Kolyan sounded pleased to hear from him. 'How are you feeling?'

'Listen,' Igor said slowly, carefully choosing every word to try and avoid sounding stupid, 'did I . . . did I turn up yesterday?'

'I can't believe you're asking me that!' Kolyan burst out laughing. 'Can you really not remember? Must have been a good night then! Of course you turned up. You were wearing some old military uniform and had obviously been drinking before you got there. You were really winding up the bouncers, you know! We managed to drag you away from them just in time. They wanted to throw you out, and it was chucking it down outside.'

'Right, I see . . . What were we drinking, in the club?'

'What weren't we drinking! You were on the brandy, mainly. You must've had a bottle and a half, maybe even two . . . We had to flag a car down to take you home. You were in such a state, we gave the guy two hundred hryvnas. So you can pay me back when you get the chance!'

'Right, I see,' Igor repeated slowly. He couldn't hear his own voice properly because of the buzzing in his head. 'What happened before that?'

'In Petrovich? You're kidding! Can't you remember any of it?'

'No,' admitted Igor. 'And I've got a splitting headache.'

'We were just drinking, having a laugh, dancing to old music . . .'

Igor suddenly felt the sharp, sour taste of cheap white wine on his tongue.

'Did I drink any wine?'

'Wine? Yeah, right at the start. You tried some French Chablis, then announced that it tasted like cheap vinegar and washed it down with some Armenian brandy.'

'All right, I'll call you again later,' said Igor, with a weary sigh.

'Take it easy, old man!' Kolyan replied cheerfully.

Igor's head was feeling calmer by the afternoon. His thoughts had finally gathered themselves into something resembling order. He went through his memories with a fine-toothed comb, searching for the slightest grain of truth or credibility. In the interests of soothing his agitated soul he was equally keen to find proof that it was merely the fruit of his drunken, and consequently overactive, imagination. But however many times he played back the evening's events, however closely he examined the details, everything still felt incredibly real – and remarkably plausible. The watch that had suddenly started ticking and showing 'Moscow time', Vanya Samokhin, the Ochakov Wine Factory, the glass of white wine . . . And, perhaps most significantly, Vanya's suggestion that Fima Chagin might be the reason a policeman from Kiev had been sent to Ochakov. The only thing on the other side of the scales of Igor's common sense was the brandy he'd been drinking before Kolyan had called. Yes, and there was something else – the party in the Petrovich club in the Podil district! Igor couldn't remember a thing about the birthday celebrations. He couldn't remember where the club was, or even where he'd seen the poster advertising the 'Retro Party'.

Igor put his hand into the pocket of the policeman's breeches and took out the gold watch. He brought it to his ear. Silence. He opened it. The hands had stopped at half past one. Igor sighed, utterly perplexed. Exhausted by his own unanswered questions, he drank a cup of coffee then went out into the yard. The shed door was still shut and padlocked. Stepan was obviously still not back.

Sparse but heavy raindrops were falling from the sullen sky.

When Igor looked up he saw a black storm cloud hanging low over Irpen, ready to unleash its contents at any moment, and he hurried back inside. The rain began hammering down on the slate roof the moment Igor entered the house.

10

The afternoon downpour lasted several hours. When it suddenly stopped, the inhabitants of Irpen had no choice but to accept that the evening was upon them. Autumn evenings are all too brief; they are followed quickly, almost imperceptibly, by night. This particular night, with its leaden, starless sky, promised to be impenetrable.

Putting aside the book he'd been staring at for the past three hours, Igor glanced out of his bedroom window and then at the clock. His thoughts returned to the night before. What would happen, he wondered, if he were to do the same again? What if he were to drink a couple of glasses of brandy, then put on the police uniform and take another walk towards the bus station? No one would be out in this weather, at this time of night. Even if they were, they wouldn't pay him any attention.

Igor went into the kitchen and poured himself a brandy. He drank it slowly, then poured himself another and drank that too. Noticing out of the corner of his eye a prescription for heart medication in the raised pan of his mother's scales, he poured a third glass of brandy and took it back to his bedroom. He swallowed a mouthful, then put the glass to one side and felt in the pockets of the breeches to check that the bundles of Soviet roubles were still there. With the next sip of brandy he felt a warmth on his tongue, which soon reached his nose and his forehead. Igor broke into a light sweat. He raised his glass to take another sip but it was already empty, so he went to the kitchen and refilled it.

About half an hour later Igor felt a heady rush of adrenalin and confidence. He smiled to himself. Approaching the police uniform more decisively, he put on the tunic and breeches, pulled on the boots and buckled up the belt. This time he deliberately kept the gun in its holster. He put on the peaked cap and lifted the round table mirror up to get a better look at himself. This cheered him up still further. What a fine figure of a man! he thought.

As soon as Igor shut the gate behind him and set off towards the bus station the darkness around him intensified, as though it were attempting to swallow him whole. But his feet kept walking straight ahead, apparently not in need of a sighted guide, and the soles of his leather boots met the concrete surface of the road with reassuring familiarity.

Fear crept up on Igor several times, surprising him from behind or from the side. Each time he would stop and look around, trusting his hearing more than his sight, but everything was quiet.

After a while a faint light appeared ahead of him, and this became a reference point. About twenty minutes later Igor recognised the illuminated gates of the Ochakov Wine Factory. He stopped under the trees, about twenty metres from the gates, and wondered what was going on. Was it really happening again? Was it going to be like that American film, where the same day repeats itself endlessly, driving the main character insane?

Just then the green gates opened. They seemed to be taunting Igor, mocking his apprehensions. He heard the rumbling of an engine, and then the same little old lorry that he'd seen before drove out of the grounds of the wine factory. It turned right and drove away from Igor, lighting up the road with its headlights. The gates closed and silence gradually seeped back to fill the space illuminated by the powerful factory lights. Strictly speaking, the factory lights illuminated everything on the other side of the concrete fence and the green gates; the square in front of the gates was lit by a street lamp.

The gates suddenly creaked again and opened slightly. A lad with a strange sack over his shoulder peeped out of them, just like the day before.

Now he's going to come out and wave back at the guard. Then the gates will close, and the metal bolt will make a loud clang, thought Igor. Then I'll come out from under these trees and walk over to him, and he'll panic, throw the sack on the ground and ask me not to arrest him.

Just as Igor had predicted, the lad waved to the guard and the bolt made a heavy, metallic noise as the gates closed. Igor walked out from under the dark trees and took several decisive and exaggeratedly stern steps towards him.

'Oh!' Vanya exclaimed happily, a smile lighting up his face. 'Where did you disappear to this morning? I brought you a cup of tea and some sliced sausage for breakfast.'

Igor continued walking, his demeanour no longer either

decisive or stern. He stopped in front of Vanya and shook the hand that was held out to him.

'Did you have some urgent business to attend to?' enquired Vanya. He adjusted the sack of wine, which had slipped down to his forearm.

'At it again, I see,' remarked Igor, ignoring the question and nodding at the wine.

'Er . . . I thought we had an agreement. I'll write the declaration right now, if you like.'

'Don't worry about it.' Igor brushed away the suggestion, irritated and confused by both this strange parallel reality and the fact that it didn't quite correspond to his expectations.

'Let's go back to my place. I've got something to tell you,' continued Vanya, with a friendly smile.

'You're Vanya Samokhin, right?' Igor asked, keen to establish beyond all doubt that what was happening right now was a direct continuation of what had happened the night before.

'That's me! Come on.'

They set off into the darkness, just as before. Only this time Igor wasn't glancing nervously around him but walking calmly behind Vanya Samokhin, who was carrying the sack of stolen wine with ease.

They went into Vanya's house, trying to make as little noise as possible. Vanya led Igor to the room with the old-fashioned sofa.

'Go ahead, get ready for bed,' he whispered. 'I'll be back in a minute.'

About two minutes later he returned with a glass of wine, again full to the brim.

'This is for you,' he said quietly. 'It'll help you sleep.'

Igor took off the peaked cap and sat down on the sofa without undressing. He felt that as soon as he lay down and closed his eyes this parallel reality would cease to exist; then he would never find the answers to the questions that were multiplying by the minute.

He took the glass from Vanya Samokhin and drank the wine, feeling the familiar sharp, sour taste on his tongue. Then he nodded at Vanya, indicating that he should sit too. Vanya sat down.

'So, you said you had something interesting to tell me,' Igor said.

'It's just that . . . I haven't written the declaration yet.'

'All right then, go and get a piece of paper,' said Igor.

Vanya left the room and came straight back bearing an exercise book and a tin inkwell with a fountain pen sticking out of it. He sat down at the oval table.

'Tell me what to write, comrade lieutenant,' he said.

Igor hesitated. It was taking him a little longer to get into character this time.

'All right,' he said after a pause. 'Write this . . . I, Ivan whatever-your-patronymic-is Samokhin, agree to cooperate voluntarily . . .'

Vanya Samokhin bent over the exercise book and started scratching at it with his fountain pen, dipping it in the inkwell every few seconds. Igor waited until the scratching stopped. Vanya raised his head and looked questioningly at the police officer.

'. . . to cooperate voluntarily with the police force,' continued Igor, 'and am prepared to risk my life to assist in the fight against criminal elements –'

Vanya suddenly looked up at Igor, panic and confusion written all over his face.

'Is there a problem?' asked Igor.

'I never agreed to risk my life,' Vanya said quietly. 'I'm happy to help you, but not if it means risking my life. My mother's not well. Her heart . . .'

'All right,' sighed Igor. 'Leave out the bit about risk, just say that you'll help.'

'You're paid to risk your life, and they give you a gun to protect yourself!' Before returning to the declaration Vanya glanced pointedly at Igor's holster.

'To assist in the fight against criminal elements,' repeated Igor. 'Date, place, signature.'

Once he'd finished writing, Vanya neatly ripped the page from the exercise book, folded it into four and handed it to Igor, who took the piece of paper and put it into the breast pocket of his tunic.

'Can I go to bed now?' asked Vanya.

'Why don't we . . .?' Igor wondered aloud.

'Why don't we what?' asked Vanya cautiously.

'Why don't we go for a little walk? You can show me the sights.'

'What sights?' Vanya was puzzled.

'Well, Fima Chagin's house, for a start.'

'Haven't you ever seen it before?' Vanya's surprise was tinged with condescension, as though he'd suddenly realised that his guest was not a police lieutenant at all but the village idiot.

'Of course! But it would be good to see it again, with two pairs of eyes!'

Sensing trust and respect in the way the police officer spoke to him, Vanya raised no further objections. He stood up eagerly and turned towards the door.

'Let's go,' he said. 'I'll show you a short cut.'

Vanya led Igor outside. They walked about thirty metres along the unlit street, then turned left. They crossed an abandoned yard and an old garden and came out onto a different street, which was evidently more important – the street lamps at the crossroads were not merely for show but actually worked. The single-storey brick buildings were more impressive too. Their dark windows reflected the night.

'There it is,' whispered Vanya, gesturing towards an unsightly building with a high socle all the way around it and a set of steps leading up to a pair of folding wooden doors.

They stopped. A motorbike roared somewhere in the distance. Igor felt on edge.

'Someone's up,' said Vanya, staring at the house.

Igor glanced at the dark windows. 'What makes you say that?'

Vanya gestured towards the right side of the house. Peering more closely, Igor noticed a glow of light that must have been coming from an unseen window at the back of the house.

Igor beckoned to Vanya to follow him. They stopped by the gate.

'Has he got a dog?' whispered Igor.

'No! It would never stop barking.'

'What do you mean?'

'There are always people coming and going . . . Dogs don't like being disturbed all the time.'

Igor nodded. Just then there was a muffled bang and he froze, listening intently. The sound of men's voices came from somewhere nearby. Igor glanced at Vanya and gestured towards a broad apple tree about five metres to the right, which stood up against the fence. They moved quickly towards it and hid under its branches, which still bore several fruit.

Fima Chagin's front door creaked open. Two men came out onto the doorstep and lit cigarettes.

'When will he be back?' asked one of them.

'Two or three years. Maybe sooner, if they knock a bit off.'

'Well, that would be great. Tell him to bring a note from you when he comes to see me.'

'Right you are, then,' said the second man. Throwing a large cloth bundle over his shoulder, he walked down the steps and headed towards the gate.

'Iosip!' called the man on the doorstep. He threw his cigarette to the ground and pressed the toe of his boot into it.

'Yes?' Iosip turned round.

'What if he doesn't come back in three years?'

'What if he does come back and you're not here? Or the house burns down in the meantime?'

'Hold your tongue, Iosip! What a thing to say! If the house ever burns down, I'd better hope that I burn with it.'

'You've got a point there,' replied Iosip. He cleared his throat. 'Don't tempt fate. He'll be back.'

The gate creaked. Iosip went out into the street, spat on the ground and walked away. The front door closed and silence descended once again. Igor and Vanya emerged from under the tree. Vanya picked an apple and bit into it. Igor glared at him.

'What?' whispered Vanya. 'They've gone now, and I'm hungry!'

'Do you know that Iosip chap?' asked Igor.

Vanya shook his head.

'What about the one who was smoking?'

'That was Fima Chagin.'

'Fima Chagin?' repeated Igor. 'But he's so young.'

'Why shouldn't he be?' Vanya shrugged.

'Anyway, what did you have to tell me?' asked Igor, referring to the comment Vanya had made when they'd been standing in front of the wine factory.

'Oh yes, my mother said that Fima's having an affair with Red Valya! She said he's always calling on her at the market.'

'Who's Red Valya?'

'She works in the fish section at the market. Everyone knows Red Valya.'

'What does she sell?' asked Igor.

'Fish, of course. What else do you think they sell in the fish section? Her husband's a fisherman. He catches it, and she sells it.'

'Will you point her out to me?'

'There's no need. You can't miss her. You'll hear her from a hundred paces.'

'All right,' nodded Igor. 'Let's go back and get some sleep. Tomorrow morning we're going to the market.'

Igor took off the peaked cap and the belt with the holster then lay down fully dressed on the ancient sofa, acutely aware of its invisible springs. He pulled the blanket up over himself. His body was exhausted and craving sleep, but his agitated mind was wide awake. Igor's main concern was that if he fell asleep he would wake up in his own comfortable bed in Irpen, thereby scuppering his chances of finding out more or of ever setting eyes on Red Valya. What then? Would he have to drink brandy again and take another nocturnal stroll? Igor realised that he didn't have a lot of choice in the matter, that at some point he would have to surrender to sleep whether he liked it or not. A plan was already in place for the following day, and as long as he didn't drive himself mad trying to reconcile the real and parallel worlds then there was still a chance that he would make it to the market in Ochakov in 1957. If this plan came to fruition, then he would even be able to buy something there! He felt both pockets of the breeches, which bulged agreeably with the bundles of banknotes. Each individual note was big enough to twist into a perfect paper bag for carrying sunflower seeds.

11

A creaking, clanging noise started up outside the window just before 6 a.m. the following morning. Igor opened his eyes and immediately looked around to see where he was. His eyes took in the high wooden back of the sofa above him, the mirror, the shelves and the black leatherette that was fastened to the sides of the sofa.

Igor was just contemplating the two porcelain figurines of children that stood on the shelves when the door opened and Vanya came in, already dressed. He was splashing cologne onto his cheeks.

'Good morning!' he greeted Igor brightly. 'So, are you ready to go to the market?'

Igor threw off the blanket and stood up. He brushed out the creases in the uniform and pulled on the boots, which were standing on the wooden floor next to the bed.

'Where's the toilet?' he asked Vanya.

'Outside, at the back of the house.'

'And the washroom?'

'That's outside too, just round the corner. There's a sink on the wall of the shed.'

Igor cleared his throat and glanced at the peaked cap.

'Where's your mother?' he asked.

'She's already at the market. People get up early here. They're at work by six . . . and drunk by three,' Vanya answered with a grin.

Emboldened by the knowledge that there was no one else at home, Igor went out into the yard and immediately spotted the sink. He washed his hands and face. The sour taste of the wine from the night before lingered on his tongue. Igor rinsed his mouth out with water, but the sour taste refused to go away. He looked at the little wooden shelf that was fixed to the wall of the shed next to the sink. It held two slivers of soap, a small tin box and several frayed toothbrushes, but there was no toothpaste.

Igor moved the toothbrushes to check underneath them, but there was definitely no toothpaste. He opened the tin box. It was full of white powder.

'Is this what they use instead?' he wondered, vaguely recalling something he'd once heard about people in the olden days cleaning their teeth with powder rather than paste.

Igor selected the least frayed toothbrush, rinsed it under the tap and stuck it into the powder. When he took it out, the brush felt noticeably heavier. He brought it to his mouth and was surprised to discover that the powder didn't taste of anything at all. He brushed his teeth, rinsed his mouth out again and noticed that the wine taste had disappeared. Not the slightest trace remained.

'I've made you some cocoa,' said Vanya, meeting him in the hallway with a white enamel mug. 'Here.'

The cocoa was far too sweet. Igor sat down with the mug at the kitchen table and looked out of the window, which was hung with a fine lace curtain. The delicate fabric featured exactly the same pattern as the cloth – either a serviette or a tablecloth, Igor couldn't tell – that was arranged neatly over the large radio on top of the chest of drawers.

'I, uh . . .' Vanya sat down opposite him. He looked like he was wrestling with his thoughts. 'You'll have to go to the market on your own. If I went with you . . . well, it wouldn't look good. Our police officers only accompany people to the market when they've been robbed. They go there to try and recover the stolen property.'

'But how will I recognise Red Valya?'

'Easy,' Vanya Samokhin waved his hand. 'You can't miss her. She's the only redhead there. You'll hear her first, and then you'll see her!'

'What do you mean?'

'Her voice is loud and distinctive,' explained Vanya. 'Perfect for the market.'

'How will I find my way back? Have you got a map?'

'What do you mean?'

‘A map of Ochakov, showing the streets and the market, so I can find your house.’

‘There aren’t any maps of Ochakov. You must know about the military aircraft, and the port . . . It’s all very hush-hush. We’re not allowed maps.’

‘All right, in that case draw me a map showing the way to the market, and I’ll work it out from there.’

‘I can do that,’ nodded Vanya. He fetched the exercise book and a pencil and busied himself with an elaborate sketch.

‘Keep it simple, so I can understand it,’ remarked Igor.

‘All right,’ murmured Vanya, without looking up.

When he eventually finished his sketch, he carefully tore the page from the exercise book and passed it to Igor. ‘There, you see . . . that’s my house, there’s the street . . . you have to go past the park and turn left, then keep going straight and you’re there.’

‘Write down your address, just in case,’ said Igor.

Vanya took the piece of paper, added his address and gave it back. Igor studied the map and found it reasonably comprehensible. He finished his cocoa and looked at Vanya.

‘Are you going to stay at home?’ he asked.

‘I’m on the second shift today. I’ll be at home till midday, then at the factory.’

‘What do you actually do there, apart from steal wine?’ Igor asked with a smile.

‘I’m a general worker,’ said Vanya, lowering his eyes. ‘They’re going to send me to the Nikolaev College of Trade and Industry in the spring, to study wine-making. When I graduate, I’ll be a wine technologist.’

‘All right, stay here. I’ll be back before twelve,’ said Igor.

He went in to pick up the peaked cap, put it on and looked in the mirror. Then he nodded goodbye to Vanya and went out onto the doorstep.

Vanya's hand-drawn map was surprisingly easy to follow. The closer Igor got to the market, the more people he encountered, and the air was filled with a joyous chirruping, twittering noise, like a chorus of human birdsong. Several young army officers cycled past, and one of them waved to Igor. He was overtaken by a brand-new brown Pobeda car with a chubby, red-faced driver at the wheel.

Igor really wanted to stop for a few minutes to look at the world around him, to watch the people and study their faces, to let it all sink in. Everything seemed slightly strange, natural and unnatural at the same time, as though old black-and-white newspaper images had been scanned into a computer and digitally coloured. Nevertheless he managed to suppress this desire and his curiosity and kept walking at a steady pace, rhythmically measuring out each step on the pavement.

Finally he noticed the gates to the market, through which a steady stream of cheerful humanity flowed in both directions – some holding baskets, others with bags. To the right of the gates two men wearing dark blue quilted jackets were gluing a colour poster to the noticeboard. The poster appeared to show a flying ball with four knives sticking out of it. A little further along a woman wearing overalls in the same colour blue, with a broom at her feet, was pinning the day's newspaper into a flat, glass-fronted display unit designed for the purpose. As Igor approached she closed the window and started wiping the glass with a cloth, enhancing its transparency in order to render the contents more accessible to the curious public.

Stopping in front of the poster, Igor realised that the 'ball with knives' he'd seen from a distance was actually the first artificial satellite in space. Several other people gathered around the noticeboard, and Igor took advantage of this legitimate opportunity to observe them more closely. He noticed a couple of police officers nearby, wearing exactly the same uniform as him. Alarmed by the prospect of a possible encounter with 'colleagues', he strode decisively into the market and instantly felt as though he'd fallen into a beehive.

'Hey, comrade lieutenant, try one of my apples!' An ample saleswoman with plump, painted lips immediately started making eyes at Igor. 'Sweet as a peach!' she cried, holding an apple out to him.

The seller's voice was also as sweet as a peach, and sticky too. Igor could almost feel it clinging to his ear and trickling down his cheek. Smiling self-consciously and shaking his head, he walked away from the woman and continued down the central aisle of the market.

The noises, sounds, voices and words began to revolve slowly around Igor's head, making it spin. He screwed up his eyes and stopped walking, then opened his eyes again. It felt like he and all the other people at the market were in a giant aquarium, except instead of water this aquarium was full of a strange, dense air, in which bodies moved slowly and words were stretched and drawn out. As they reached your ears the words became louder then gradually faded again into silence as they receded into the distance, like aeroplanes high up in the sky.

Igor tried putting his hands over his ears and contemplating the world without sound. Everything looked perfectly normal, including people's faces and their expressions. The only indication that he was in the previous century was the way people were dressed – that and a few other details, such as the old-fashioned scales.

'Comrade lieutenant, can you change fifty roubles for me?' A woman turned towards him holding a banknote between her chubby fingers. She had a plump face and curly chestnut hair pulled into a chignon.

'I'm afraid not,' said Igor, increasing his pace.

He noticed that he was in the vegetable section. Someone bumped into him accidentally and apologised. Igor began to feel claustrophobic. Spotting a passageway between the stalls, he quickly moved into the adjacent trading aisle. This aisle was less crowded, and the sellers seemed to have a calmer approach to business. They stood patiently at their stalls, waiting for customers to come to them rather than calling out.

Igor approached an old woman selling bunches of succulent, freshly washed carrots. 'Where's the fish section?' he asked.

'That way,' she gestured further down the row, to the right. 'Before milk and cheese.'

The air began to smell of fish, both pickled and fresh. The smells mingled together, and there seemed to be a salty sea breeze in the air.

Igor heard a woman's voice up ahead, loud and melodic. 'Sardines and herring, from Astrakhan and the Don River! Take a look, they're delicious!'

It's her! he thought. He almost broke into a run but stopped himself just in time.

Then there was the fish section, right in front of him. The peaked roofs of the stalls were decorated with clusters of dried gobies and sea roaches. The sun shone in and the flies buzzed about deliriously, luxuriating in the fish-saturated air. The woman whose voice continued to resound throughout the entire section stood behind four open barrels of salted herrings. She was using a little bundle of birch twigs to swat away the flies, but she was doing it almost gracefully, without even looking at the fish. She only had eyes for potential customers as she repeated her mantra, the same words over and over again: 'Sardines and herring, from Astrakhan and the Don River! Take a look, they're delicious!'

'Three herring.' An old woman had stopped in front of her, holding a string bag. The string bag already contained several beetroot, a head of cabbage and a jar of horseradish.

The seller took a brief respite from her sales pitch, but this made no difference to the general noise levels.

Suddenly Igor heard another voice, a little further on. 'Black Sea flounder! Black Sea flounder!' This voice was stronger and more melodic than the first.

Igor stood on tiptoes, peering in the direction of the voice. He saw a queue of about five people ahead of him. As he approached the head of the queue, Igor spotted the striking red-haired young woman behind the stall. She was tall, maybe even taller than Igor himself. He wondered if she were wearing heels.

'Black Sea flounder! Caught this morning! You won't find fresher unless you catch them yourself!' she continued, her penetrating gaze sweeping over the passing shoppers. 'Hey, Brown-Eyes! Take a look! Your wife will thank you for it!'

Brown-Eyes was a bald man of about fifty, wearing glasses and a suit and tie and holding a bulging brown briefcase. He stopped and approached the stall obediently, like a tame rabbit.

'How much?' he asked.

'For you, I'll sell them at a loss,' said the seller. 'Five for five roubles!'

'But that's more expensive than herring!' Brown-Eyes was disconcerted but made no move to walk away.

'The market's awash with herring! Barrels of them, everywhere . . . But only a handful of fresh flounder! You should try catching them – it's not easy!'

'All right, I'll take five,' said the man, nodding his assent.

The seller took a newspaper from under the counter and spread it open. She tossed a flounder into the air, catching it deftly in her other hand.

'See how beautiful they are!' she said.

She wrapped five fish up in the newspaper and took the money. Brown-Eyes regarded the newspaper parcel with suspicion.

'It's bound to leak,' he said. 'And my accounts are in there.'

The seller smiled. She produced another newspaper and wrapped it tightly around the parcel of fish, before holding it out to her customer again.

'It won't leak now!'

The man opened his briefcase and hesitated, considering the matter, then clicked it shut and walked away, holding the newspaper parcel in his other hand.

Igor moved closer to the stall and pretended to be interested in the flounder as well.

'Go on, treat yourself,' the seller said to him. 'You won't regret it! Your wife will thank you!'

'I'm not married,' replied Igor, looking boldly into the young woman's pretty freckled face. Now, standing in front of her, he had the impression that they were the same height.

'In that case your mother will thank you,' she retorted cheerfully. 'Women like fish more than men do!'

'How much?'

'To an officer of the law, five for ten roubles!' A mischievous smile lit up the seller's face.

'Why so expensive?' he asked, returning her smile.

'You're a figure of authority,' she replied, spreading her hands. 'A pillar of the community. Is ten roubles really too much to ask?'

'Fine,' said Igor, feeling his latent machismo awaken. He took out one of the bundles of hundred-rouble notes in such a way that his affluence was visible to her and her alone. He peeled a note from the bundle and handed it over. The smile fell from the seller's face, but this didn't detract from her beauty. She looked anxiously at the note.

'Haven't you got anything smaller?' she asked.

'Figures of authority don't carry small change,' joked Igor, still looking directly into her green eyes.

'I'm going to tell my husband he ought to join the police force,' she declared, the smile returning to her face. 'You get paid well, and you get a gun!' She glanced at the holster.

'You get a gun,' nodded Igor. 'But not everyone gets paid well!'

'Only the bosses?' The seller's voice was playful, teasing. She seemed to have forgotten all about the fish.

'What's your name? It wouldn't by any chance be Valya, would it?'

'Why "by any chance"? Cats are named by chance, not people! So, five Black Sea flounder, was it?' she asked briskly. Her face had lost its light-hearted look.

Igor nodded. The seller wrapped the fish in newspaper and took the note from Igor's hand.

'I'll be right back,' she said.

Igor watched her walk to a neighbouring stall. He saw her friends change the money for her and listened to her laughter. When she came back she put some coins and a pile of notes into Igor's hand, placing two ten-rouble notes on top.

'If you enjoy them, come back for more!' she said. Her eyes were already over Igor's shoulder, looking for new customers.

'Would you like to go for a coffee?' Igor asked cautiously. Her green eyes immediately looked back at him, wide with surprise.

'Go where? What do you mean, for a coffee?'

'Or tea, or cocoa,' stammered Igor, growing flustered. He could feel his cheeks burning in the heat radiating from her eyes. 'Or champagne?'

'Oh!' she exclaimed, temporarily nonplussed. 'Why?'

Igor spread his hands helplessly.

'So we can talk . . . Get to know one another . . .'

'Is this part of your job?' she asked warily.

Igor shook his head. 'No! I'm . . . new here, in Ochakov . . . I don't know anyone.'

'Where do you usually work?'

'In Kiev, mainly. I'm here on business.'

'Well, people don't go for coffee round here,' she smiled.

'Or cocoa. And as for champagne – you have to go to a restaurant for that, and I don't go to restaurants.'

'All right then. Never mind,' replied Igor, desperately wishing that the ground would open up and swallow him. 'Goodbye . . . and thanks for the fish!'

'I'll pass your thanks on to my husband. Come again!'

Igor made for the exit, feeling a surge of awkward emotion. He felt as though he'd behaved inappropriately. Was it the feisty redhead who had made him feel so unsettled? He walked quickly and restlessly, full of pent-up energy, as though he were trying to get away as fast as he could without breaking into a run, but he let his feet lead him back to the street where Vanya Samokhin lived. Igor recognised certain familiar landmarks on the way – a particular house, a dark blue fence, the 'Fashion Studio No. 2' sign affixed to the cracked plaster of an imposing building that extended right out onto the pavement, while the other buildings stood modestly back from the street, behind fences and front gardens where traces of green still remained.

When he spotted Igor lingering by the gate, Vanya went out onto the front porch and beckoned him inside.

'I thought you'd get lost,' he said, closing the front door behind Igor. 'What have you got there?' he asked, nodding at the newspaper parcel.

'I bought some fish,' said Igor. 'Can I put it in the fridge?'

'We don't have a fridge,' grinned the lad. 'This isn't a meat-processing factory! I can take it down to the cellar, if you like?'

'No, don't worry about it,' Igor replied. He looked pensively at Vanya. 'Is your mother here?'

'Why would she be here? She's still at the market.'

'In that case, I'm going to lie down for a bit,' said Igor. 'But first, we need to have a little chat. Can you put the kettle on?'

'Wouldn't you prefer wine?'

'I thought you had to go to work this afternoon.'

'The whole factory smells of wine. They never smell it on us!'

'All right then, why not?' agreed Igor. 'After all, you usually drink it before you go to bed, don't you?'

They sat down together in the little kitchen. Igor took a hundred-rouble note from the bundle in his right-hand pocket. He laid it on the table between them. Glancing at Lenin's portrait on the banknote, Vanya immediately tensed up.

'Do you have a camera?' asked Igor.

'Why would I have a camera?' Vanya shrugged. 'I'm not a photographer.'

'How much do cameras cost in Ochakov?'

'Same as where you're from, I expect.' Vanya scratched his forehead with the fingers of his right hand. 'They're not cheap. Maybe five hundred, maybe a thousand . . . I don't know.'

'Do you know how to use one?'

'I can learn, if you want me to. It's not complicated, is it? You just have to focus, then press a button. My friend showed me once.'

Igor took ten more notes from the bundle in his pocket and placed them on the table.

'There, use that to buy a camera and a film.'

'And then what?'

'Then, when you've got some free time, find yourself somewhere to hide near Chagin's house and photograph all the people who come and go. I'll pay you for every photograph. Understood?'

'How much?'

'If the person's face is visible, then . . . twenty roubles.' Igor paused, checking Vanya's reaction to his proposal. Vanya was nodding gravely, indicating his acceptance of the terms. 'And if not, then nothing. I need faces.'

'I could take a picture of you and Red Valya, if you like?'

'Good idea,' agreed Igor. 'Get one of her husband too!'

'Why do you want one of him? That would just be a waste of film.' Vanya gave a condescending smirk.

'What do you mean?'

'Well, he's just a fisherman. Belarussian Petka calls him an "old rag". He's not a real man. He's always ill, never drinks—'

'I see,' Igor interrupted his garrulous host. 'Well, to your good health!' He raised his glass, which Vanya had filled generously with wine.

They drank.

Igor stood up. 'Right, I'm going to bed,' he announced.

'You won't be here when I get back, will you?'

'No, I'll be gone by then,' Igor confirmed. 'But I'll be back in a couple of days. What's your mother's name? Just in case?'

'Aleksandra Marinovna.'

Igor left the kitchen and went into living room, where he put the parcel of fish on the floor next to the bed and began to undress. He folded the uniform neatly and put it on the stool, placed the belt with the holster and the peaked cap on top of it, and lay down under the quilted blanket. He still had the trace of a sour taste in his mouth from the local wine. He saw an image of Red Valya, her green eyes ablaze. Her voice rang in his ears. Unable to find a way out, the warmth of Igor's body began to accumulate under the heavy blanket. Once his energies were restored he would emerge like a butterfly, full of life, ready to make the most of the new day.

12

'Why are you still in bed?' cried Elena Andreevna, standing over her son. 'You'll suffocate in your sleep one of these days!' She pulled back the blanket that was covering Igor's head. 'It's nearly half past twelve!'

Igor raised his head and looked at his mother.

'What's the matter with you?' she asked in surprise. 'Were you drinking yesterday?'

He could feel the sour taste of the Ochakov wine in his mouth and there was a rocking, swaying sensation inside his head, which was preventing him from thinking clearly. Igor lay back down on the pillow. Out of the corner of his eye he noticed the newspaper parcel on the floor by his bed.

'Take that,' he mumbled, pointing at the parcel. 'We can have it for lunch.'

'I'm cooking buckwheat for lunch,' said Elena Andreevna, but she picked up the parcel and sniffed it.

'Why didn't you put it in the fridge? It's fish, isn't it?'

Igor nodded. 'I was too tired,' he admitted in a slightly hoarse voice.

'All right, you stay in bed,' his mother said graciously. 'I'll call you when it's ready. What's that doing there?' Elena Andreevna's eyes had come to rest on the peaked cap and the neatly folded police uniform. 'Have you got a job as a security guard?'

'No, I just wore it for a laugh.' Igor waved his hand dismissively. 'Kolyan had a retro birthday party.'

This explanation seemed to satisfy Elena Andreevna's curiosity. She left the room, taking the parcel of fish with her.

As soon as he was alone again, Igor got out of bed. First he hid the police uniform in his wardrobe, then he put on a tracksuit and a pair of fur-lined leather slippers. They were soft and comfortable, and this pleasant sensation spread from the soles of his feet throughout his entire body; even his head started to feel better. Everything was back to normal. Apart from the taste in his mouth.

Igor spent a full five minutes cleaning his teeth. He brushed them with a hard toothbrush and thought about the tooth powder he'd used at Vanya Samokhin's house.

Should I tell Stepan about everything? wondered Igor, glancing at himself in the mirror above the sink as he listened to the flow of water. He decided Stepan would never believe him. Unless he could prove it . . .

His face broke into a smile. He felt rather pleased with himself.

'Lunch is ready,' his mother called from the kitchen.

As soon as Elena Andreevna tasted the fried fish, her face softened.

'Oh my goodness, that's incredible! Just a minute, I'll be right back,' she cried, jumping up from the table.

'Where are you going?' asked Igor in surprise.

'I'm just going next door to fetch Olga. It's so delicious! Just like it used to taste when I was a little girl!' Muttering to herself, she hurried out into the hallway. Igor shrugged as he heard the front door slam. He put some butter on his buckwheat, then wrapped a crispy piece of fish skin around his fork and put it into his mouth.

She's right, he thought. It is pretty good. But it's hardly worth running off like that!

His mother returned with their neighbour Olga about three minutes later and immediately started bustling about, placing another plate and fork on the table. She spooned some buckwheat onto Olga's plate and placed a fried flounder next to it.

Olga tried the fish first, and her face froze in an expression of deep concentration. Or rather, most of her face froze. Her lips were moving slowly, indicating the focus of her attention. Olga swallowed her mouthful and nodded.

'Where did you buy this fish? At the market?' she asked. 'Was it still alive?'

'No, but it was freshly caught,' explained Igor.

'How can it have been freshly caught? It's a sea fish, it would need to be transported.' Olga beamed at him. 'They must have seen you coming! It's obviously been frozen.'

'What about the flavour?' asked Elena Andreevna, mildly disgruntled. 'What do you think of the flavour?

Olga shrugged. 'They've probably added something to it. They put all sorts in food these days. Chemicals, MSG . . . They can make it taste like something else altogether!'

Elena Andreevna sighed heavily and put her fork down on the table. Igor glared at their neighbour.

'Please forgive Mama for bothering you. I'm sure you were

busy before she came round and interrupted you, and for something so trivial too . . . Why don't you go back to what you were doing?'

'Don't worry about it. I'm here now, aren't I?' Olga waved Igor's concerns away, oblivious to the sarcasm in his voice. Unable to hide her enthusiasm, she turned her attention back to the food.

Igor finished his fish and helped himself to another from the frying pan in the centre of the kitchen table.

His mother picked up her fork, but she seemed to have lost her appetite.

Igor glanced at their neighbour. He noticed that she was eyeing the last remaining flounder. Igor stood up and took the frying pan from the table, covered it with a lid and placed it on the hob.

As Igor sat down, he and Olga looked at one another.

'Sorry,' he shrugged. 'Mama thought you'd like it.'

'But I do!' said Olga, pursing her lips. 'I love plaice!'

'It's not plaice, it's Black Sea flounder,' Igor corrected her irritably.

Olga looked down at the unfinished buckwheat on her plate.

'How are things working out with the gardener?' She asked suddenly, hoping to steer the conversation in a more favourable direction by alluding to her own part in the arrangement.

'He disappeared a couple of days ago and we haven't seen him since,' Igor replied on his mother's behalf. 'He's probably found a drinking buddy somewhere.'

'But he doesn't drink!' exclaimed Olga.

'He's been a great help,' said Elena Andreevna, turning to her friend. 'Thank you for introducing him to us.'

Olga smiled, mollified, and on that positive note she decided that it was time for her to leave. Igor and his mother drank their tea together.

'It's a shame you didn't buy more,' said Elena Andreevna.

Igor stood up. He took the lid off the frying pan, put the last fish onto a clean plate and placed it near his mother.

She smiled, put her cup of tea to one side and began eating again.

'It wasn't too expensive, was it?' she asked.

Igor shook his head. 'I'll buy more next time,' he promised.

In the afternoon, Elena Andreevna went round to Olga's house to make sure there were no hard feelings after their lunchtime disagreement over the fish.

Igor went out to the shed and contemplated the padlock on the door with irritation. He thought about breaking it, but he couldn't justify actually doing so. There wasn't anything in the shed that he specifically needed. Besides, the fact that Stepan had padlocked the door seemed to suggest that he was planning to come back at some point. The treasure – or at least part of it – must still be inside.

The sun made an unexpected appearance the following morning. A few birds that had not yet flown south for the winter started singing. As Igor's mother moved about the house, the wooden floor creaked beneath her feet. The morning was fresh and full of life. Igor got out of bed. Just at that moment, he heard a familiar cough from outside, although he couldn't be sure whether it came from the yard or from the street. He looked out of the window and saw Stepan walking towards the house. He was wearing a new dark green jacket, and a half-empty canvas rucksack hung from his shoulders. Stepan didn't notice Igor looking out of the window. Whistling a Russian folk song, Stepan went straight to the shed.

Igor got dressed and sat down at the kitchen table. He waited for his mother to make him tea and heat up some leftover buckwheat for breakfast.

'It's a pity you didn't come to Olga's with me yesterday.' Elena Andreevna glanced quizzically at her son. 'We had a lovely time. She'd baked a gooseberry pie, and it was delicious. She sent a piece for you too – it's in the fridge.'

'Stepan's back,' said Igor, nodding at the window as though the gardener were standing right there, on the other side of the glass.

The news seemed to distract Elena Andreevna. She fell silent.

'Why don't you warm something up for him? I'll take it out,' said Igor.

Armed with a plate of buckwheat, Igor approached the shed. He stood and listened outside the door for a moment, but he couldn't hear a sound. The shed seemed to be empty.

Igor knocked once and opened the door. The gardener was standing in front of the shelf unit, wearing a short-sleeved T-shirt and looking into a square mirror that was resting on the top shelf. He was holding his hand to his chin and the side of his face, as though he'd been contemplating whether or not to shave.

'Good morning,' said Igor. He looked around, wondering where to put the plate.

'Good morning to you,' nodded Stepan. 'Though it might not have been,' he added darkly.

Igor suddenly noticed that the gardener's left hand was wrapped in a bandage.

'You can leave it there,' Stepan said, nodding at the shelf unit. To Igor's great astonishment he proceeded to turn his rucksack upside down, emptying bundles of 200-hryvna notes all over the bed.

'There,' he said with a sigh. 'Now my life can begin again, with a clean slate. It's just a pity I'm not eighteen years old any more!'

He thought for a moment, then he picked up one of the bundles and held it out to Igor.

'There you go. That's for your motorbike . . . For all your help.'

Igor weighed the bundle in his hands. 'How much?' he asked expectantly.

'Depends how you look at it. There might be more where that came from . . . It might include an advance payment,' smiled the gardener.

'For what?'

'Various things. I've got a daughter. She lives in Lviv. I want you to go and visit her, for a start. Take her a letter from me. See what her place is like, who she's living with. And tell her something good about me.'

Igor was delighted by Stepan's proposal, although he didn't show it. He thought about the two bundles of Soviet roubles in the pockets of the police uniform. Having a wad of cash in your pocket, does that make you rich? he wondered, stuffing the bundle of 200-hryvna notes into one of his tracksuit pockets.

'When do you want me to go?' he asked, looking up at the gardener.

'You might as well go today. There are plenty of trains to Lviv. Get an overnight train from Kiev, and another one back the following night. You'll be home the day after tomorrow.'

Back in the house Igor took his time counting the money Stepan had given him. Not because he was interested in the total amount, but because he was fascinated by the sheer number of notes. He'd never had so much money at one time before. The banknotes were crisp and new and seemed to whisper when Igor flicked through them with his fingertips. He enjoyed playing with the money so much that he decided to take out both bundles of Soviet roubles too. The Soviet hundred-rouble notes were bigger and more impressive than the Ukrainian 200-hryvna notes, but that seemed to make sense: the USSR had been much bigger than Ukraine. If they printed banknotes in proportion to the size of the country, then Igor would probably have been able to fit several bundles of Ukrainian money in the palm of his hand, not just one. This thought amused him. Comparing the two currencies again, Igor decided that the Soviet notes were more pleasant to touch and hold. The way they rustled in his hand felt somehow more impressive, more authentic.

Late that afternoon, before setting off for the station, Igor called Kolyan.

'Hey, I'm getting the overnight train to Lviv. Why don't you come and see me off? I've got something to tell you. You'll never guess what it is.'

'I can't,' answered his friend. 'The bosses have asked me to investigate one of the clients, and it's going to take me until at least midnight to hack into his email account. He's applied for a big loan using dodgy documents. Let's meet up when you get back, though. A new club's just opened . . . we could check it out, if you like?'

'OK,' Igor agreed reluctantly. 'Why not? See you soon.'

13

After an almost sleepless night on the train, Igor splashed his face with water from the sink to wake himself up before stepping out onto the platform at Lviv station.

The station was a hive of human activity. Trunks, suitcases and rucksacks flashed past him. The square outside the station surprised him with its modest dimensions. A tram, far skinnier than those in Kiev, loomed into view then rang its bell and disappeared off down a straight track that clearly led to the centre of the town.

'You looking for a taxi? Good price!' declared a sprightly old man with a thick regional accent.

Igor took Stepan's letter out of his jacket pocket and glanced at the address.

'How much to Zelenaya Street?' he asked.

'Forty hryvnas, if you can spare it!'

'And if I can't?' grinned Igor.

'In that case, thirty-five.'

The old Lada creaked and groaned for the duration of the journey. Every now and then Igor was thrown up into the air as the car lurched over the tram tracks that criss-crossed the cobbled streets. They left the beautiful old houses in the centre behind, and a winding road took them past a series of Khrushchev-era five-storey blocks. After that they passed a number of large industrial plots, with factory and warehouse fences stretching out into the distance on either side, before eventually reaching a district of neat, well-maintained private houses.

'Number 271,' Igor said to the driver.

When they arrived, Igor's first impression was that the building didn't look particularly grand. It consisted of two houses joined together; three steps led up to a green wooden door on the left, and three steps led up to a dark blue door on the right.

Igor went up to the dark blue door. He couldn't see a doorbell, so he knocked three times. The door was opened by a young woman who was about thirty years old, wearing jeans and a dark blue sweater. Her hazel eyes looked at him enquiringly.

'Are you Alyona Sadovnikova?' Igor asked cautiously.

'Yes.'

'I've got a letter for you. From your father.'

Alyona hesitated, a fleeting look of concern in her eyes.

'Come in.'

She led Igor into a room that was furnished neatly and modestly. Indicating that he should sit on the sofa, she took the envelope from him and walked over to the window. She moved the curtain aside. Taking out a piece of paper that was covered with fine handwriting, she read it several times. Then the hand holding the letter dropped to her side and she sighed with relief.

'I'd started to think something bad must have happened,' she said. 'Does he want me to reply straight away?' Alyona looked pensively at her guest.

'No. He didn't say anything. Just asked me to deliver it.'

'Doesn't he trust the postal service?'

She left the room and returned a few minutes later, holding a piece of paper torn from an exercise book, which she had folded in half and then in half again.

'Give this to him,' she said. 'How is he? Is he well?'

Igor nodded.

'I don't suppose you have any photos of him?'

'Photos?' Igor repeated in surprise. 'No.'

'Why did he ask you to come?' continued Alyona, her curiosity piqued. 'Are you a friend of his? Or did he pay you?'

'It's not like that, he's staying with us . . . He and I are . . . well, I suppose we're friends.'

'Why's he staying with you?'

'He's helping us around the house,' explained Igor. 'It's too much for my mother and me to manage by ourselves.'

'Your mother?' repeated Alyona. Then she gave a strange nod, as though everything suddenly made sense.

Igor noticed this and frowned. He knew what she was thinking, but for some reason he had no desire to clarify the situation. On the contrary he felt like asking her a few questions himself, although it somehow seemed like the wrong moment.

'Do you ever come to Kiev?' asked Igor.

'Me? To Kiev? No,' she replied, shaking her head. 'Why would I want to go to Kiev?'

'You should come,' Igor shrugged. 'You could see your father. You could come and visit us, although we don't actually live in the city. When did you last see him?'

Alyona's eyes widened. She paused before answering.

'When did I last see him?' she repeated slowly. 'It feels as though I've never seen him . . . although I know that's not true. He came a couple of times, when my mother was still alive. The last time was about fifteen years ago.'

'I'm sorry,' Igor lowered his eyes. 'I didn't know . . . I shouldn't have asked.'

'I've got to go to work now,' Alyona said apologetically.

Igor stood up and said goodbye. They went out into the hallway and stood there looking at each other in silence.

'Where are you going to stay tonight?' Alyona asked suddenly. 'I'm afraid I can't put you up here.'

'Don't worry, I'm going back tonight,' said Igor.

'You mean you came just to deliver the letter?'

'Well, I'll have a little walk around the town too . . . My train doesn't leave for hours.'

'Yes, the town's certainly worth a visit,' said the young woman, nodding in approval.

Igor walked down the street, recognising the buildings and fences he'd driven past in the old Lada just half an hour previously and feeling the eyes of this attractive young woman on his back. Her reaction to the letter that Igor had brought had been so subdued. But when he thought about it, that wasn't really so strange. She'd answered Stepan, hadn't she?

She'd given Igor a note to take back to him. A folded piece of paper.

When he reached the Khrushchev-era blocks, Igor stopped and took the piece of paper out of his pocket. If it had been in an envelope, even unsealed, he probably wouldn't have dreamt of reading it. But it wasn't in an envelope. Igor had no idea what Stepan's letter to his daughter had said, but maybe her answer would somehow enlighten him.

He unfolded the piece of paper. There were just four words: 'Nothing is impossible. Alyona.'

Igor spent the rest of the day wandering the old alleys and cobbled streets of Lviv. He went into a church, browsed the shops, even got his hair cut for thirty hryvnas in a little salon. He spent the last two hours of his visit at the train station, remembering at the last minute that he'd forgotten to buy a present for his mother.

The following morning the sun was shining over Irpen again. Only the puddles in the street gave any indication that it had been raining during the night.

The first thing Igor did was to give Stepan the note from his daughter.

'How is she?' asked the gardener.

'Fine,' Igor shrugged. 'She was on her way to work, so we couldn't really talk.'

'Does she live alone?'

Igor thought about it. He recalled the living room, the hallway, the slippers by the front door.

'I think so,' he said.

Stepan nodded a few times. Then he read the note. To

Igor's surprise, her brief answer made the gardener smile. There was something touchingly childlike about the look on his face.

'Thank God,' breathed the gardener, looking at Igor. 'She's not ruling it out.'

'Ruling what out?' asked Igor.

'The idea of coming to live with me,' said Stepan.

'What, here?' Igor looked around the shed in astonishment.

Stepan burst out laughing. 'Oh, you do surprise me sometimes,' he said. 'Don't forget, I paid you an advance, didn't I? You're *my* gardener now!'

'But I don't know anything about gardening!'

'Don't worry, I'm joking. I've got another job lined up for you. Have a little rest. You need to recover from your trip. Then I want you to start asking around, find out whether there's a house for sale near here. Or, even better, two houses right next to each other. All right? I'll ask around as well. Hopefully we'll be able to find something between us.'

Igor nodded, and his eyes came to rest on Stepan's left hand. It had been bandaged up last time he'd seen him, but now it wasn't.

Following the direction of Igor's gaze, Stepan held up his left arm and looked at the cuts that had been rubbed with iodine.

'Sometimes you even have to raise your hand against old friends,' he said. 'In order to jog their memories. Pashka the Jeweller, he and I go way back – known each other for thirty years, we have. But he seemed to have forgotten that. Didn't offer the right price for our treasure. Trying to cheat his old friend, he was. But he changed his mind eventually.'

Igor's tiredness caught up with him at around lunchtime, and he went to bed. It took him a long time to get to sleep. He was thinking about Stepan and his daughter, about the money he'd got from Pashka the Jeweller, whoever he was, and his request to find two houses somewhere nearby. Igor couldn't shake the strange feeling that he was somehow related to Stepan, even though he knew virtually nothing about him.

Suddenly it began to pour with rain. The air filled with an autumnal humidity, and the hushed, monotonous patter of the rain on the tenacious leaves outside the window finally lulled Igor to sleep. The last thing he thought about was the attractive, melancholy face of Alyona and the way she'd held his gaze when they were saying goodbye in the intimate hallway of the house on Zelenaya Street.

14

First thing the following morning Stepan went outside to have a look at the fence. He was in a good mood and seemed to have taken it upon himself to improve Elena Andreevna's mood too. Either that or he was just trying to make up for his absence as best he could. The fence was his idea.

'That fence seems a bit rickety,' he said over breakfast. 'When I shut the gate yesterday, the whole thing wobbled. A couple of the fence posts must have started to rot.'

Igor's mother nodded and looked at him gratefully.

'Those scales of yours are beautiful,' remarked Stepan, looking over at the windowsill. 'Every time I see them, they make me think about my life.'

'They belonged to my grandmother,' said Elena Andreevna. She looked lovingly at the copper scales. 'She took them everywhere with her, even when she was evacuated to Siberia during the war. She lived to be almost ninety.'

Stepan looked at Igor's mother thoughtfully.

'You're a good woman,' he said.

As soon as Stepan finished his tea he went back outside and resumed his inspection of the fence. He walked along the entire length of it, on both the yard side and the street side. Igor stood by the window in the kitchen with his second mug of tea, watching the gardener apply himself enthusiastically to his task.

After a while Stepan came into the house. 'We need to change three of the fence posts,' he said matter-of-factly. 'That'll be 150 hryvnas.' Igor was taken aback.

'You mean, we have to buy them?'

'Well, we're not going to steal them, are we?' Stepan spread his hands. 'There's a chap selling building materials not far from here. He's got a few fence posts.'

Still taken aback by the unexpected outlay, Igor went into his room and took a 200-hryvna note from the bundle that Stepan had given him.

'I'll bring back the change,' promised Stepan.

Alone again, Igor succumbed to an autumnal mood. The sky was cloudy and grey. It didn't look like it was going to rain, but there was no chance of sunshine either. You had to make every day count, whatever the weather. In his heart Igor knew that whether the days of his life were filled with events or inactivity was entirely down to him.

Although it was autumn in the parallel world of Ochakov too, everything had been so vivid, so full of life. Not like here.

Igor called Kolyan on his mobile and asked what his plans were for the evening.

'Why, do you want to go for a drink?' asked his friend.

'Yes, and I've got some news for you.'

'Meet me at six, and we'll decide where to go then,' said Kolyan. 'I've got some news for you too. I've just made two thousand dollars, without even taking my fingers off the keyboard!'

The conversation cheered Igor up. He only had a few hours to kill until the evening. But why wait? He could go to Kiev earlier and wander round for a bit.

Igor was on his way out of the yard when Stepan called to him.

'Shall we go and pick up the fence posts then?'

'I can't, I'm already late. I'm meeting someone in Kiev,' Igor answered hurriedly. The last thing he felt like doing was helping Stepan fix the fence. It was his idea, he can sort it out! he thought as he walked away.

According to its driver, the minibus would be leaving for Kiev 'when it was full', as usual. Igor looked irritably at the ten vacant seats. It was a quiet time, the lull between the morning crowds and the evening rush hour. He looked out of the window, mentally urging anyone contemplating a trip to the city to get a move on. Half an hour later, the last place in the minibus – the front passenger seat – was finally occupied by a young woman with a laptop bag, which she placed carefully on her knees. The driver, who had also been waiting impatiently for his final passenger, started the engine immediately and set off.

The young woman turned round and began looking at each of the passengers in turn. Igor's suspicions were instantly aroused. As if to emphasise her strangeness, the young woman took out a folder containing a stack of paper and a bag of cheap ballpoint pens. She attached a pen to every piece of paper, then counted them and looked around at the other passengers again, ignoring Igor's questioning look.

She's counting us! thought Igor.

As the minibus taxi left Irpen the road began to straighten out. Pine trees flashed past on both sides of the highway.

'Ladies and gentlemen,' the young woman suddenly began, with the practised delivery of a sales agent, 'you have been selected to enter a draw to win a Korean vacuum cleaner. All you need to do is fill out these questionnaires . . .' She held up the pieces of paper to show the 'ladies and gentlemen', who were looking at her with interest. 'It's an official market research survey. And the pens are yours to keep!'

She leaned over the back of her seat to hand out the questionnaires. What Igor found most surprising was that all the passengers reached out to take one. Even Igor himself took one automatically when it was handed to him. He scanned through the information requested: name, address, telephone number, email address, monthly salary, number of pensioners in the family, size of accommodation.

What a cheek! thought Igor. I might as well give her my house keys! He handed the questionnaire and the pen back to the young woman.

'Is there a problem?' she asked, with a supercilious smile.

'The problem is that I don't like people trying to find out what I'm thinking,' replied Igor, with what he hoped was a similar smile.

'The questionnaire doesn't ask you what you're thinking. Or what your religious beliefs are,' she calmly pointed out. 'Nor does it ask how much beer you drink, or what brand.'

Igor glanced at the other passengers. They were all diligently filling out the questionnaires.

She's just a con artist, thought Igor, but he managed to refrain from answering back. He knew she'd get the better of him and he'd probably just end up making a complete fool of himself.

If only I were an undercover police officer, thought Igor. I'd ask her for some ID. I bet that would wipe the smile off her face!

But Igor wasn't a police officer, although he did feel a certain duty to maintain law and order. Or at least to uphold the cause of social justice. Maybe it was because he liked what he saw in the mirror when he was wearing the old police uniform. When you feel comfortable wearing a certain uniform, you find yourself adapting to suit it.

There was a cool wind blowing in Kiev, but otherwise the weather was unremarkable. Constant traffic noise. Early twilight. Street lamps coming on. Huge billboards, buzzing gently as one advert was replaced by another.

Igor met Kolyan at his office in the Podil district and they walked to Sahaidachny Street. They stopped in front of a cafe they both knew, but the music was far too loud. So they took the bus one stop to Kreshchatyk Street and went to an

Irish pub on Malaya Zhitomirskaya Street, which was nice and quiet. Fake school blackboards hung about the pub, with details of upcoming football matches chalked on them, targeting customers who liked both beer and sport. Thankfully, there didn't seem to be a match on that evening.

'I need something to warm me up,' said Igor, biting his lower lip as he looked up at the young waitress who had stopped at their table. 'A double shot of Khortitsa vodka and a Chernigivske beer should do it.'

'Mixing your drinks, eh?' Kolyan smiled. 'I prefer to drink one or the other. Either vodka or beer, but not both together.' He looked at the girl. 'I'll have a Lviv beer and some bar snacks, please.'

The girl left. Kolyan looked at his friend.

'So, what's up? Come on, tell me.'

'Let's have a drink first,' said Igor, brushing Kolyan's request aside. It had suddenly occurred to him that it might sound like he'd made it all up. If Kolyan had told him a similar story, that's what he would have thought anyway.

'Right,' nodded Kolyan. 'I knew it. You're bored out of your mind, aren't you? Stuck out there in the sticks . . . Just admit it! Irpen's not the same as Kiev, is it? You don't even have anyone to go for a proper drink with. No intellectually stimulating conversation. "What are you looking at? No, what are *you* looking at?" That's the only kind of conversation you get out there!'

Igor shook his head, but Kolyan's mind was already on other matters.

'I'm feeling rather proud of myself today, you know. You'll never believe it . . . For the first time ever, I actually made some money out of my hacking skills. Two thousand dollars!'

'How come?' asked Igor, surprised. 'Did you take it out of someone's account?'

'Of course not! It was all above board. I hacked into some rich guy's email account and copied his email correspondence with his lover, and then sold it to his wife. She was delighted.'

Igor raised his eyebrows. 'Delighted?' he repeated.

'Well, not delighted, obviously, but . . . Well, anyway, she wasn't disappointed, that's for sure! She's going to take him to the cleaners. He'll definitely be paying for his bit on the side.'

A slender female hand placed the long-awaited vodka shot on the table in front of Igor, then a large glass of beer next to it. The light in the bar made the beer glow an appetising amber colour. Igor knocked back his shot and chased it with a gulp of beer. There was a bitter aftertaste in his mouth, which was both pleasant and refreshing.

'Excuse me . . . Another double, please!' he called, smiling as he caught the waitress's eye. She brought it straight over.

'Hey, slow down, old man! At least have something to eat,' said Kolyan, nodding at the saucer of salted croutons on the table.

Igor took a handful and started crunching them noisily between his teeth.

'You won't believe what I'm about to tell you,' he said, casting a sly glance at his friend.

He thought about the way Kolyan had made him wait before showing him the printout of Stepan's tattoo.

'Why, what is it?'

'No, you'll never believe it . . . Oh, I'll tell you later,' continued Igor, deliberately taunting his friend. 'After all, you don't believe in fairy tales.'

'Depends what kind . . . Come on, tell me.' Kolyan took a large swig of beer. 'Don't keep me hanging on!'

'Remember I got drunk at your birthday, in the Petrovich club?'

'How could I forget?!'

'Right, well, I wasn't actually there at all,' declared Igor. 'I was in Ochakov . . . in 1957!'

Kolyan looked at the two empty shot glasses. 'Doesn't take much, does it?' he grinned.

Igor sighed heavily. 'Can you remember what I was wearing?' he asked.

Kolyan thought about it. 'I'd had a fair amount myself, you know . . . Birthday boy's prerogative, and all that!'

'Right,' nodded Igor. 'Well, I got dressed up in an old police uniform, put my jacket on and left for your party. Actually, I left for the bus station but ended up at the Ochakov Wine Factory . . .'

And Igor went on to tell his friend all about his first trip back in time. Kolyan listened attentively, with an incredulous smile on his face. His expression only changed when Igor told him how he and the wine thief Vanya had watched Fima Chagin's house. As though he'd suddenly made the connection with the tattoo.

'So, do you believe me?' asked Igor, noticing Kolyan's reaction.

'Of course not,' replied Kolyan. 'But it's a great story. Have you considered recording your fantasies?'

'Oh, piss off,' muttered Igor. He was a bit annoyed, but he wasn't really angry with Kolyan. He turned towards the bar again. 'Another double, please, and another Chernigivske.'

'And I'll have another Lviv,' added Kolyan, taking advantage of the fact that they had the waitress's attention.

'Right, well, I'll shut up then!' declared Igor.

'Why?' Kolyan shrugged. 'Drinking in silence is bad for your health. Now I'm wondering whether or not I should make a move on the wife of the businessman whose accounts I hacked into . . . She's just found out her husband's cheating on her, maybe she'll want to get her own back? With me, for example? Why not, eh?'

'If I were a girl, I might be able to rate your chances more accurately.'

'Good job you're not then,' laughed Kolyan. 'We need an expert opinion,' he added, looking at the waitress as she walked past. 'When you've got a minute!' he called after her.

The girl was concentrating on carrying three glasses of beer to another table, but she looked their way and nodded.

'So is it something you drink that enables you to travel back in time?' asked Kolyan, turning back to his friend. 'Or are you smoking some new kind of blend? Seems to be very popular these days.'

Igor cleared his throat, but it didn't sound as exasperated as he'd meant it to. His mood was improving. The double shots of vodka, washed down with beer, had warmed his soul, and he felt relaxed and amiably indifferent to the world.

'This is how it works,' said Igor. 'First you drink two glasses of brandy, then you put on an old police uniform and go outside, around eleven o'clock at night. Then you leave the yard and turn right.'

'Excellent!' exclaimed Kolyan. 'If you dressed up as an astronaut, do you think you'd end up in space? Look, now you've got me talking nonsense too!'

'And you're not even mixing your drinks,' Igor smiled.

'Can I get you anything else?' The waitress had stopped near their table.

Kolyan looked at the little name badge that was pinned to her white blouse.

'Lena . . . Lenochka,' he said, his tone familiar but not overly so. 'Please bring me another Lviv beer, and he'll have five' – he glanced at Igor – 'no, six shots of vodka! Out of interest, can I ask you a personal question? What do you think of me? You know, from a woman's perspective. Be honest. I really want to know!'

The girl smiled. 'You seem like a typical man to me,' she shrugged. 'An armchair football fan.'

'What do you mean?' Kolyan seemed genuinely baffled, and Igor couldn't keep the smile from his face.

'You men are all the same. You like watching football on TV, and drinking beer . . . I bet you work with computers, don't you?'

'How do you know that?' asked Kolyan.

'You look like you're typing on the table. See, you're doing it now,' laughed the girl.

Alarmed, Kolyan looked down at the fingers of his right hand, which were drumming on the tabletop. He frowned, and his hand stopped moving.

'She got you there!' said Igor, not entirely unsympathetically, as he watched the waitress walk away.

Kolyan didn't answer. He finished his second beer and put the glass to one side.

Instead of six shots Lena the waitress brought a whole bottle of vodka, and another beer for Kolyan. Igor filled his shot glass and knocked it back. He looked at his friend with a mischievous gleam in his eyes.

'Don't worry about it,' he said. 'You'll have better luck with the wife of that businessman . . . As long as he doesn't catch you at it!'

Kolyan only sulked for about five minutes. Once they stopped winding each other up the conversation flowed easily, interspersed with stories and jokes. The emptying of the vodka bottle was admirably methodical.

There were two young women sitting a couple of tables away, both about thirty years old. One of them had bright red dyed hair, cropped short. She was wearing jeans and a tight-fitting red polo shirt. Her friend had brown hair and was wearing tight leather trousers and a leather waistcoat over a black blouse. There were no other customers.

Igor peered at the red-haired woman, scrutinising her sharp-featured but attractive face.

'I'm going to go over and say hello,' he said, standing up with some difficulty.

He went over to their table and stared at the woman with red hair.

'You're not from Ochakov, are you, by any chance?' asked Igor, with a drunken attempt at a charming smile.

Both of them looked up at him, amused.

'No,' answered the red-haired one. 'We're from Mariupol, actually. Would you like to join us for a drink?' She nodded at an empty chair.

Despite his advanced state of inebriation Igor knew it was time to leave.

'As you're not from Ochakov, I'm sorry for bothering you,' he slurred, returning to his own table.

'Will you be all right getting home?' asked Kolyan.

'I'll be fine,' Igor assured him.

Before they went their separate ways Kolyan, who had managed to stay relatively sober due to not mixing his drinks, helped Igor to flag down a car. He even sat him in the rear seat of the red Lada and gave the driver precise instructions on where to drop him off, so Igor was able to doze off in the back of the car. They arrived at the Nivka metro station just as the last minibus to Irpen was getting ready to leave.

Whereas Igor's journey in the red Lada had lulled him to sleep, the jolting and swerving of the minibus to Irpen was more of a rude awakening and soon sobered him up. He left the minibus in Irpen with the other late-night passengers and surprised himself by setting out towards home with a light spring in his step. The minibus driver may have succeeded in shaking the alcohol out of his system, but his head still felt cloudy.

After a traumatic labour, the thought was born in Igor's mind that maybe the whole thing really was just nonsense. Maybe I've turned into an alcoholic and I'm seeing things that don't exist in real life? he thought. It could be a withdrawal symptom, without the fever or the nightmares. But what about the red-haired woman at the market? And the one in the bar?

Why am I being haunted by red-haired women? It's like a new version of scarlet fever!

Igor thought about the woman from the bar. She was the spitting image of red-haired Red Valya from the Ochakov market. Only if that Valya didn't really exist, then who did she look like?

It's all too weird, thought Igor. I'll have to do a bit of research . . . And then find out whether or not it can be cured!

He went into their yard, carefully closing the gate behind himself. He stopped and looked at the fence, which Stepan had been so determined to fix. Peering at it closely, Igor noticed that three of the fence posts were brand new. He walked round behind the house and looked at the shed. A strip of light was visible beneath the closed door, and light was also coming from the little window to the right of the door.

Why isn't he asleep? wondered Igor. Well, let's find out!

He clambered carefully onto the bench by the door. Straightening up, he stood on tiptoe and pressed his left cheek to the window.

Stepan was sitting on a stool directly underneath the light bulb that hung down from the ceiling, poring over a large book. After staring intently at the book, Igor recognised it as the one they'd taken out of the first suitcase.

Igor climbed down from the bench and spat on the ground. He walked over to the house and, trying not to make a sound, carefully let himself in. He went into the kitchen, opened the cupboard and took out a bottle of brandy and a glass.

'Well, here goes,' he whispered, before downing it and pouring another.

The warmth of the brandy remained on his tongue. He

walked along the dark hallway to the dining room, then into his bedroom. He changed into the police uniform, put on the peaked cap and pulled on the boots. He put the heavy gold watch into one of the pockets of the breeches and walked over to the window. It was pitch black outside, like the inside of a cellar.

'Right then,' he whispered to himself. 'Research time!'

15

The dark part of the road from Irpen to Ochakov seemed to go on for ever this time. Maybe because Igor was walking slowly, belatedly feeling the after-effects of his drinking session with Kolyan. Time had become a fluid concept in his mind: minutes and hours had been replaced by this dark time of day, defined only by its darkness.

A sudden rush of anxiety seized Igor, making him stop for a moment. He patted the pockets of the tunic. Then his hands moved down to his breeches, brushing against the holster before coming to rest on the bundles of Soviet roubles. The nocturnal time traveller was instantly reassured and continued on his way.

As soon as Igor saw the familiar gentle glow from the factory in the distance, the gold watch came to life and began ticking in the left-hand pocket of the breeches, like a vibrating mobile phone alarm. Keeping his eyes fixed on the gates, which were still three hundred metres away, Igor increased his pace.

Any minute now that lorry's going to leave, he thought. Then Vanya will come out with his sack of stolen wine . . .

Just then the gates opened slightly and Vanya Samokhin slipped out onto the square. He stopped and looked around furtively, adjusting the sack on his right shoulder. Then he waved back at the guard and set off towards the town, away from Igor.

Igor sensed that the darkness was about to swallow Vanya. He knew he wouldn't stand a chance of finding his way round Ochakov at night, so he quickened his pace. The accelerated rhythm of the soles of his boots on the road spurred him on, and he was already thinking more clearly than before. He thought specifically about the room in Vanya's house where he'd gone to sleep several times but only woken up once. He could only just make out Vanya's back. He began to panic and eventually started running.

'Vanya!' he called.

Vanya Samokhin stepped to one side and looked over his shoulder. At the sight of the police officer running towards him, he threw the sack of wine under some nearby trees and automatically raised his hands.

'What's the matter?' asked Igor, stopping alongside him and catching sight of his frightened face.

'Oh!' The lad wiped his forehead with the palm of his hand. 'You scared me, comrade lieutenant!'

He retrieved the sack of wine from under the trees and threw it over his right shoulder again.

'I haven't seen you for a while,' he said.

'What do you mean?'

'About four days, isn't it?'

Igor didn't answer. 'Aren't you bored of stealing wine?' he asked instead.

'God helps those who help themselves, and the police help everyone else,' Vanya said with a sigh. 'Shall we go back to my place?'

'Where else?' replied Igor.

'I've taken the photographs you wanted, but I don't know how to develop them . . . You'll have to take the film to a photography studio.'

'You can do that for me,' said Igor, catching up with Vanya and falling into step alongside him.

'I can't,' Vanya said in a low voice. 'The photographer is a Jew. He'll tell Fima that I've been taking secret pictures of him and his friends.'

'Why would he tell him? Are they good friends or something?'

'No. Because he's a Jew.'

'Don't you trust Jews?' asked Igor, surprised.

'No one does! Our head technologist, Efim Naftulovich, was arrested and imprisoned for sabotage.'

'You're talking nonsense!' exclaimed Igor, shaking his head emphatically as he walked. 'Did you take photographs of many people?'

'About seven . . . And Valya.'

They ran out of things to say and walked in silence for about ten minutes, until Vanya opened the gate to his yard and then the door to his house.

Igor sat down on the sofa with the high wooden back and removed his boots. When Vanya came into the room holding a glass of wine, Igor drank it in two gulps and nodded his thanks.

‘Is it true that they’re introducing a new police uniform?’ Vanya suddenly whispered.

Igor was instantly on edge.

‘Where did you hear that?’

‘On the radio.’

‘It must be true, then,’ Igor replied uneasily. ‘Wake me at nine if I’m not up by then. What time does the photography place open?’

‘Everything opens at eight here, except the market. That opens at six,’ said Vanya. ‘But you should take the film to Kiev to get it developed. Otherwise the old man will tell Fima and all the others that the police are taking photographs of them. Here, take it.’ Vanya placed the film in Igor’s outstretched hand and left the room. Igor looked at the small black cartridge protecting the undeveloped film from the light. He rolled it back and forth in his palm, then put it in his pocket.

It was a surprisingly resonant morning. The footsteps of people hurrying past in the street mingled with the sound of doors slamming and the creaking of the wooden floorboards in the house. Igor pulled on his boots, just as Vanya looked into the room. He was already dressed.

‘Why are you up so early?’ he asked, surprised. ‘It’s only six. I thought I’d just go to the market, then come back and we could –’

‘Why are you going to the market?’ asked Igor, adjusting his tunic.

‘I’m going to carry the wine for Mother. It’s too heavy for her to manage alone.’

'Well, I'll come with you,' said Igor. He could tell from Vanya's face that he wasn't keen on this idea.

'If you want to go to the market, you'll have to walk behind us. Otherwise people will wonder what's going on – Mother, me with the wine, and a police officer. They all know . . .' His voice trailed off.

'You mean, they know where the wine's from?' smiled Igor.

'Not everyone, of course, but it's a small town. I know how Bartenyuk gets hold of the ox tongues that he sells at the market, and he knows where my wine's from.'

'OK, OK,' Igor reassured him. 'I'll give you a head start. I'm only going to wander round for an hour or so, then I'll come back here.'

'Going to wander round, eh?' Vanya smiled. 'Are you going to see Red Valya?'

'I might drop by while I'm there,' admitted Igor. 'Maybe I'll buy some more fish. Her fish isn't stolen, like your wine or the ox tongues. It's the product of honest labour.'

'Yes,' Vanya nodded pensively. 'All right, just leave the house about three minutes after you hear the door close. Make sure you pull the door shut too, so that it closes properly.'

Vanya left the room. On the other side of the door Igor could hear bustling sounds, a woman's voice urging Vanya to hurry up and the monotonous burbling of the radio.

Igor heard the door shut while he was standing at the window, looking past the fence at the street beyond. This was how he got his first glimpse of Vanya's mother – a large, stout woman carrying two capacious shopping bags. Her skinny son was walking behind her, also carrying two bags. She was walking confidently and seemed to be carrying her burden with ease – unlike her son. As soon as they went through the gate and turned left along the street, Igor moved away from the window.

No one took any notice of Igor at the market, and he liked it that way. Like an accomplished spy, he revelled in his successful infiltration of this alien environment. His nose captured strange smells, which in actual fact were strange to him alone. He was amused by strange details in the clothes people wore – the shape of their collars, the unusual fabric of their coats – but what made the greatest impression on Igor was the look on people's faces, the way their eyes seemed to shine with joy, with passion and spirit. This was something he'd never seen before, either in Kiev or in Irpen.

The air began to smell of fish and the names of various fish began forcing their way through the other market sounds, which had already merged into a kind of white noise.

'Black Sea flounder, Black Sea flounder!' cried a woman's voice he didn't recognise.

Igor quickened his pace as he approached the fish section.

'Herring from the Danube!' sang a short, plump saleswoman in a clean white overall, as soon as she spotted the handsome young police officer.

Igor walked on. Suddenly he heard a cheerful, familiar voice up ahead.

'Gobies, gobies, come and get your gobies!'

Igor's heart swelled with joy and he grew flustered, certain that other people would notice. He came to a stop when he saw the owner of the voice. He decided to watch her for a while, but sharp-eyed Valya immediately spotted the police officer.

'Hey, lieutenant!' she called. 'Come and buy some fresh fish . . . You've already tried my flounder!' She smiled broadly at him.

Igor approached obediently and looked closely at the stall. A birch twig was swishing from side to side above the counter with the steady rhythm of a conductor's baton, chasing the persistent flies away from the fish.

'Look at my gobies!' The seller directed his gaze to a row of ugly-looking fish. 'Why don't you try some? Get your mother to fry them for you. You'll love them!'

'Haven't you got any flounder?' asked Igor, looking up at Valya.

'Why have you left it so late? I've already sold them all. I never have many. I can put some aside for you tomorrow, if you like – just let me know many you need!' The seller smiled.

'I'll take a kilo,' said Igor. His eyes were involuntarily drawn to Valya's chest, which was conspicuously curvaceous beneath her white overall.

'I don't remember you wearing an overall last time,' said Igor.

'We're having a sanitary inspection today, and there's a prize for the best stall,' explained Valya, adjusting her red hair.

Igor thought back to their previous conversation. 'What are you doing after work?' he asked.

'Are you going to invite me to a restaurant again?' asked Valya, smiling. 'I would say yes, but people will see!'

Igor was delighted.

'We could go somewhere else, if you prefer?'

Valya thought for a moment, fish forgotten.

'Go out that way, turn right and you'll see some benches

in the park,' she said, looking in the direction of the entrance to the market. 'We can sit there for a while. Meet me at six, and don't wear your uniform!'

'I'm afraid I have to wear my uniform,' Igor said apologetically. 'But I'll be there at six o'clock. On the dot!'

Valya nodded and immediately turned her attention to an old woman who had stopped nearby and was looking at her gobies.

'Try some! Buy some! Either for yourself or your cat. They're tastier than sanderling, you know they are!'

Igor walked away with a self-satisfied smile on his face. Suddenly he heard the shrill sound of a whistle. He looked around and spotted a commotion in the adjacent trading aisle: a young boy was running away from a police officer with puffed-out cheeks, who was blowing his whistle with all his might and waving his arms about frantically. It wasn't clear whether he was trying to move people out of the way or appealing for help in catching the thief.

Igor bowed his head and walked in the opposite direction. He found the side entrance to the market, which led out onto a short, narrow street. The two-storey brick building opposite the market just so happened to have a bar on the ground floor. When Igor came face to face with the apprehensive woman behind the counter, he changed his mind about ordering a double shot of vodka. He ran his eyes along the bottles, then looked around the bar. The only table was occupied by two pensioners in drab clothing.

'Do you have any mineral water?' he asked cautiously.

'Only sparkling,' said the woman, and her face softened. 'Twenty kopeks a glass.'

Igor took a hundred-rouble note out of his pocket and held it out to the woman.

'Haven't you got anything smaller? We've only just opened!'

Igor thought about it, and then he remembered Red Valya giving him change when he bought the fish. He took a handful of coins from his pocket and she helped herself to the correct change from his outstretched palm. The mineral water hissed as it was poured into the glass.

As he left the bar Igor wiped his mouth on the sleeve of his tunic, ignoring the old man who was staring at him in surprise. He walked to the end of the street and came to the park. The benches were painted bright green. He stood and looked around for a few minutes, lost in thought, then trudged back to Vanya Samokhin's house.

After idling the afternoon away in Vanya's house, Igor had no trouble making his way back to the park near the market to meet Valya as arranged. He strolled up and down the concrete paths, inhaling the autumnal sea air and glancing at the people who passed him, each of them burdened with their own lives and their own thoughts. He sat down on the third bench from the path that led from the market and inspected his uniform, which looked clean and smart. He glanced down at his boots. They were as comfortable as if they'd been custom-made by an experienced cobbler, although Igor could remember them being a couple of sizes too big when he'd first put them on. He shrugged. The fact that the boots seemed to have shrunk was not the most surprising thing that had happened to Igor recently. No, the most surprising thing was that he was sitting on a bench in 1957, waiting for a married woman who worked at the market – a beautiful woman with red hair, whose mischievous spirit was evident in both her looks and her personality.

Igor glanced towards the market. He took the gold watch out of his breeches and opened the engraved cover. It was exactly 6 p.m. His other hand brushed the bundle of hundred-rouble notes in his right-hand pocket.

'Where shall I take her?' Igor wondered. The money wouldn't let him relax. He knew he would only be able to spend this money here, only now. Back in the future – or wherever 2010 was in relation to now – the notes might be worth something to a collector, but the most you could buy with them would be a smile. Assuming, that is, that the salesperson had a sense of humour.

A woman wearing an elegant, pale grey felt coat with the collar turned up glided past him with an air of importance. Seeing the police officer, she stopped and gave him a friendly smile.

'How's Pyotr Mironovich?' she asked.

'He's fine,' he said, smiling back at the woman, his smile concealing his sense of panic. He was dreading the thought of her asking another question.

'Tell him Irina Vladimirovna said hello! He promised to send us someone to talk to the children.'

'I will,' promised Igor.

The woman in the felt coat went on her way. Igor took a deep breath as he watched her go. He had no idea who Pyotr Mironovich was, of course, but it seemed reasonable to assume that he was the head of the police force.

Igor stood up and walked along the path, away from the

market. He looked back the way he'd come. Still no sign of Red Valya.

Igor's good mood gradually dissipated and was replaced with a growing sense of apprehension and unease.

'I'll walk to the end of this path and back twice more, and then I'll give up and go back to the house,' he decided.

Turning round, he set off slowly in the direction of the market. The path was suddenly overcrowded. Two army officers were walking towards Igor, and there were other people just behind them. The officers saluted him as they walked past, without interrupting their conversation, and Igor saluted in return. He was surprised by how naturally the gesture came to him.

'You don't look very happy to see me!' said a woman in a headscarf, who had stopped just in front of him. Igor looked into her eyes and broke into a smile.

'Oh, I'm sorry! I didn't recognise you in that disguise!'

Red Valya burst out laughing. 'It's so easy for me to disappear. All I have to do is put a scarf over my hair and no one recognises me, no one even notices me. But without a scarf, you can't miss me. Shall we take a seat?' she asked, nodding at the nearest bench. Without waiting for an answer, she sat down and adjusted her knee-length beige raincoat.

'I was worried you weren't going to come,' admitted Igor, sitting down and casually resting one foot on the opposite knee.

'Did you arrest anyone today?' Valya asked playfully.

Igor shook his head. 'I don't like arresting people,' he said, adopting the same tone. 'I wouldn't mind arresting you, though!'

'You cheeky devil!' She smiled again. 'And where would you take me once you'd arrested me?'

Igor shrugged. 'Not to prison, obviously!'

'Well, I suppose I ought to be grateful for that! Have you been here long, in Ochakov?'

'No, it's just a short visit . . . I'm here on business.'

'Ah, that explains it! Business travellers are always bold when they're away from home. If you were from Ochakov, you would have thought not just twice but a hundred times before inviting me anywhere!'

'Why, are the police officers in Ochakov afraid of you?'

'Not me,' said Valya, adjusting her scarf and tucking a lock of red hair back under it. 'My reputation! But really, I'm no different from any other woman.'

'Come on, let's go for a walk,' suggested Igor. 'You can show me the town. I don't even know my way round yet.'

'So get the local police officers to show you!' Valya got up from the bench and looked around. 'Maybe we can walk over to the trees, there aren't too many people over there.'

'Let's do that,' agreed Igor.

They wandered companionably through the park then along a narrow street, past squat single-storey buildings where the windows were already glowing with light. It wasn't only the windows that had been set ablaze by the evening but the street lamps too, which burned brightly at every corner. Their light-hearted conversation about nothing in particular was relaxed and unhurried, as though it had fallen into step with their slow-paced stroll. Igor didn't realise that they'd left the last city street behind until allotments began to appear along the sides of the road. Then several trees emerged from the twilight and the wind began to rustle their leaves. Igor glanced up. A scattering of stars had already pierced the sky and were shining down through the tiny holes they had made. Igor found Valya's hand and took it gently in his own, as though he feared she might resist. But she didn't. They continued on hand in hand, without looking at one another, as though their shared enjoyment of this evening walk was all either of them needed.

Half an hour later Igor heard the sound of the sea. Waves were rolling and breaking on the unseen shore. Valya's hand was very warm. Igor gave it a little squeeze and immediately felt Valya squeeze his hand, hard, in response.

'Be careful here,' warned Valya, leading him to the right.

They went down a narrow gully. They were walking on sand, which gave way beneath their feet.

When they reached the shore, Igor looked back and saw a cliff hanging over the narrow strip of beach. Valya sat down on the sand. Igor sat down next to her. He put his arm around her shoulders, and she leaned in towards him.

'It's nice sitting here with you like this,' she said. 'That uniform suits you. So does the gun!'

'May I kiss you?' asked Igor, turning to face her.

'No,' said Valya. 'It would be inappropriate. We're still on formal terms.'

'But you keep switching between formal and informal! Shall we just decide to address each other informally?' he suggested.

'Well, we would need to toast each other to seal our friendship, and I bet you haven't brought anything to drink!'

'No, I haven't,' agreed Igor, disappointed.

Valya put her hand on his shoulder in a gesture of consolation.

'You're all so indecisive now, after the war,' she said. 'All the brave ones must have died.' She smiled in mock sympathy.

'I'm usually decisive,' said Igor, who was immediately embarrassed by the timidity in his own voice.

'You mean, when you're catching bandits?' asked Valya, suddenly serious.

Igor nodded.

'Are there that many of them?'

'Who?'

'Bandits,' said Valya, looking straight into his eyes.

Igor thought about Fima and remembered what Vanya had told him about his relationship with Valya. He shrugged. He couldn't quite see the two of them together.

'There'll be more in about fifty years' time,' he said after a pause.

'Fifty years?' Valya's eyes widened. 'But the newspapers say that they'll all be gone in twenty years. They're going to train them as teachers and engineers, so that they can serve the country.'

'You shouldn't believe everything you read in the newspapers,' Igor began but stopped short, realising that he was in danger of saying too much. 'I mean, you should. Of course you should believe the newspapers. But you need to understand things for yourself.'

'I prefer books. Newspapers are full of boring facts, whereas books contain facts *and* romance. I like Vadim Sobko.'

'Who?'

'Haven't you heard of him? He's famous all over the world. He was awarded two Stalin Prizes before Stalin even died!'

'I've never read anything of his,' admitted Igor.

'What a shame I've already taken it back to the library . . . You ought to go and get it out. Otherwise you'll be like that police officer in the joke.'

'Which joke?' asked Igor, with mock indignation.

'Sorry! The one where two police officers are deciding what to give the third for his birthday. One of them says, "Let's buy him a book!" And the other says, "No, he's already got one!"'

'I've got more than one book at home,' said Igor, smiling.

Valya's eyes and lips were so close, so alluring and seductively aloof. Igor took her hand and pulled it towards him. He tried to kiss it but immediately felt her move his face firmly aside.

'Don't,' said Valya, her voice soft and apologetic. 'I'm sick. You might catch it too.'

'What do you mean? What is it?'

'I don't know what it's called. It's a disease that humans can catch from fish. Sometimes it makes me cough, leaving a bad taste in my mouth, and sometimes it makes my eyes water . . . It also means I can't have children.' These last words burst from Valya in a rush of emotion, as though she were on the point of tears.

She managed to compose herself and was silent for a few minutes. Then she looked up at the sky. The stars were shining down on them. In the distance a half-moon was floating on the surface of the sea, and the crest of a small wave could be glimpsed fleetingly in its light.

'But,' began Igor, cautiously breaking the silence, 'can't it be cured?'

'Probably. The doctor says he'll cure me if I leave my husband for him. Can you believe that?'

'You should report him!' Igor said indignantly.

'What's the point?' Valya's eyes and lips were very close again, but her eyes looked so sad that it didn't even occur to Igor to try and kiss her.

'What's the doctor's name?' asked Igor, feeling like a real police officer.

'Don't worry about it,' said Valya, waving her hand dismissively. 'Maybe he's just pretending that he knows how to cure me.'

It was after midnight by the time Igor returned to Vanya's house. The light was on in the kitchen and his young host was sitting at the table, reading the newspaper. When he heard footsteps on the porch he put the newspaper down and stood up.

The front door was open. Igor let himself in, went through to the kitchen and nodded at Vanya. They sat down at the table together.

'Would you like some wine?' asked Vanya. 'I'm not having any. I've already had two glasses.'

'Tell me,' Igor put his hand in the pocket of his breeches and took out a hundred-rouble note, 'is there a clinic or a hospital round here?'

'A hospital.'

'I want you to find the doctor who saw Valya. Give him this and get him to tell you the history of her disease, or at least the diagnosis. All right?'

Vanya shook his head.

'You will find the doctor who treated Red Valya and find out what she's got! All right? Get him to write it down.'

This time Vanya understood what was being asked of him. He nodded and slipped the hundred-rouble note into his jacket pocket.

'I'm going to bed,' said Igor, getting up from the table. 'I'm leaving early in the morning, but I'll be back in a couple of days. Goodnight.'

Igor didn't need to put the light on in the living room. He already knew exactly where everything was – the ancient sofa with the high wooden back, the chair and the little table. He got undressed, folded the police uniform and placed it on the stool, then lay under the warm quilted blanket and fell asleep.

16

The following morning Igor had a headache. His mother put her head round the door to his room, saw him lying in bed and retreated. A tractor rumbled past the house and the noise revived Igor, forcing him out of bed. His face was contorted in a painful grimace. The world was becoming increasingly full of unpleasant, irritating noises, and Igor's head was like a vacuum cleaner – sucking them in, tossing them about, mixing them together so that they merged into a continuous drone.

Igor reached out and felt the police uniform that lay on his stool, neatly folded as usual. The bundles of roubles were still there, and the gold watch, but there was something else too.

Igor took the breeches from underneath the tunic and gave them a shake. He found the film cartridge and took it out, staring at it with a look of utter perplexity.

'You're back then, are you?' His mother's face had appeared at the door again. 'Do you want anything to eat?'

Igor turned round to face his mother. She looked worried and upset.

'You've started drinking too much,' she said. It was more of an observation than a reproach, but her voice was trembling.

'No,' he protested, shaking his head. 'Not that much . . .'

'I can smell it on you.' His mother shook her head too. 'Have you got a new group of friends?'

Igor thought about it but didn't answer.

'I'm just popping out for an hour. I've got a few things to do,' she said. 'If you want anything to eat, it's all in the fridge.'

'Ma, where's Stepan?' Igor suddenly asked.

'Stepan? He was in the yard earlier, sharpening the spades.'

'I might go to Kiev today,' said Igor. He glanced at the wooden floor, which would soon need of a coat of paint. 'I won't be long . . . I just need to get a film developed.'

'I thought you had one of those digital cameras,' said his mother, surprised.

'I bought an antique one that uses film,' he lied.

'Why are you so interested in antiques all of a sudden? And what about that old uniform?' His mother nodded at the stool.

'It's no big deal. Everyone's into retro parties and vintage these days.'

Elena Andreevna left her son's room. Igor placed the film cartridge on the stool and got dressed. He stood at the window for a few minutes, looking out at the grey autumn day, which was about to burst into rain. His headache had subsided.

I wish I lived alone, he thought suddenly. Then I wouldn't be constantly under surveillance.

Igor smiled. He'd just remembered the bundle of 200-hryvna notes that Stepan had given him: 20,000 hryvnas! That was more than he needed to keep himself in beer and coffee . . . but not nearly enough for a place of his own. What if he were to invest it, though? Igor stopped smiling and grew serious as he contemplated this idea. There's no point investing in someone else's business, he decided. I'd never get it back. But what do I know about starting my own business? Nothing.

Igor decided to take the commuter train to Kiev. Although the sky hung low under the weight of the storm clouds, it still wasn't actually raining. He used to do this journey more often, taking the commuter train to Kiev and then walking to Victory Square. His route took him across the other platforms via the pedestrian bridge and down into Starovokzalnaya Street, which had been turned into a kind of market for suburban commuters. As well as kiosks and shops there were all kinds of little workshops, where you could prolong the life of an old pair of worn-out shoes, get the batteries in your watch changed or even fix the lock on a suitcase. Igor could remember seeing a little photo-processing place here. To Igor's delight, it was still there and the door was open. However, after inspecting the film the boy behind the counter shook his head.

'Can't do anything with that,' he said, handing the cartridge back to Igor. 'It's an old Svema film. Black and white, too. You need to take it to a proper lab.'

'What do you mean, a "proper lab"?' Igor asked in dismay.

'Fuji or Kodak. Let me think where the nearest one is . . .' He paused. 'You'll have to go to Khmelnitsky Street. Or Lviv Square, that would be a better bet. It's only five minutes by minibus from the circus. There are a couple of places past the House of Artists.'

Igor put the film cartridge in his jacket pocket, glanced up at the sky and started walking towards the circus.

The slick Fuji salon on Lviv Square was a far cry from the little shack on Starovokzalnaya Street. The man behind the counter wore a solemn expression and an expensive suit; a large printing and processing machine, which evidently originated from Japan or one of its neighbouring countries, was humming busily away behind him. Nevertheless, he couldn't help either.

'A Svema, eh?' He seemed surprised. 'I'm afraid I can't help you.' He looked back at the machine. 'It's programmed to work in colour. If we were talking a hundred black-and-white films, then we might be able to come to some arrangement.'

'Right,' said Igor, his voice a mixture of disappointment and despair. 'So isn't there anywhere in Kiev I can get it developed?'

'I didn't say that!' The man gave a guilty smile. 'You need to go to a professional. Try number 26 Proreznaya Street.'

Igor stuffed the cartridge back into his jacket pocket, nodded despondently at the man in the suit and went outside.

A light rain had begun to fall, apologetically, as though embarrassed by its own inadequacy – the heavy storm clouds were clearly capable of thunderous downpours, and yet all they had managed to produce was this pathetic drizzle.

The photography studio on Proreznaya Street had large windows facing the street. Several oversized prints of black-and-white photographs were on display behind the glass, and Igor stood there for a while admiring them. Even the tiniest details were clearly visible. Everything about the photos was contemporary – the people, the buildings – but the absence of colour emphasised the timelessness of the images and made Igor look at them more closely to see what he was missing. Colour photos can make you smile. They're great for holiday snaps but they rarely inspire you or make you think. Black-and-white photos are a different matter, and Igor felt this as soon as he set eyes on them.

When he'd finished admiring the photographs, he looked for the door to the studio. He found it in the courtyard.

This studio didn't have a counter or any processing machines. It reminded him more of a private apartment. The door to the room on the left was wide open, and the twin aromas of coffee and menthol cigarettes indicated that this was the kitchen. Further inside, down two little steps and through a set of open double doors, was a spacious room with two sofas and two armchairs, all arranged around a large coffee table with a thick glass top. A couple of photo albums lay on the table. One was still wrapped in cellophane, and the cover of the other featured one of the photographs from the studio windows.

'Can I help you?' A quiet female voice behind him made him jump.

Igor spun round and saw a short woman of about forty

years old, holding a cup of freshly brewed coffee in one hand. She had cropped ash-coloured hair and was wearing earrings inset with turquoise, a dark blue housecoat and fluffy slippers. Igor felt extremely uncomfortable, as though he'd barged into someone's home uninvited.

'I must have made a mistake,' he said hurriedly, taking the film out of his jacket pocket. 'I thought this was a . . . photography studio.'

Igor thought about walking straight past the woman and out of the door, but she'd already caught sight of the film cartridge and stopped him with a look.

'Can I see?' she asked, holding her free hand out towards him.

'Of course!'

'Take a seat,' she said, leading the way to the sofas and chairs. She placed her coffee on the table and sat in an armchair, then held the film cartridge up and inspected it more closely.

'So it hasn't been developed yet?' The woman looked at Igor.

'I don't think so.'

'Are they family photos?'

'What?' Igor didn't understand what she meant.

'I assumed you'd found it among your parents' things,' she said. Her voice became softer, more velvety. 'I once found three undeveloped films in the bag where my mother kept all her documents . . . One of them turned out to be full of pictures of my brother and me in Yevpatoriya in the 1970s. He was seven years old, and I was five.'

Igor listened attentively, nodding his head.

'Can you develop it for me?' he asked.

'Of course,' said the woman. 'My husband will be back in half an hour. He's the photographer, I just help out. You need to talk to him.'

The woman's husband was also called Igor – a short, wiry man with a pleasant demeanour. He was wearing a threadbare grey jacket and a checked shirt, which was tucked into his jeans. The top two buttons of the shirt were undone.

'I pride myself on the high quality of my work, and my prices reflect that,' he said immediately. 'You can take the film along to an amateur photography club and come to some arrangement with one of the old boys who use antique cameras, or you can leave it here with me – it's up to you. The price for developing and printing will be a hundred dollars.'

'A hundred dollars?' repeated Igor.

'Actually it should be at least two hundred and fifty. The chemicals are all imported, and then there's the special paper and so on. I'm offering you a one-off special price, an introduction to the world of professional photography.' He nodded at the film. 'You don't even know what's on there. And in any case it might already have been exposed to light. So think about it carefully – are you sure you want to go ahead?'

Igor-the-photographer stared searchingly into his visitor's eyes, as though he were hoping to dissuade him. Igor found himself momentarily reconsidering. He didn't have a hundred dollars on him, for a start.

'Yes,' said Igor. He looked down at the little plastic container. 'I'm sure. How long will it take?'

'Well, I can probably do it in a couple of days. I need to check I've got all the right chemicals, and then it's a question of finding the time. I'm working on various commissions and projects . . . Art for art's sake does not pay the rent!'

'Do I need to pay up front?' Igor asked warily.

'Of course,' sighed the photographer. 'If you just leave it with me, I might never see you again. But if the work's paid for I'll do it, then it's your choice whether or not to come back for the photos.'

Igor nodded.

'Fine, in that case I'll leave it with you,' he said, handing the cartridge to the photographer. 'I haven't got the money on me right now, but I . . . I'll call my friend. He might lend it to me.'

'Go ahead.'

Igor called Kolyan on his mobile.

'Hey, can you lend me a hundred dollars for a couple of days? I've got the money, but it's at home and I'm in Kiev.'

'No problem, come and get it!' Kolyan sounded particularly cheerful. 'I can lend you a thousand if you like. Just say the word!'

'I don't need a thousand, thanks.' Igor rang off and turned to the photographer. 'I'll be back with the money in an hour,' he promised.

'If I'm not here, just give it to my wife,' replied the photographer.

Kolyan bounded out of the bank. 'So what's it to be – beer, coffee, cappuccino?' he asked playfully, spreading his hands as if to indicate that in order to drink beer they would have to go one way, but in order to drink coffee they would have to go the other.

'You seem a bit weird today,' Igor observed cautiously.

'I'm not the same man I was yesterday.' Kolyan smiled and lowered his hands. 'I've just been given five thousand dollars! Come on, let's go.'

They headed to a cafe they both knew, five minutes' walk from the bank. They ordered a couple of espressos and sat down at a little table in the corner.

'Here you go!' Kolyan made a big show of taking a bundle of hundred-dollar notes out of his pocket. Peeling one off, he handed it to his friend. 'Do you need another one?'

Igor put the money in his pocket.

'One's enough. I need it to get a film developed.'

'A hundred dollars, just to develop a film? What's so special about it? What's it going to cost you to get it printed, another two hundred?'

'A hundred covers developing and printing. Remember I told you about Ochakov in 1957 and you didn't believe me? Well, that's where the film's from! You'll be able to see for yourself when I get the photos back.'

'What is it, you and Khrushchev with your arms round each other? Been having fun with Photoshop, have you?!'

Igor threw his hands up in exasperation.

'I'm only kidding.' Kolyan smiled. 'But I'm afraid I do have some bad news . . . The government's about to ban smoking blends!'

Igor scowled at him, and Kolyan decided to change the subject.

'You might not believe my news either, but I'm getting richer by the day. I've got the proof right here!' he said. He produced the bundle of hundred-dollar notes again.

'Is that from the wife of the businessman whose accounts you hacked into? For services rendered?' Igor asked sardonically.

Kolyan shook his head. 'It's from a friend of hers, who wants me to hack into his business partner's emails.'

Igor eyed the bundle of dollars then looked around to see whether anyone was watching them.

'Put it away, will you? It's making me nervous.'

'Tell me first, do you believe me?'

'Given the evidence, yes, I believe you,' Igor answered calmly. 'Why do you care so much what I think anyway?'

'It helps me believe in myself. That's just an advance, by the way. I'll get the same amount again once the deed is done.'

'I take it you're going to quit your job at the bank . . . They pay you peanuts!'

'What would I gain by leaving? I might as well stay. I enjoy the work, and I have access to the latest computers. Anyway, what's up with you today?' Kolyan leaned towards Igor, trying to get a closer look at his face.

'I'm fine!' Igor tried to smile. 'I'm just not too keen on the sight of big piles of cash. It probably reminds me of the day we sold the apartment in Kiev.'

'Ah, I get it,' said Kolyan, nodding sympathetically. 'You're missing Kiev. Never mind, when you make your fortune you'll be able to buy yourself another apartment. You know what? I envy you. You've got the forest right on your doorstep, the perfect venue for shashlik whenever you feel like it . . . In fact, how about this weekend? I'll bring the meat if you sort out the barbecue equipment and the beer.'

'Good plan!' Igor readily agreed.

After they went their separate ways, Igor wished they'd gone for a beer instead. It might have led to a very different conversation.

It took Igor about half an hour to walk from Podil to Proreznaya Street. The door to the photography studio was shut, so Igor rang the bell. Igor-the-photographer opened the doors but didn't invite his visitor inside.

'I'm with a client,' he said, tucking the hundred-dollar note into the breast pocket of his checked shirt. The top two buttons were still undone. 'Leave me your mobile number, and I'll call you when it's ready.'

The sky above Kiev had brightened and was no longer hanging quite so low. The wet concrete shone beneath his feet.

17

Igor checked his phone to see whether he'd missed any calls. He was pleased with the way things had gone in Kiev, and his buoyant mood had continued to improve as the evening wore on. Now it was time for bed, but he didn't feel remotely tired.

Maybe I should take another trip to Ochakov, thought Igor. Vanya might have some more films for me. I could even get him to take some photos of me out and about in the town . . .

Daydreaming in the evening often leads to sleep, and Igor drifted off without even realising it. Some internal anxiety caused him to wake suddenly at 12.30 a.m. It was completely quiet, both inside the house and out.

Igor got up and put the police uniform on. He tiptoed into the kitchen and drank a glass of brandy. With the taste of the brandy still on his tongue, he crept out of the house and closed the front door quietly, acutely conscious of the sound his boots made as they met the road.

He peered ahead, his eyes already used to the darkness. Finally the familiar lights appeared in the distance. The green gates grew closer. Igor stopped at the edge of the square. There was complete silence on both sides of the gates.

He stood there for about five minutes before setting off again. His feet already knew the way to Vanya Samokhin's house. Igor was delighted to see that the light was on in the kitchen window – someone was still awake, which meant that someone would let him in!

Vanya was sitting at the kitchen table, reading *The Wine-Maker's Handbook* in preparation for his studies at the Nikolaev College of Trade and Industry. He wasn't at all surprised to see the police officer at the window; he simply got up and went into the hallway to let him in. The first thing Igor did was remove his boots and stand them against the wall.

'You're late tonight,' said Vanya.

They went into the kitchen. Vanya tore a page from the calendar to mark his place in the book. He took a wine bottle from under the table and poured two glasses.

'Any news?' Igor asked him.

'Yes,' Vanya replied with a nod. 'I got a note from the doctor. Only it's written in medical language, so I can't understand what it says.'

'Have you got any more films for me?'

'Yes, two.'

'Have you got any left to take?'

'Yes, three,' said Vanya.

'Tomorrow morning . . . I want you to follow me. Take some photographs of me.'

'Photographs of you?' Vanya was surprised. 'Why?'

'Why do you think? As a souvenir of my trip,' Igor replied sharply.

'All right,' Vanya shrugged. 'Shall we do it first thing?'

'Yes. You'll be going to the market anyway, won't you?'

'Yes.'

'So let's start with the market. Right, I'm off to bed.' Igor stood up, feeling the weight of a long day on his shoulders.

'Don't you want some wine to help you sleep?' asked Vanya, surprised and a little dismayed. He glanced pointedly at the glasses of wine.

Igor took one of the glasses and brought it to his lips. The familiar sour smell hit his nostrils. Vanya picked up the other glass and gave a cautious smile.

'Let's drink to your studies,' Igor said quietly, indicating *The Wine-Maker's Handbook*.

'We can drink to that later,' Vanya whispered back. 'Let's drink to my mother's health instead!'

'All right,' agreed Igor. He took a large mouthful.

Vanya emptied his glass in one go and took a deep, contented breath, filling his lungs with air. Igor carried his glass into the living room, where he drank the rest of his wine before lying down, fully clothed, on the lumpy leather sofa.

He was woken early the following morning by the

cacophonous medley of birdsong and human voices outside Vanya Samokhin's house. The sounds were already familiar, but so different from his own home. Igor felt different too – full of energy and impulsive enthusiasm. He got up, brushed the creases out of the uniform and put on the belt and holster. Then he heard Vanya's footsteps on the other side of the door.

'Mother and I will head to the market first,' said Vanya, looking into the living room with shaving foam on his cheeks and a razor in one hand. He had obviously heard his guest getting up and rushed in to tell him the plan.

'But you're supposed to be taking photographs of me!'

'I'll take the camera with me. I just need to drop the wine off at my mother's stall. I dare say you'll be going to the fish section first anyway.' A sly smile spread across Vanya's face.

'Fine. I'll pull the door shut, like last time,' said Igor, choosing to ignore both the insinuation and the smirk.

He rolled up the blanket and put it at one end of the sofa. Then he went over to the window and looked out through the white lace curtain. The sound of a bicycle bell caught his attention, and he watched a man in a grey suit cycle directly towards two women, each of whom was carrying a three-litre milk churn. The women didn't seem to mind, though – on hearing the bell they jumped apart, and when the man had passed they came together again and resumed their animated conversation.

Igor soon saw Vanya Samokhin and his mother leave the house. They were both carrying heavy shopping bags. Igor felt quite sorry for them, while simultaneously marvelling at the impracticality of their system. Why not use a trolley or, as he'd seen numerous times in the provinces, an old pushchair?

Both Vanya and his mother were moving relatively swiftly in spite of the obvious weight of their loads. They turned left out of the gate and soon disappeared from view. Half an hour later Igor himself went through the gate and turned left.

He could feel salt on his lips from the light wind that was blowing into his face, reminding him of the proximity of the sea. Igor quickened his pace as though he were heading towards it. He even imagined that he could hear waves crashing to the shore. But real sounds took over as he approached the market. Igor strode through the familiar gates without even glancing at the fruit and vegetables on display. He was heading straight for the heart of the market in any coastal town – the fish section. He could already hear the voices of the sellers exalting their husbands' catches of herring, or mussels, or whatever else they had hauled from the waters.

'Damn!' Igor stopped suddenly, realising that he didn't have anything in which to carry the fresh flounder home. He looked around and saw an old woman selling string shopping bags, the kind he remembered from his childhood. He went over and bought one from her, then looked around again. Unable to spot Vanya, he continued on to the fish section at a more leisurely pace.

Red Valya was at her stall. Her face lit up when she saw Igor in his police uniform.

'Have you got any Black Sea flounder left?' Igor asked affably.

'I put some aside for you,' she said, smiling sweetly. Brazen sparks flashed in her eyes. 'Will five be enough?'

'Yes,' said Igor.

Valya spread a piece of newspaper on the counter, lay the flounder on top and deftly wrapped them up.

'How much do I owe you?' asked Igor.

'Ten roubles.'

'Are you doing anything this evening?' he whispered as he paid.

'Why do you keep pestering this married woman?' she whispered back playfully. 'If that bench suits you, I'll be there again at six.'

Igor tried to look around discreetly, hoping to see the camera lens trained on him and Valya, but he couldn't see anything. He put the parcel of fish into his string bag, smiled at Valya and walked slowly away from the counter. He stopped about five metres away, near some barrels of herring, to see whether Vanya was taking photos of him as agreed. Try as he might, he couldn't spot him among the colourful human chaos of the market.

Igor wandered about for another half an hour, sampling home-made salami, lightly salted pickles and fresh lard, before leaving the market via the side entrance. It was calmer there. He called into the little bar opposite the entrance for a glass of mineral water, then continued walking in the direction of Fima Chagin's house.

His feet seemed to be taking him there of their own accord. Unless it was the boots, which had been discovered in Fima Chagin's house . . . Maybe they wanted to go home?

Igor smiled. He stood outside the gate, looking at the house. Suddenly the front door opened and Chagin himself appeared on the threshold, a cigarette hanging from his mouth. He was about the same age as Igor. He stared at the police officer standing on the street outside his house. Igor, meanwhile, was rooted to the spot – his brain was telling him to leave, but his body refused to obey. Chagin walked up to the gate and fixed Igor with a cold, hostile glare. Then he took a deep drag on his cigarette before demonstratively stubbing it out against the gatepost and flicking it into the street.

Igor finally broke free of Chagin's stare. Lowering his eyes and keeping his face free of expression, he walked purposefully away. The bag of fish swung in his right hand and bumped awkwardly against his knee. Sensing Fima Chagin's eyes on his back, he didn't look over his shoulder or even slow down until he'd turned the corner into a different street.

Later that evening – after his date with Valya, during which he'd been seconds away from his first real kiss – he sat down at the kitchen table and once again interrupted Vanya's preparation for his future wine-making career.

Vanya laid five films on the table. His face bore an expression of naive and unabashed self-satisfaction, like a peasant who has managed to dupe someone into buying lame livestock.

Igor gave Vanya one hundred roubles to buy new films and two hundred roubles as a bonus. Vanya's expression changed to one of pride.

'Looks like I'm on the early-morning shift this week!' he joked as he tucked the money away in the pocket of his trousers, which looked like they had seen better days.

'Take as many as you can!' urged Igor, trying to curb Vanya's enthusiasm.

Vanya composed himself and nodded.

'Would you be able to bring me a couple of burnt-out light bulbs? I broke one by accident, and –'

'What do you want burnt-out light bulbs for?' interrupted Igor, surprised.

'Mother uses them to darn socks and tights. It's easier if you put a light bulb inside them.'

Once again they concluded the evening, and their conversation, with two glasses of dry white wine. Then Igor went through to the living room where he undressed, placed the uniform on the stool, put the bag containing the fish on the floor and lay down on the sofa.

18

Sleep deserted Igor at about midday, chased away by his mother's cheerful humming and the appetising smell of fried fish.

Igor wandered into the kitchen barefoot, wearing just a pair of boxer shorts.

'Thanks, son!' Elena Andreevna looked up from the spitting frying pan.

'A promise is a promise,' said Igor with a nod. 'You haven't invited Olga to lunch this time, have you?'

His mother shook her head.

'Stepan's coming, though,' she said. 'He's bought himself a suit!'

'A suit?' Igor's brain had trouble processing this piece of

information. 'For lunch? That's a bit over the top, isn't it?' he added with a smirk.

Elena Andreevna was offended, apparently on Stepan's behalf.

'You should think yourself lucky. I bought you your first suit when you graduated from school. Some people never get the chance to wear a suit!'

Igor shrugged. 'I've got nothing against suits,' he said calmly. 'Would it make you happy if I wore mine for lunch too?'

'Get out of here, you and your smart remarks!' His mother waved him away mildly and began turning the fish in the frying pan.

Half an hour later the flounder were melting in their mouths. They ate them with marinated cucumbers and boiled potatoes with dill, which complemented the fish perfectly. Stepan wasn't wearing a suit after all – he'd come wearing his normal clothes, although Igor couldn't help noticing that the gardener had shaved before joining them. So, he thought, his mother's invitation to lunch must have meant something!

'Is there any news from your daughter?' asked Igor, helping himself to boiled potatoes.

Stepan raised his eyebrows and turned to look at Igor.

'There will be, when the time is right,' he answered brusquely.

Elena Andreevna put another piece of fish on Stepan's plate.

'No, no, I've had plenty!' he protested.

'Isn't she married?' she asked cautiously.

'No. It's not easy to find a good husband these days.'

'Or a good wife, for that matter,' agreed Elena Andreevna, looking at her son.

Stepan also stared thoughtfully at Igor. Acutely aware of both sets of eyes upon him, Igor choked and began coughing. Stepan leapt up and thumped him hard on the back. Igor raised a hand to try and stop all the fuss.

'I swallowed a bone,' he said quickly, trying to suppress his cough.

When Elena Andreevna stood up and began collecting the plates from the table, Stepan looked at Igor again.

'Do you know anyone who might make a good husband for Alyona?' he asked. 'She's got a dowry now.'

'I don't know that many people,' confessed Igor. 'And I've only really got one friend – Kolyan.'

'The one who works in a bank?'

'That's the one.'

'Will you introduce them?'

Igor was taken aback by the request. 'Well, he was planning on coming out here soon for a barbecue . . . But I should warn you, he likes a drink or two!'

Stepan thanked Elena Andreevna for lunch and went out into the yard. A little while later Igor's mobile phone rang. It was the photographer's wife, letting him know that the prints were ready for him to collect. Igor was delighted by the news and quickly got ready to leave, taking the next lot of films with him.

The autumn sun was shining over Kiev, and Igor couldn't help feeling pleased – as though the sun were trying to support and enhance his good mood. People tend to walk faster when they're anticipating miracles. Igor had indeed quickened his pace, but he showed no sign of exertion – he wasn't at all tired or out of breath, even though he was walking up Proreznaya Street this time instead of down.

He reached the studio, turned into the courtyard and rang the doorbell. The photographer's wife opened the door and let him in. She was wearing the same dark blue robe and slippers as before. The air inside was different this time. It no longer smelt of freshly ground coffee or menthol cigarettes but of certain chemical compounds. The smell itself wasn't particularly offensive – just overtly professional, which was at odds with the domestic surroundings.

Looking through to the room with the sofas and armchairs, Igor could see a number of large-format black-and-white prints hanging from lines across the room, where they were drying.

Are they really mine? thought Igor, and his heart skipped a beat.

He took a step towards them, to get a better view. Without saying a word, the photographer's wife disappeared behind the kitchen door. The black-and-white prints featured naked girls sitting astride broomsticks, pretending to be witches. There was no way Vanya Samokhin could have taken those, especially not in Ochakov in 1957!

Igor walked over to the kitchen and looked through the door. The photographer's wife was standing with her back to him, facing the coffee machine. She seemed to sense Igor's presence and turned round.

'Would you like some coffee?'

Igor nodded.

'Take a seat in there,' she said, nodding towards the

reception room. She followed him in, carrying three cups of coffee on a tray.

There was the sound of curtains being pulled back vigorously, followed by the sound of running water. Then the photographer came through another doorway into the room. He was wearing a checked shirt with the top two buttons undone, as before, although the shirt was a different colour. Igor noticed that it was hanging out of his jeans. Following the direction of his gaze, the photographer tucked it in.

'I'll be right back,' he said, then went behind a screen that was covered in black cloth and started making rustling noises.

'There you go. See what you make of those,' he said, holding a padded envelope out to Igor and sitting down in one of the armchairs.

Igor reached into the envelope and took out a pile of photographs. He was hit by the same chemical smell he'd noticed on entering the studio. His hand automatically reached for his coffee cup, and he took a reassuring sip of thick, aromatic espresso.

Igor saw that the photographs were shaking in his hand. He placed them on the glass tabletop in front of him, then picked up the first one. It showed a plump woman standing in front of a gate, holding two bulky shopping bags. A single-storey building was clearly visible behind her. It seemed a bit odd that she was just standing there holding the bags, when she could have put them down on the ground . . . Not even her smile could conceal the weight of the bags, or rather the effort required to carry them, which was written all over her face. Puzzled, Igor held the photograph up to take a closer look.

The photographer stood up and moved a floor-standing spotlight over to Igor's armchair. He angled the lamp so that it was pointing at the photograph and switched it on. Igor's hands were immediately bathed in a warm glow. Furthermore, the photograph suddenly seemed to come to life, as though infused with colour.

That's Vanya's mother! realised Igor, peering at the woman's face. And I paid a hundred dollars for *this*?

Somewhat apprehensively, he picked up the second photograph. The spotlight spared him having to screw up his eyes or hold it inches from his face. This photograph showed a middle-aged man with prominent cheekbones walking down the steps at the front of Chagin's house. The man's lips were twisted in a dissatisfied grimace, and he was looking down at his feet. Igor decided that Vanya must have been lying or squatting down to the left of the gate. Igor recalled seeing a tree there. The next twenty or so images were of various other men, all of whom were sombre and unsmiling, defeated by life. Three individuals had been photographed several times. The profile of Chagin himself was visible in one of the shots.

Then suddenly there were three photographs of Red Valya at the market. In one of them she was extolling the virtues of her fish to a customer; in another, she was talking to a short man with a guilty look on his face.

'She's rather striking!'

Igor turned round at the sound of the photographer's voice. Igor-the-photographer pointed to Valya.

'I bet she's got red hair,' he said, sipping his coffee.

'Why do you say that?' asked Igor, surprised.

'I can tell by her face,' the photographer replied calmly.

'Redheads have distinctive facial features and a particular way of using their hands – they're more emphatic, more expressive.'

Igor thought about it. Did any of his contemporary acquaintances have red hair?

'Is she a relative?' asked the photographer.

'Yes . . . Well, not mine, my friend's.' Distracted by his own thoughts, Igor wasn't really paying attention.

'They're good,' the photographer went on. 'You could make a bit of money out of them, if they were family photos.'

'What do you mean?' Igor snapped out of his reverie.

'Some of my clients collect old family albums.'

'It's not a family album,' sighed Igor, looking through the photos again. He laid them out on the table in front of him. As he was doing so he suddenly remembered the name of the man with the prominent cheekbones, the one Vanya had photographed four times – it was Iosip. He and Vanya had seen him coming out of Chagin's house that evening, when they'd hidden under the apple tree.

'I've got five more films,' said Igor, looking up at the photographer. 'The thing is, five hundred dollars is a lot of money . . .'

'I haven't poured the reagents away yet,' said the photographer. His eyes were smiling. 'You'll just need to pay for the paper. Are these films the same as the last one?'

Igor placed the five plastic containers on the glass tabletop.

'Three hundred hryvnas,' said the photographer. 'German paper.'

'It's a deal,' Igor nodded.

* * *

When he got home Igor went into his bedroom, moved the reading lamp to his bedside table and looked through the photographs with a magnifying glass. They sent shivers running down his spine – the people, the buildings, even the trees in the photographs seemed so familiar. Magnified by the lens, Iosip looked exactly like Stepan, but it wasn't just him – Red Valya reminded him of an ex-girlfriend of Kolyan's called Alla, and also of the salesgirl in the kiosk at Irpen bus station where he always ordered an instant coffee.

'I must be tired,' Igor said to himself with a yawn. He stuffed the photographs back into the cardboard envelope and switched off the lamp. As he did so he remembered Vanya's request to bring him a couple of burnt-out light bulbs for darning socks, and his lips parted in a smile.

19

The following morning Stepan came to the house and asked Elena Andreevna to adjust the knot in his tie. When Igor came out of his room into the hallway, he found the two of them occupied by this very task.

Igor thought Stepan looked extremely strange. His tanned, weather-beaten face contrasted starkly with the new grey suit, and the expression on the gardener's face implied that he was all too aware of this – Stepan's eyes were full of uncertainty, and his thin lips were frozen halfway between a smile and its opposite.

After spending several minutes trying to align the knot in the tie with the top button of Stepan's shirt, Elena Andreevna gave a heavy sigh and lowered her hands.

'This knot isn't right,' she said, shaking her head.

Stepan's expression grew even more strained. He glanced in irritation and dismay at Igor, who was watching them both attentively.

'Could you possibly tie it again for me?' he asked eventually. 'Seems I've forgotten how to . . . It's not every year I wear a tie.'

Elena Andreevna hesitantly loosened the tie, undid the knot and turned up the collar on Stepan's shirt. She paused for a moment, then her hands began to weave a new knot. She seemed to be observing them objectively, marvelling that they still remembered how to tie a man's tie.

'There you go. That's better!' Igor's mother took a step back.

Stepan broke into a relieved smile and suddenly came to life. He rushed into the bathroom to look in the mirror, then out again.

'Are you off on a date?' asked Igor, with a hint of derision.

'No,' replied Stepan, looking intently at his landlady's son. 'I'm going for a walk.'

Without waiting for Igor to respond, the gardener went straight to the front door and disappeared outside.

Igor shrugged. He hitched up his tracksuit bottoms and went into the kitchen, where his mother was sterilising glass jars in a large pan on the stove. The air was hot and steamy, almost tropical. A bag of sugar sat in the left-hand pan of the scales on the windowsill, and Igor almost bumped into a basket of small tomatoes awaiting their fate.

'Did you want some breakfast?' asked his mother, turning round.

'No, I'm fine,' said Igor, retreating into the hallway.

The sun had migrated from the capital to the suburbs and hung in the very centre of the sky, almost directly over the bus station. Glancing up at the blue sky, Igor smiled. So what if it was raining in Kiev? Irpen was enjoying a golden, sun-drenched autumn!

Igor had originally planned to go to the local clinic and speak to a genito-urinary specialist about Red Valya's diagnosis, but he changed his mind before he even got there. Someone's bound to see me and report back to Mother, and then I'll never hear the end of it! he thought. At that moment, as luck would have it, he spotted a pharmacy. Igor waited outside while an old woman in a quilted jacket pushed her prescription through the little window at the counter; as soon as she left, he dived inside. The elderly female pharmacist smiled expectantly at him.

'A friend of mine has been given this diagnosis,' said Igor. 'I'm not even sure what medicine she needs. She's too embarrassed to come herself.'

The woman in the white coat took the piece of paper from him. She put her glasses on and peered at the writing on it.

'I can see why,' she said, looking up at Igor. 'She'd be better off going to the clinic and getting it treated properly. Or is she too embarrassed to do that as well?'

Igor panicked.

'No, she can't go to the clinic . . . She's worried she'll lose her job.'

The pharmacist browsed the array of medicines in the cabinet behind her.

'Well, if you're able to personally supervise the dosage,' she said, 'then –'

'I will,' promised Igor, who wanted to escape from this medicinal cornucopia as soon as possible. He was terrified that someone else would come in and overhear their conversation.

'Don't you need treating yourself, young man? It's not the sort of disease to be taken lightly.'

'No, definitely not,' Igor answered hurriedly, with a glance at the door. 'We're just friends!'

The pharmacist nodded, then sat down and began writing something on a piece of paper. Igor's nerves were stretched to their limit. Just then the door opened and a young woman came in. Her cheeks were unnaturally flushed, and her eyes were watering.

The woman in the white coat finally finished writing. 'Here,' she said, passing the piece of paper to Igor. 'I've written down the instructions for each medicine – there are thirteen altogether. So, that'll be eight hundred hryvnas.'

Igor was flabbergasted. He automatically felt his pockets. He knew he only had about a hundred hryvnas on him.

'I'll have to come back in half an hour,' he said, glancing at the woman behind him, who was holding her hand over her mouth and coughing discreetly. 'I didn't realise it would be quite so much. Can you put them aside for me?'

'It's the antibiotics that cost the most. I'm afraid they're the only option these days.' The pharmacist spread her hands sympathetically. 'So, are you going to take them?'

'Yes, definitely,' Igor assured her, backing away from the counter. 'I just need to get the money.'

Igor had planned to spend the afternoon 'loafing around the house', as his mother sometimes put it, but things didn't turn out that way. No sooner had he picked up the TV guide to plan his viewing schedule for the rest of the day than Kolyan called.

'I hope you're at home,' he exclaimed cheerfully.

'Er, yes.'

'Well, I'm in a minibus taxi on my way to your place. I've got meat and vodka! Although, come to think of it, you were supposed to provide the drinks . . .'

'Meat and vodka?' repeated Igor, sounding somewhat less enthusiastic than his friend.

'Aren't you pleased?'

'Of course I am!' declared Igor, managing to sound genuinely enthusiastic.

'Well, you'd better get the skewers, the matches and the glasses ready!'

In less than five minutes Igor had reconciled himself to the change of plan and was looking forward to the barbecue. He checked once more that it wasn't going to rain, then selected two large shot glasses from the kitchen cupboard and took a couple of onions from the basket under the table, in case they needed them. Two plates, for the sake of propriety, and a couple of forks. By the time he'd finished getting everything together, he'd managed to fill two carrier bags.

⋆ ⋆ ⋆

'You take after your mother all right!' remarked Kolyan, when he saw his friend standing there armed with the bulging carrier bags, ready for the afternoon.

They decided to base themselves in a small birch grove about three hundred metres from the nearest house. It had the added bonus of an abundant supply of firewood. Igor spread a square of oilcloth and laid out the plates, then started preparing the fire.

Meanwhile, Kolyan wandered about singing to himself. As chief benefactor, having provided the meat for the shashlik, he was fully entitled to do so. Suddenly he cried out. Squatting down in the undergrowth, he turned and called out to Igor.

'Hey, bring me a knife and a carrier bag!'

Kolyan cut two sizeable orange-cap boletus mushrooms and put them into the carrier bag. From that point on his energies were entirely devoted to mushroom hunting and he no longer paid any attention to his friend, who was busy assembling a small grill for the shashlik over the roaring fire.

Neither of them bothered to keep an eye on the time. It was irrelevant, anyway. They had the whole afternoon ahead of them and it was going to revolve around quality leisure time, in which shashlik and vodka would play a critical role. The only limits on such occasions are the energy and stamina of the participants. As the birch firewood turned to coals, Kolyan returned to the fire with his bag full of mushrooms and opened the bottle of Nemirov vodka. Given the success of his spontaneous foraging Kolyan decided on the first toast.

'To the mushroom harvest!' he declared, raising his glass in a jubilant mood.

Kolyan didn't even chase his first shot of vodka, simply

sniffing a piece of bread instead. He did, however, start eyeing up the plastic bucket of marinated meat that he'd brought with him. Reaching for the skewers, he set about skilfully threading pieces of pork onto them.

'You know what, it takes me an hour's trek by metro and minibus taxi to get to the nearest forest . . . but you've got it all right on your doorstep. I ought to buy a dacha round here.'

'Business is booming then, I take it,' remarked Igor.

Kolyan smiled. 'It's only a matter of time. A good hacker will always be in demand – everyone needs information!'

Igor thought about it. 'I don't,' he said, smiling back at his friend.

'Yeah, but what do you matter? You've got no *ambition*. By Soviet standards you're a parasite and a sponger. I bet you'd love to be a landlord! Letting something out and living off the money you earn, without having to actually do anything . . . Trouble is, you'd need something to let out in the first place, which you don't have. If you want to buy an apartment or an office, you need to be making five to ten thousand dollars a month, or more. That's why people need information!'

'Well, if you happen to come across any information worth ten thousand dollars a month, do me a favour and send it my way!' retorted Igor, not at all offended at being called a parasite and a sponger. 'The thing is, I'm just not a natural businessman. I see myself as more of a treasure hunter – always have done, really, ever since I was little.'

'Well, I'm happy to drink to you finding your next treasure trove!' Kolyan burst out laughing and filled their glasses. 'So, what are we drinking to? A pot of gold, or a chest full of diamonds?'

'A suitcase full of diamonds and guns.'

They clinked glasses and downed their shots. Kolyan placed the skewers of meat over the glowing birch coals. Igor felt a sudden and overwhelming urge to bring up the subject of his trips to Ochakov again, but two shots of vodka were not enough to loosen his tongue. Particularly since all previous attempts to tell Kolyan about Ochakov had been crushed by the scathing sarcasm of his response.

The shashlik was cooked to perfection, so much so that they soon ran out of vodka to wash it down with. The empty bottle lay near the campfire, dampening their mood.

Igor volunteered to rescue the situation. 'I'll go back for more,' he declared, swallowing the piece of meat he'd been chewing.

'Needs must,' said Kolyan with a nod. 'Your country will thank you for it!'

The journey home took about ten minutes. Igor went straight to the kitchen and took a bottle of brandy from the cupboard. The door creaked behind him.

'Are you back, then?' asked his mother.

'No, we've just run out of supplies. You used to have a bottle of homebrew in here somewhere, didn't you?'

'In there, under the sink.'

Putting the brandy back in the cupboard, Igor bent down and opened the little wooden door. He took out a two-litre jar of home-made vodka and looked around in search of a smaller container.

'You could pour some into a smaller jar,' suggested his mother, pointing at a bag that contained her spare preserving jars.

'We're not tramps!' Igor shook his head. 'We used to have some empty beer bottles, didn't we?'

'I took them out to the shed.'

Igor went outside and glanced into the shed. Stepan wasn't there. He took an empty bottle and went back into the kitchen, where he filled it with vodka and sealed it with a wine cork. As he was doing so he had an idea for a stunt he could pull on Kolyan, which might finally convince his friend that he really had been to Ochakov in 1957. He went through to his bedroom and put the old police cap on his head, then fastened the belt around his waist and inserted the gun into the holster. He went back into the kitchen, grabbed the beer bottle from the table and left the house.

It was already getting dark outside. At the gate Igor bumped into Stepan, who stopped and stared at him in surprise, glancing ironically at the cap, belt and holster.

'You look like you're enjoying yourself,' he said, then smiled and went into the yard. The gardener's voice floated back to him. 'Just make sure you don't get too attached to that uniform, or you might find you won't be able to live without it!'

The white trunks of the birch trees created the illusion of prolonged twilight. At the point where their little grove merged with the coniferous forest, night had fallen and darkness reigned.

Kolyan was staring into the campfire. 'Oh!' he exclaimed when he saw Igor. 'Is it a retro picnic now?'

'Yeah, something like that.' Igor sat down next to the square of oilcloth that was serving as a table. He held the beer bottle out to his friend. 'I'm afraid we're going to have to switch to home-made vodka, though.'

'Did you make it yourself?'

'No, my mother gets it from the next-door neighbour.'

'Your neighbour wouldn't poison you!' Kolyan took the bottle, removed the cork and inhaled. 'Oh! It smells of the earth! The art of the people! A celebration of the unbreakable spirit of the nation!' He brought the bottle to his nose once more.

As everybody knows, it's impossible to drink home-made vodka without food to chase it. Fortunately Kolyan never did things by half and had brought no less than a kilo and a half of meat. They'd already eaten three skewers each, and six more skewers of meat were still cooking over the mellow embers of the fire.

As he knocked back the first shot from the beer bottle, Igor felt his appetite return. The shashlik meat was not as tender as before, but it still tasted delicious. Kolyan devoured another skewer too.

'Oh, I still owe you a hundred dollars,' exclaimed Igor, suddenly remembering. 'Come back to mine later and I can give it to you then.'

Kolyan waved his hand dismissively. 'Some things are worth more than a hundred dollars,' he said, nodding at the bottle. He picked it up and refilled their glasses.

The homebrew ran out after about twenty minutes. Igor and Kolyan kept eating until they'd finished the meat, more out of a sense of duty than because they were actually enjoying it.

Igor casually took the gun out of the holster and started looking at it.

'What's that you've got there?' Kolyan leaned towards his friend.

'Oh, just something I found in a treasure chest,' replied Igor, with a drunken smirk.

'Is it real?'

'Yes, and there's a uniform to go with it.'

'Let me see.'

Igor gave the gun to Kolyan. He could still feel the cold metal grip in his warm hand.

'Put the empty bottles on that tree stump over there,' said Kolyan.

Igor placed both bottles on a birch stump about five metres away from where they were sitting. Kolyan took aim. He pulled the trigger, but no shot was fired. Surprised, he took aim and pulled the trigger again. Another empty click.

'Isn't it loaded?' asked Kolyan, looking at Igor.

'Yes, it is,' said Igor. 'I checked.'

'I've got an idea,' said Kolyan. 'Why don't you let me have it? You never gave me a present for my birthday!'

'You said the best present people could give you was to come dressed in "retro" fancy dress. Anyway, why do you want a gun that doesn't shoot?'

'It might come in handy. You and I know it doesn't shoot, but other people don't know that. It could still save my life.'

'As if anyone's bothered about your life,' smiled Igor, taking the gun back from his friend. 'Do you want to scare all the drunks with it?'

Kolyan waved his hand dismissively and seemed to forget all about the gun.

'Right! Let's head back,' he said, struggling to stand up. 'What time's the last minibus?'

'You might as well stay over at my place,' said Igor. 'You're in no fit state to travel.'

'What are you saying?' Kolyan cried indignantly. 'It's impossible to get drunk if you're eating as well as drinking – and we had plenty of food!'

Apparently true to his word, Kolyan managed to pull himself together. He helped Igor pack up and even remembered the carrier bag full of mushrooms that he'd gathered at the start of the afternoon. Stumbling and swaying, they left the forest and shuffled along the road – past houses lit only from within, past windows that stood out like egg yolks, beyond which the inhabitants of Irpen were getting ready for bed.

They stopped at Igor's gate. Kolyan flatly refused to stay the night. Igor had neither the strength nor the desire to walk his friend to the minibus stop, but Kolyan didn't ask him to.

'I know where it is,' he said, and set off in the direction of the bus station.

20

The photographer called at around 11 a.m. the following morning. Igor thought he sounded almost too friendly.

'Everything's ready! The quality is magnificent, I'm sure

you'll be delighted,' he said. 'You're welcome to come and collect them, preferably before two o'clock as I need to leave then – I've been commissioned to do a family portrait for one of the deputies.'

Why did he tell me that? thought Igor, surprised. Did he think I'd be impressed?

He slipped his mobile phone back into his pocket and looked at his watch. It would take him about an hour to get into town, to be 'delighted' by the 'magnificent quality' that awaited him there, and it was a full three hours until the photographer had to leave. Time was very much on his side, so there was no need to rush. The day felt like an echo of the night before – he didn't have a headache or any other sign of a hangover, as such, but was consumed by listlessness.

He made himself a cup of tea, with three spoonfuls of sugar instead of his usual one. Then an instant coffee. Eventually he started preparing to leave, but when he was ready he looked at his watch and felt another wave of inertia – he didn't even feel like moving, let alone going into town. He wandered out into the yard. The sky was gloomy and grey. He glanced over his shoulder then walked towards the shed. The door was slightly open, and there was a quiet, muffled noise coming from inside. He looked through the gap in the door and saw Stepan extracting nails from wooden boards with the end of a hammer. There were three separate piles of boards lying on the concrete floor.

Stepan glanced up at his landlady's son.

'You look rather the worse for wear,' he remarked indifferently. 'I dismantled an abandoned fence. I'm going to make a couple of storage crates. They might come in handy.'

First a new suit, now storage crates, mused Igor. 'Where were you off to yesterday, dressed so smartly?'

'I just went for a walk around the town. The first of many! I want people to get used to seeing me around. I'm starting a new life, and I'm here to stay.'

'With us?'

Stepan smiled. 'No, I've had enough of sleeping in sheds. I'm going to buy a house. I can afford it now. I seem to remember that you were planning on buying a motorbike, weren't you?'

'In the spring,' said Igor, waving his hand airily. 'There's no point at the moment.'

'True, a motorbike isn't much use in winter,' agreed Stepan.

By a stroke of luck, Igor was the last passenger the minibus taxi been waiting for, and it set off as soon as he got in. There was no Radio Chanson this time, but Igor barely even noticed. He was quite happy to let his mind wander – first he imagined himself buying a motorbike in the spring, then he started thinking about the photographer and his wife.

The photographer greeted Igor with a smile and offered him brandy with his coffee, which was rather unexpected. It would have been foolish to refuse such hospitality. Igor sat down on one of the soft leather armchairs and looked around the room. Over by the black screen he saw some photographs attached to a nylon cord with little multicoloured pegs. They were somebody else's studio portraits.

'My wife's gone to visit her mother,' said the photographer, approaching Igor from behind. He was carrying a tray containing two coffee cups, two brandy glasses and a bottle of Hennessy, which he placed on the coffee table. He poured brandy into the glasses, then fetched a long-handled copper coffee pot. Igor thought the coffee, as it was poured from the *cezve*, looked unusually thick.

The photographer brought five large envelopes over and put them on the table, then sat down in the other armchair.

'I'm beginning to find you very interesting,' he said. He picked up his brandy glass and turned to Igor, indicating that he should follow suit.

Igor lifted the glass to his nose and inhaled. It had a distinguished aroma, particularly after the home-made vodka he'd been drinking with Kolyan – although that hadn't been at all bad! Igor smiled, remembering the previous evening.

'These films,' began the photographer. He sipped his brandy. 'Look, I'm a professional and I know everything there is to know about photography. Well, almost everything. But I have to admit, I'm completely at a loss here. I'd love to know how you do it. You're using old films, and taking old-fashioned photos, right?'

'What do you mean?' Igor stared at the photographer.

'I assure you, my interest is purely professional. If someone showed me pictures like this on their computer, I would congratulate them on their Photoshop skills. But you brought me real films. Everything appears to be set in the past – at least the decor and costumes appear to be authentic – yet you're in the photos yourself . . . Were they taken on the set of some historical drama? Do you work in cinematography?'

Igor shook his head and smiled.

The photographer took a sip of coffee and poured some more brandy into his glass. Then he pushed the envelopes across the table to his client. Igor took the photographs out of one of the envelopes and looked through them. He saw himself standing in front of Red Valya's counter. He saw her wrapping the fish up in newspaper. He saw a man standing behind him, staring at Valya.

'You could turn this lot into an excellent, and highly original, photography exhibition.' Smiling broadly, the photographer looked at his client again. 'You could use the same method in your advertising . . . I think you could make a decent amount of money, as well as a bit of a name for yourself. You seem to be quite an ambitious young man!'

Igor burst out laughing. Me? Ambitious? he thought happily.

'It's just a hobby,' he said after a few moments, keen to maintain the good-natured atmosphere over the coffee table. 'Maybe I'll take a few more, and then we'll see!'

'What camera do you use?'

The question caught Igor off guard.

'An old one,' was all he said.

His answer was obviously music to the photographer's ears. 'I'm willing to develop and print your next films for free,' he said. 'On one condition.'

'What?'

'That if you do decide to put on an exhibition of your pictures, you come to me first. I'll arrange everything for you. You clearly have an exceptional talent, and a great imagination.'

'All right,' agreed Igor. He reached for the bottle of Hennessy and poured some into his glass. 'It's a deal.'

With the envelopes tucked under his arm, Igor walked down Proreznaya Street to Kreshchatyk Street. When he got to the metro station he called Kolyan.

'Hello?' said a woman's voice.

'Oh, sorry, I must have got the wrong number –'

'Don't hang up!' said the voice. 'Who are you trying to reach?'

'My friend Kolyan. I mean, Nikolai.'

'He's here, but he can't talk right now. Can I give him a message?'

'Where's "here"?' asked Igor.

'The Accident and Emergency hospital on Bratislavsky Street. Your friend was the victim of a violent assault yesterday. He's recovering in one of the wards.'

'This is Igor. Tell him it's Igor! I owe him some money,' said Igor, then he stopped abruptly. 'Can I see him?'

'Of course,' said the woman's voice. 'Fifth floor of the main building, Ward Seven.' The woman gave Igor directions to the hospital, and the escalator carried him down to the metro.

Kolyan's bed was up against the wall on the left-hand side of a six-bed ward. The door to the ward was wide open. Two large top windows were also open, and Igor was struck by a gust of wind that carried the smell of rotten autumn leaves. A length of clear plastic tubing, twisting and coiling like a snake, connected an intravenous drip bag to Kolyan's right wrist. Igor was shocked by the sight of his friend – Kolyan's face was partially covered with bandages, but the exposed parts were swollen and dark blue. His eyes were closed.

Igor noticed Kolyan's mobile phone lying on the bedside cabinet. Fetching a chair from the entrance to the ward, Igor placed it next to his friend's bed and sat down. He reached out a hand, wanting to wake Kolyan up, to let him know he was there, but then he hesitated. Igor went out into the hospital corridor and looked around, hoping to see a doctor or a nurse, but there was no one about. He walked along the corridor, glancing through the open doors of the other wards. Some patients were reading books or newspapers; one young man with a bandage around his head was wearing earphones, his eyelids twitching in time with music only he could hear. Igor walked up and down the corridor several times, until he heard a mobile phone ringing in the ward next to Kolyan's. Curious, he looked in and saw a phone vibrating on a bedside cabinet next to a patient with both arms in plaster, a bandaged head and mottled bruising around his eyes. When the man in plaster saw Igor, he jerked his chin up and tried to speak. Understanding immediately, Igor walked over and picked up the phone.

'Hello,' he breathed.

'It's Varya. Is that . . . the doctor?'

'No. I'm just visiting a friend in the next ward.'

'Is Kostya there?' The woman's voice sounded scared.

Igor turned to the man in plaster.

'Is your name Kostya?' he asked, reading the answer in the man's eyes.

'Yes, he's here, but he can't talk right now.'

'I know. Just tell him . . . tell him that Varya called. I'll come and see him this evening. Tell him that I love him!'

'OK,' Igor promised and put the mobile phone back down.

'Varya called,' he said to the owner of the phone. 'She said she loves you, and that she's coming this evening.'

The man's face did not show any sign of joy. Nodding goodbye, Igor left the ward and noticed the sign on the outside of the door: Ward No. 5. That was strange – why wasn't Ward No. 5 followed by Ward No. 6? He checked the numbers of the wards on the opposite side of the corridor, but they were all double digits.

'Are you looking for someone?' came a woman's voice from behind him. It sounded familiar.

He turned round. Finally, a nurse! She was young and cheerful-looking, with dark hair. She was like an idealised image of a nurse, but for the colour of her uniform, which had been washed so many times it had long since lost its snow-white purity.

'Yes. My friend's here . . . in Ward Seven.'

'Ah, the one they brought in last night?'

'Yes. What happened?'

'He's got a CHI, concussion, bruises and suspected broken ribs.'

'A CHI?' Igor repeated in alarm.

'A closed-head injury,' explained the nurse.

'Is he going to be all right?'

'Yes. He'll have to stay here for a couple of days, and then we'll send him home,' the nurse said gently. 'Under supervision.'

'Is he asleep at the moment?'

'Why don't we go and see?' The nurse turned round and started walking towards Ward No. 7. Igor hurried after her.

Kolyan was lying with his eyes open, staring at the ceiling. He tried to smile when he saw the nurse and Igor, but instead his wounded lips grimaced in pain.

'How are you?' asked Igor, leaning over him.

The look in Kolyan's eyes told him all he needed to know. Igor nodded and put the photo envelopes down on the floor.

'I brought you the money I owe you, a hundred dollars . . . Shall I leave it with you?'

Kolyan shook his head. 'No,' he murmured. His swollen, cut lips were making it difficult for him to talk.

Igor waited until the nurse had left the ward, then sat down on the chair next to the bed. 'Who did this to you?' he asked urgently.

'I didn't see,' whispered Kolyan. 'They got me from behind.'

'After you left my place? In the street?'

'No, in Kiev, in the lobby of my apartment building.'

'Did they take anything?'

Kolyan moved his head slightly from side to side. 'Not even my phone.' He looked at the bedside cabinet.

'They could tell it was a cheap one,' said Igor.

Kolyan tried to smile again, without any luck.

'My jacket's in there,' he murmured. 'Take it out.'

Igor opened the bedside cabinet and took out the black canvas jacket that Kolyan had been wearing the day before. It was covered with pockets and rivets. He unfolded it and looked at his friend.

'There's some cash in the pocket,' whispered Kolyan.

Igor started uncertainly groping the front of the jacket.

'No, not there,' his friend whispered urgently. 'In the lining.'

Perplexed, Igor looked inside the jacket and found a secret pocket. He opened it and took out a thick bundle of hundred-dollar notes.

'This?' he asked.

Kolyan gave a barely perceptible nod. 'Take it. You can give it back later,' he said.

Igor put the money in his pocket, then folded the black jacket up again and put it back in the bedside cabinet.

Suddenly his ears were assaulted by the sound of Kolyan's mobile phone. In the hushed silence of the hospital, the cheerful ringtone sounded farcical. Igor picked up the phone.

'You're still alive, then?' asked a slightly affected male voice, almost playfully.

'Are you calling to speak to Kolyan?' asked Igor. 'He can't talk right now. Can I take a message?'

'Tell him I'll finish him off. He'll know who it is. Who are you?'

'A friend,' said Igor, disconcerted.

'Will you be coming to his funeral?'

'What?' gasped Igor. He hung up immediately and put Kolyan's phone back on the bedside cabinet.

'He said that he was going to "finish you off",' said Igor, looking directly into Kolyan's eyes. 'He said you'd know who it was.'

Kolyan was silent. He looked up at the ceiling, then closed his eyes.

'Do you want me to leave?' asked Igor.

'Stay for a while,' whispered Kolyan.

'Who was it?'

'One of three.'

'Which three?' Igor didn't understand.

'One of the three whose systems I hacked into,' answered Kolyan. 'Probably that woman's husband.'

'The one whose emails you copied?'

'Yeah,' sighed Kolyan.

'Did you sleep with her?' hissed Igor, bending down to his friend's ear.

Kolyan didn't answer.

'I'm going,' Igor said firmly. 'I don't like what you've been up to lately.'

'Neither do I,' mumbled Kolyan. 'Will you come tomorrow?'

'Yes. Bye.'

Igor picked his envelopes up from the floor. He looked closely at his friend, waved goodbye then went out into the corridor. He bumped into the nurse again outside the next ward.

'Are you leaving already?' she asked.

Igor nodded.

'Can I ask you a question?' He went right up to her, as though there was a chance she might not hear him otherwise. 'Why do you have Ward Five and Ward Seven, but no Ward Six?'

The nurse beamed at him.

'You noticed!' she exclaimed, delighted. 'Most people don't. If we did have a Ward Six, we'd be inundated with complaints. One of the doctors arranged it that way. You know how planes don't have a row thirteen, because no one would want to sit in it . . .'

'Don't they?' Igor wasn't convinced.

'Of course not,' the nurse assured him. 'Well, Ward Six is the hospital equivalent.'

Still feeling confused, Igor walked down the concrete stairs to the ground floor and left the building. He looked back up at the window of the casualty department, then walked to the tram stop. He could hear rooks cawing loudly in the tall pine trees nearby. The smell of rotten leaves, stronger now, was a constant reminder of the proximity of the forest.

21

Evenings in Irpen are darker than they are in Kiev. Igor noticed this every time night fell as he was on his way home, which seemed to happen often. He couldn't stop thinking about the sight of Kolyan's swollen lips. He could still hear the man's taunting tone as he promised to finish Kolyan off. Igor was scared for his friend.

The familiar windows of his home appeared ahead of him. Igor went inside and took off his shoes, then went into the kitchen. He poured a shot of brandy, took a sip and sat down at the little table, expecting the brandy to calm him down straight away. He glanced at the scales. The left-hand pan was empty – no tablets, no bills waiting to be paid. Igor got up and moved several weights from the right-hand pan to the left, trying to balance them, but he couldn't get it right. His glass soon ran low, but he still felt agitated. Never mind, good things come to those who wait, thought Igor, smiling as he filled his glass again. After his third glass of brandy Igor stopped fiddling with the scales. He started thinking instead about the strange conversation he'd had with the photographer. Yes, it would be good to earn a bit of money out of them, thought Igor. If only I knew how!

He spread the photographs out in front of him and started

trying to put them into some kind of order. The ones that were easiest to arrange were those that Vanya had taken the day he'd photographed Igor in his police uniform at the market. There was a logical sequence to them, and in any case Igor could clearly remember being at the market that day – which stalls he'd stopped at, what he'd looked at. Three photographs that had been taken of him talking to Red Valya drew his attention like a magnet. They deserved to be framed and hung on a wall. She really is beautiful, thought Igor. So full of life. Those mischievous eyes, that smile that makes you want to kiss it, those dimples in her cheeks . . . They were more noticeable in the photographs than in real life. And what about the way she'd agreed so boldly to a date with an unknown police officer? She might be beautiful, but it was still foolish, all the more so because she was a married woman. Igor thought about it for a moment, then shook his head. No, it wasn't foolish, he decided. Things were just different back then, including police officers. And she was obviously bored with her husband.

He looked at her lips again, her smile. I can see her tomorrow if I want to, he thought. And give her the medicine . . . I can cure her! It doesn't matter whether I'm doing it for her, for myself or for her husband. Igor filled his glass again.

'To me!' he whispered, because he had to drink to something.

He swallowed some brandy, and a self-congratulatory smile spread across his face. Igor felt happy. Furthermore, he was brimming with every good quality he could think of. He was almost as virtuous as Mother Teresa! And there was nothing to stop him performing another good deed. All he had to do was put on the old police uniform, and it would instantly stop being old.

'Ma, have we got any burnt-out light bulbs?' he asked, glancing into the living room.

Elena Andreevna looked up from the television.

'What do you need them for?'

'I just do.'

'They're in the shed, in the far right-hand corner.'

When Igor opened the shed door, the bright light inside almost blinded him. Stepan was sitting on a stool directly beneath the light bulb that hung from the ceiling, reading a book. Igor stared at him, puzzled.

'Good evening,' said the gardener.

'Good evening,' answered Igor. 'Sorry, I won't be a minute . . .'

He went to the far right-hand corner of the shed and immediately saw a bag containing about a dozen burnt-out light bulbs. What's she keeping them for? he wondered, bending down. He chose two foreign bulbs with a matt finish, because their glass seemed a little thicker. Then he heard Stepan's voice behind him.

'I was thinking about going to a cafe a bit later. Would you like to join me?'

'What do you mean?' Igor didn't understand.

'We could have supper together,' suggested Stepan.

'No, I can't, I've got to be somewhere.'

'That's a pity,' said Stepan. 'Well, can you recommend a good cafe?'

'All the good cafes are in Kiev. As for round here,' shrugged Igor, 'I really don't know what they're like.'

'Well, you should know! You live here, as do a thousand other decent people, all of whom are entitled to good cafes and restaurants.'

Igor stared at Stepan, trying to work out whether the gardener was reprimanding him or simply being naive. Meanwhile, Stepan was eyeing the two matt light bulbs in Igor's hands and wondering what his landlady's son was up to.

Back in his room, Igor got dressed in the old police uniform, fastening the belt and holster around his waist. He took the gun out of the wardrobe, where he'd hidden it from his mother's curiosity. After trying it out at the barbecue, he now knew that it was a useless fake. On the other hand, if Igor had given Kolyan the gun when he'd asked, it might have frightened off his attacker.

Igor turned the gun over in his hands, trying to decide whether or not to take it with him. He brought it to his nose and inhaled. Igor liked the smell of gun oil, and it was a good feeling holding this heavy toy, even if that's all it was. Eventually Igor slipped the gun into the holster and found a bag for the light bulbs. He put Valya's medication into the bag too, along with the pharmacist's handwritten instructions. Holding the carrier bag, he glanced into the living room to let his mother know that he was going out. His mother wasn't sitting in front of the television for once; she was at the ironing board, carefully ironing creases into a pair of trousers.

'Ma! I've told you before! Nobody wears creases in their trousers these days!' exclaimed Igor.

'They're Stepan's,' answered his mother. 'He's going somewhere in his suit this evening. It must be something important!'

'Yeah, I bet it is.' Igor smiled. 'I'm going out now, and I'll be back tomorrow or the day after. Don't worry about me.'

As soon as he'd said this he closed the door and walked briskly down the hallway, the heels of his police boots knocking against the wooden floorboards. He heard his mother's voice behind him but couldn't make out what she was saying, nor did he try to.

It wasn't long before he'd left the house behind. The evening was wrapping the street in its dark cotton wool, muffling sounds and thickening the air. An old Moskvich car drove past, overtook Igor and turned into another street, disappearing from view.

Igor quickened his pace. He wore a tense smile and all his thoughts, all his feelings, were focused on his impending immersion in another world. There was a different kind of meaning behind the windows and faces in this world, a different energy in its gestures and movements. The eyes of its inhabitants burned with a unique spirit, in both solemnity and joy.

Drunken excitement seemed to accelerate the dark time of day. The familiar lights of the Ochakov Wine Factory soon appeared in the distance. When Igor was about two hundred metres away, the green gates opened and the old lorry came out. It turned and drove off towards the town, its headlights illuminating the road ahead. Just as Igor reached the edge of the square, the gates creaked again and opened slightly. A young lad carrying a sack of wine over his shoulder stuck his head out. He turned and waved to the guard, and the gates closed again after him.

Igor peered closely at him. The lad was about the same

height and build as Vanya, but there was something different about his posture and the way he was moving. It wasn't Vanya. The lad carrying the leather wineskin took several steps towards the road, then stopped and adjusted his burden. Igor emerged from under the trees.

'Hey!' he called out to the lad. He wanted to ask him about Vanya.

Turning round sharply at the sound of his voice, the lad threw the wineskin from his shoulder and leapt into the darkness.

'Come back!' called Igor. 'There's nothing to be afraid of!'

Everything was quiet. The only sound to be heard was the crackling of branches coming from the direction in which the lad had disappeared, and it was growing more and more distant.

'Little devil!' Igor shook his head, annoyed. He walked over to the abandoned leather sack. He prodded it with the toe of his boot and watched it wobble as the wine sloshed about inside. He looked around again.

He was holding a carrier bag full of light bulbs and medicine, and there was a sack of stolen wine at his feet. Everything was dark and quiet. What was he supposed to do now? Should he leave the wine there?

Igor sighed deeply and placed the carrier bag next to the wineskin. Then he squatted down, lifted the leather sack and hoisted it onto his shoulder. He was sure he felt his shoulder joint crunch under the sudden and unfamiliar burden. Igor grabbed the carrier bag and stood up with a jerk. The wineskin heaved and trembled as though it were alive, and it seemed to be trying its best to slip off his shoulder.

'Not a good start,' Igor muttered to himself and set off along the familiar road to the town. His right shoulder ached. Igor tried to carry the wine over his left shoulder, but the sack just wouldn't stay on it.

Giving the familiar gate a shove, Igor went into Vanya Samokhin's yard. He put the sack down carefully on the doorstep and caught his breath, then looked up at the dark, sleeping windows of the house.

He went round behind the corner of the house and rapped on the glass with his knuckles. Vanya's sleepy face appeared in the window. He rubbed his eyes with his hands and peered out.

'Open up, it's me!' Igor said quite loudly, bringing his face as close as he could to the glass.

Eventually Vanya spotted his guest and went to let him in.

'Where did you get that?' he asked in surprise. His eyes were fixed on the sack of wine that Igor had lowered onto the wooden floor in the hallway.

'From your factory,' said Igor, with a tired smile. 'I was waiting for you there, and another lad came out instead of you, carrying that.' He nodded at the sack. 'I was going to ask him about you, but when I called out he just ran off. I couldn't leave evidence of the misappropriation of socialist property there in front of the factory gates, could I?'

Igor was surprised at how easily the right words flew out of his mouth this time.

'So, did I do the right thing?' he asked Vanya.

Vanya shrugged. 'It must have been Petka, my co-worker,' he said. 'It's his sack.' He squatted down near the wine. 'We need to give it back. A leather sack like that costs more than a hundred roubles.'

'Return stolen goods to a thief? Maybe you'd like me to hand this embezzled wine back to him in person, right now?'

Vanya didn't answer. In the dim light of the hallway, Igor could see him pouting childishly.

'If he's your friend, you can give it back to him yourself,' said Igor.

'No, I'll tip the wine out first, then give the sack back,' whispered Vanya. 'I feel bad for him, though, he's really unlucky.'

'And you're lucky, are you?' Igor asked snidely.

'Yes, I am,' Vanya answered firmly. 'I've got my own camera, and Mother and I eat cutlets on Sundays. We're doing well.'

'Ah, that reminds me . . .' Igor looked into the carrier bag and took out two light bulbs. 'Here, these are for your mother.'

'Oh, I've never seen this kind before!' Fascinated, Vanya examined the matt white glass of the light bulbs. 'Are they really bright?'

'They were,' said Igor.

'Thank you, Mother will be delighted! Why don't you go through and lie down? I'm just going to sort this wine out.'

Igor went into 'his' room, took his boots off and put the bag containing Valya's medication on the floor next to the sofa. Then he fetched the quilted blanket, which was folded up on a nearby chair, and settled down on the familiar protruding springs.

The door creaked open and Vanya's silhouette appeared.

'Here,' he whispered. 'Take this, to help you sleep.'

The contents of the glass shone with a strange matt gleam.

Igor took the wine and drank it in two gulps. As he felt the familiar sour taste wash over his tongue, he was suddenly overcome with the desire to sleep. The springs seemed to yield beneath him, until he no longer felt them at all.

The dawn chorus infiltrated Igor's subconscious early the following morning. He opened his eyes. Several bicycles went past the house, then he heard the creaking of a cart's wheels. The snorting of the horse was replaced immediately by two women's voices, approaching rapidly then fading away.

Igor stood up, smoothed down his uniform and pulled on his boots. He walked over to the window. The world beyond was bathed in bright golden sunlight, giving the impression that it was still summer. Only the yellowing leaves on the trees gave the true season away.

'Igor,' Vanya said from the doorway, 'Mother says breakfast is ready.'

Igor turned round. Vanya was already dressed.

He and Vanya sat down at the kitchen table, and Igor introduced himself.

'Thank you so much!' Aleksandra Marinovna turned from the stove to look at her guest. 'Thank you so much! I can't tell you how grateful I am! I've got so much darning to do, and it's funny but the light bulbs never seem to burn out. The shop took a delivery of Azerbaijani light bulbs a year ago, so I stocked up, and they're still going strong. It's quite astonishing! Here, I've made semolina and crackling.'

She ladled out three helpings of thick semolina, then added pieces of crispy pork fat from a small frying pan.

'Would you like some more salt?' she asked.

'No, thanks,' said Igor, picking up his spoon.

'Well, I'm having some – that's how I like it!' She took her place at the table and seasoned her semolina generously.

'It's time for me to start my shift,' said Vanya, glancing at Igor. 'Will you be here this evening?'

'Yes,' said Igor, savouring the taste of the semolina and crackling.

'I wanted to talk to you,' Vanya went on. 'I've really enjoyed using the camera. I've taken five more films for you.'

Igor stared at Vanya in surprise. An idea suddenly occurred to him.

'Is there a film in the camera at the moment?'

'Yes.'

'You can take some photographs right now!'

'The semolina needs to cool down anyway,' said Vanya, getting up from the table.

He came back with the camera and took a photo of Igor. Then he took one of Igor at the table with his mother, then his mother took one of Vanya and Igor. Finally Igor took one of Vanya and his mother, but only after Vanya had adjusted the lens.

'I'll be back by nine o'clock tonight,' said Vanya. Then he stood up, nodded and left the kitchen.

Aleksandra Marinovna brewed some tea.

'I'm being so lazy today,' she said with a smile. 'I should have left for the market two hours ago, but then I saw the light bulbs. I couldn't believe it! I wanted to thank you straight away but Vanya said that you arrived late last night, so we didn't want to wake you . . . But now I really must go. Don't forget to pull the door shut when you go out.'

Still smiling gratefully, she finished her tea then went out into the hallway and started getting ready to go to the market. Igor followed her and was surprised to see four heavy bags, full of three-litre bottles of wine.

'You're not planning to carry all that by yourself, are you?'

Aleksandra Marinovna glanced indifferently at her burden.

'Why not? It won't be the first time!' she said with a shrug.

'Why don't you buy a cart or some kind of trolley?' suggested Igor. 'It would be a lot easier.'

'Oh, no!' Vanya's mother waved her hand dismissively. 'People would judge us for it. They'd accuse us of having ideas above our station. It's harder this way, but at least we know our money is earned honestly.'

This line of reasoning seemed strange to Igor, but also made a kind of sense.

Igor tried to lift two of the bags. They were so heavy! He felt pathetic. How on earth did she plan to carry all four of them? Two in each hand?

'I'll help you,' Igor nodded at the bags. I don't see how you're going to manage them by yourself.'

They left the house five minutes later. Unlike her son, Aleksandra Marinovna clearly had no qualms about accepting help from a police officer. She carried her two bags easily. Unaccustomed as he was to physical exertion, Igor barely managed to keep up with her. He was carrying the other two bags, each of which contained three three-litre bottles of wine, plus the carrier bag with Valya's medication. His wrists and shoulders were already aching, and he eyed Vanya's mother enviously from behind as she took it all in her stride. Several passers-by greeted her courteously and glanced sideways in his direction, which made Igor feel even more uncomfortable – as though he were this capable woman's poodle or dachshund, doomed to follow her everywhere, wagging his little tail.

He wanted to pause and catch his breath, but she showed no sign of stopping, and Igor couldn't bring himself to ask for a break. That would have meant admitting defeat, capitulating before a woman. Just then he noticed a group of about twenty schoolchildren coming towards them, all holding little red flags. They were being led by their teacher, who was young and pretty in an earnest, respectable way. She had an honest face and a neat little nose, and her eyes were shining. Her lilac dress was tied at the waist with a sash of the same fabric, accentuating her slim figure.

'Detachment, halt!' she commanded, and the children stopped at once.

'Can you see what our police officers do?' she asked, looking warmly at Igor, who was struggling to keep the smile on his face.

'They help the elderly,' answered a little girl with two big white bows in her hair.

'Exactly!' answered the teacher. 'Who wants to be a police officer when they grow up?'

Several of the boys immediately put their hands up, holding their red flags aloft. Igor noticed that they had gold hammers and sickles on them.

'What about you, Kashenko?' asked the teacher.

Her question was directed at a chubby boy with slightly bulging eyes. Igor glanced at him as he drew alongside the group and continued walking.

'I'm going to be a builder,' answered the boy.

'Detachment, march!' called the young woman, once Igor had passed.

The children's chattering faded away – or, rather, was drowned out by the approaching noise of the market. Aleksandra Marinovna reached her stall, put her bags down and pushed them under the counter with her foot.

'Oh, thank you so much!' she breathed.

Her face was damp with sweat. This was some consolation to Igor, whose hands were buzzing like high-voltage wires.

'If you need to go back to the house during the day,' whispered Vanya's mother, 'just lift the door up a bit by the handle and give it a push. Then it'll open.'

'It's all right, I won't be back until this evening,' replied Igor. He said goodbye and moved away to the side. As he caught his breath, he watched Aleksandra Marinovna take her white overall from one of the bags and put it on. She adjusted her hair, glanced into a little mirror, then took three bottles out of one of the bags and put them on the counter in front of her.

'Home-made red wine, natural home-made wine!' she cried, casting a proprietorial eye over her little section of the market, as though she were personally in charge of it. 'Perfect for parties, perfect for funerals! Try before you buy! You won't find better!'

Igor looked along the wine section. Vanya's mother seemed to be the youngest and most animated of all the sellers. There were several old women on either side of her, all of whom had bottles or jars of wine on the counters in front of them.

At the end of the row an old man was hunched over two old-fashioned glass demijohns.

Once he was fully recovered, Igor headed for the fish section. The sellers there were more vociferous, and in the chorus of voices he immediately recognised Valya's. His feet automatically quickened their pace.

'Good morning,' said Igor, stopping at her stall. A thin woman of about forty with braids wound tightly around her head stood directly in front of Valya.

'Good mornings start at six o'clock, not nine!' Valya retorted with a smile. She looked back at the woman with the plaits. 'I'll let him know,' she assured her. 'Don't worry, he'll bring it back!'

'It simply won't do,' grumbled the woman with the plaits. 'I can't go around chasing people like this. I ought to report it to the police,' she said, looking pointedly at Igor. 'They'll put his name on the board of shame, then the whole town will laugh at him.'

The woman turned round and walked off.

'Problems?' grinned Igor.

'My husband lost a library book. Unfortunately, it appears that this particular book has been requested by the Party organiser at the jam factory.'

'Have you got any Black Sea flounder?' asked Igor, keen to change the subject.

Valya shook her head. 'Just gobies, and I've only got a few small ones left. My husband's got a bad back. He can barely walk. He went out in the estuary yesterday and was only gone for two hours. I've got hardly anything to sell.'

Igor noticed that Valya's usual zest for life was missing.

'You should find a cure,' he said.

'Well, there's a woman on Kamenka Street, but she charges a hundred roubles.'

Igor took a hundred-rouble note from the bundle in his right-hand pocket, rolled it up and held it out to Valya.

'I'll have ten gobies, please,' he declared loudly. 'And keep the change,' he added in a whisper.

Valya wrapped the gobies in newspaper.

'Oh yes, I nearly forgot!' Igor put the carrier bag on the counter. 'Here are all your medicines, and there's a note that tells you what to take and when.'

'My medicines?' repeated Valya, perplexed.

'Yes, for your disease.'

'How do you know what I've got?' she whispered.

'You told me yourself,' Igor whispered back. 'The bench in the park, this evening?'

'Six o'clock,' she said.

'Shall I bring some champagne?'

'How could any woman refuse?' she replied, with warmth in her eyes but confusion written all over her face.

22

After wandering round the town for a while, Igor came across a workers' canteen. He went in, ordered borshch and a breaded cutlet with a side order of buckwheat, washed it down with fruit juice and paid seven roubles for the lot.

The sea breeze teased his nostrils. The morning sun had taken refuge behind the clouds that filled the sky above Ochakov, chasing and bumping into one another.

It began to grow cooler as the evening approached. Igor went into a grocery shop and bought a bottle of Soviet champagne and a large bar of Leningrad chocolate. Then he went into a hardware shop and bought two glasses and a cloth bag emblazoned with the slogan 'A Holiday Souvenir'. He put everything into the bag and walked back to the park near the market. He sat on the bench. There was a rustle behind him, and suddenly a pair of warm, strong hands covered his eyes. Igor froze in alarm. If the hands had been soft and gentle he would have played along, but they had such a firm grip!

'Valya, is that you?' he asked guardedly.

He felt a warm exhalation on the back of his neck. Then he heard a familiar laugh. Igor relaxed.

'You made me jump!' he exclaimed.

The hands released his eyes, leaving their warmth on his eyelids. Igor turned round. There, behind him, stood Valya. She was wearing a pale green scarf over her red hair, a green dress and white patent shoes, and she held a white bag. She walked round the bench and sat down next to him.

'Shall we go to the sea?' suggested Igor.

Valya looked up at the sky. 'It might rain,' she protested. Then she waved her hand dismissively and added, 'So what if it does? We're not made of sugar – we won't dissolve! And it'll be more private.'

She got up decisively from the bench and looked down at Igor. He stood up quickly and the glasses clinked in his bag.

Valya led Igor along a narrow, overgrown path, which

seemed to have been trodden down specifically for secret lovers amid the adjacent islets of bushes and gullies that were bordered by private allotments and abandoned factory fences. Several times the path joined the main road, which was equally deserted. Then after twenty or so metres it would veer off to the side again. Twice they had to climb through holes in fences.

Finally their path came out at the bottom of a steep slope, and they found themselves standing beneath a sombre, overhanging cliff. Ahead of them the dark sea gently lapped the shore. Unusually, there were no lights in the distance, no trembling moon or stars on the surface of the water. There was nothing to reflect in the water that night.

They sat down on the sand. Igor took out the glasses and the bottle of sparkling wine, then opened the chocolate and broke it into squares.

'Won't your husband miss you?' he asked suddenly.

'No,' sighed Valya. 'He's confined to his bed, poor thing. His back is really troubling him. I'm taking him to that woman on Kamenka Street tomorrow. Hopefully she'll be able to fix it. If he can't go fishing, then I'm out of work too.'

'You'll find another job,' said Igor. He picked up the champagne and held the cork down as he started untwisting the wire.

'What kind of job?' Valya laughed softly. 'I left school at fourteen! Once I fell in love, I lost all interest in studying. Such passion! It's a good thing my father lost both hands in the war, otherwise he'd have beaten me to within an inch of my life. He smashed my mother's elbow with his army belt before he went off to fight.'

'Do your parents live in Ochakov too?' asked Igor.

'They're buried here, in the cemetery.'

Igor removed the wire and shook the bottle, causing the cork to explode into the sky. He filled both glasses with bubbles, then quickly covered the neck of the bottle with his thumb. With his free hand he gave one glass to Valya and then picked up the other.

'To you.' Igor leaned towards Valya, looking into her eyes.

'What's so special about me?' She gave a playful shrug, then raised the glass to her lips and took a sip.

Igor held the champagne in his mouth for a moment before swallowing. What's so special about her? Her voice repeated itself in his head, as though he'd rewound it and played it again.

'Why are you looking at me like that?' Valya frowned at him, suddenly serious.

'Why not? We're friends, aren't we?' teased Igor.

'Then let's drink a toast to our friendship,' said Valya, laughing.

They drank. Igor stuck the bottle into the sand. He took his boots and socks off and rolled his breeches up as best he could, then he walked down to the water's edge and went in up to his ankles.

'It's not cold!' he said, surprised.

'Of course not!' said Valya. 'The boys will be bathing for another two months.'

'What about the girls?' joked Igor.

'The brave ones will join them.'

'Are you one of the brave ones? Or one of the others?'

'Those who leave school early are always braver than those who graduate from university.'

'I take it that's based on your personal experience?'

'Just pour the champagne,' replied Valya.

Igor returned and filled both their glasses again.

'So, what are we drinking to?' he asked.

'To my husband, Petya, making a full recovery!'

Igor returned and managed to hide his surprise. Even if he hadn't, the darkness would have hidden it for him.

'Do you love him?'

'I did. Now I feel sorry for him.'

'Doesn't he mind you feeling sorry for him?'

'Why should he?' Valya shrugged and sipped her champagne. 'Pity is stronger than love! You can fall out of love with anyone, but there isn't even an expression for "falling out of pity". You pity someone for as long as they live – the feeling doesn't die until they do. So it's better for my husband if I feel sorry for him with all my heart.'

'I wouldn't like you to feel sorry for me,' reflected Igor. He reached for the chocolate, took a square and put it in his mouth. The chocolate was hard and bitter.

'That's probably because no woman has ever really felt sorry for you before.'

'No woman has ever really loved me before,' said Igor, suddenly sensing considerably more life experience in Valya's words than his own.

'You're still so young!' Valya slipped her arm around Igor's shoulder. She moved closer to him, and he felt the warmth of her body pass through the tunic to his skin.

'Take your holster off, it's pressing into me,' said Valya, pretending to be annoyed.

Igor obediently removed his belt and holster and put them on the sand.

'Shall we go for a swim?' she suggested.

'I didn't bring anything with me,' said Igor, flustered.

'Oh, but you did!' Valya let out a peal of laughter so loud and resonant that Igor looked around in alarm. 'You brought champagne, you brought chocolate, you brought me! Come on, take your clothes off, let's go skinny-dipping! We'll dry off easily enough, as long as it doesn't rain.'

Igor unbuttoned his tunic and watched out of the corner of his eye as Valya took her dress off. Her patent shoes showed up white on the sand. When she was completely naked she turned to look at Igor, but he was still sitting on the sand in his tunic.

'Have you gone all shy on me?' she smiled.

Igor wished the ground would just open up and swallow him. Besides, if he took off the uniform he might really disappear, leaving this beautiful woman alone on the beach. He could just imagine how frightened she would be.

'Not really,' said Igor, standing up. He managed to put the packet of roubles into the cloth bag without her noticing and strode into the water.

'You're so funny!' She burst out laughing and began to walk into the water with him.

Her body was worthy of the five-pointed star that they used to place on the very best goods: the State Quality Mark of the USSR. Everything about her was perfect – her face, her breasts, her waist and her thighs. Yet she had nothing in common with the naked beauties on the covers of *Playboy* and other men's magazines. In those images, and in the minds of millions of men, beauty had been replaced by sex appeal. Whereas here, in the dark water of the Black Sea, Igor could reach out his hand and touch real, living beauty. He touched Valya's shoulder. She turned round, and her smile seemed to say, There's nothing to be afraid of. Igor put his arms around her, brushing her breasts with his hand in a way that wasn't entirely accidental.

Valya pretended to push him away.

'You'll scratch me with your tunic!'

Igor took a step back, without taking his eyes off her.

She lowered herself up to her shoulders, holding her hair above the water. In the distance, little lights were pulsating in the darkness.

'Is that the town?' asked Igor, pointing at the lights.

'No, the port,' said Valya.

They came out of the water. Igor's clothes clung to his wet body. He stood and listened to his own skin, to the seawater running from his body. It wasn't a very pleasant feeling. He looked at Valya. She was wiping her neck with something.

'What's that?' asked Igor, surprised.

'A handkerchief,' she said, showing him.

Valya twisted the handkerchief in her hands and started wiping herself with it again. Carefully, apprehensively, Igor took his tunic off and squeezed it out. Water streamed onto the wet sand. He took his wet T-shirt off too, wrung it out and immediately put it back on. He put his tunic back on too, although he didn't button it up. Valya was standing motionless, in profile, and her beautiful breasts reminded him of a statue, as though they'd been carved from stone or sculpted from clay. He walked over to Valya and put his arms around her, pressing her to him so that the warmth of her breasts was conducted straight into his heart.

'I haven't started taking the medicine yet,' she said softly, her hands reaching up to Igor's shoulders.

They stood there with their arms around each other, sharing the warmth of their bodies. After what seemed like no time at all, Igor realised that Valya's smooth back was completely dry.

The warmth of Valya's whisper caressed his left ear.

'When I get better, I'll take pity on you – I promise!'

Igor poured the last of the champagne into their glasses and picked up the chocolate.

'Shall I show you a trick?' he asked, handing Valya her glass.

'Yes, please!'

Igor dropped a square of chocolate into both glasses.

'Watch the chocolate,' he said.

'Oh!' she exclaimed in delight. 'Look, it's rising to the surface!'

'It'll keep sinking and rising until you eat it. Best to drink it all in one go, just make sure you catch the chocolate in your mouth.'

Concentrating hard, Valya drank her champagne in one go. She immediately began snorting, coughing and laughing, all at the same time.

'So, how did you get on?' asked Igor, bringing his lips close to her nose.

She nodded, gently pushing his face away with her hand. Then she parted her lips and showed him the piece of chocolate between her white teeth. Her eyes were laughing.

'Well done!' exclaimed Igor, leaning towards her face again as though he wanted to bite off a piece of the chocolate. Their lips brushed, and his tongue was enveloped by the taste of bitter-sweet chocolate.

Suddenly they heard a noise above them and fragments of dry clay began to fall from the overhanging cliff. Igor grabbed Valya's hand and pulled her aside. They peered upwards, into the leaden darkness. Everything between them and the sky had merged together.

'Someone's up there,' Valya whispered.

Igor shook his head. Silence had descended again, but the feeling of unease remained. Igor buttoned up his tunic and fastened the belt and holster around his waist. He was about to take the bundle of roubles out of the cloth bag and put it back in his pocket but stopped himself just in time. The insides of his pockets were still wet. He sat down on the sand to put on his dry socks and boots then stood up, ready to leave. Valya stood nearby, fully dressed, already wearing her scarf and her white shoes and clutching her white bag.

When she saw that Igor was ready, she led him to the path and they scrambled awkwardly up the slippery crevice to the top of the cliff. The path ran along the cliff towards the bushes. When they reached the bushes Valya suddenly stopped, as though she were rooted to the ground.

'Someone's there,' she whispered.

Igor looked around her and saw two figures silhouetted in a narrow gap between the bushes.

'So, bitch, drinking champagne with coppers now, are you?' The voice was coarse. 'Well, let's see if it's their lucky night . . . Go on, Sanka, launch your blade!'

One of the figures made a sudden sharp gesture with his hand and a knife whistled past with a dull, sinister gleam, barely missing Igor's face.

'I'll shoot!' cried Igor, instantly embarrassed by the fear in his voice.

'Good shot, are you?'

Igor took the gun out of the holster and looked at it. Suddenly he wasn't just scared, but petrified. He imagined the men hearing the gun misfire. What would they do to them then? No, he had to scare them without actually pulling the trigger.

Igor held the gun out in front of him, stepped around Valya and pretended to take aim.

'Look, he's got his gun out!' hissed a second voice.

The silhouettes disappeared. They had stepped back into the bushes.

'Hey, Valya,' called the first voice, 'I'm going to drop by later, to see whether you're sharing your bed with a copper or a fisherman. We'll have a little chat then!'

Igor could sense Valya's fear.

'One more word and I'll finish you off!' he exclaimed in a fit of rage, feeling his own fear ebb away.

'Coppers don't talk like that,' hissed the second voice. 'Did you hear, Fima?'

'Yeah, I heard,' the first voice cut him off. 'I think this calls for my special blade!'

Valya put her arms around Igor from behind. She was trembling, and he felt his fear creeping back. Igor thought he could see the two men again, and they seemed to be approaching. Quietly, heads bowed and shoulders hunched, they looked like they were getting ready to pounce.

'Stop, you bastards!' cried Igor, but they just ignored him.

Igor held the gun out in front of him and lowered his head. His finger pressed the trigger, and a shot rang out. One of the men wheezed and fell to the ground. The other man froze for a second before jumping into the bushes, and the ensuing rustling and snapping of twigs, receding into the distance, told them that he'd decided not to hang around.

Valya crouched down and began sobbing. Igor stood over her, not knowing what do to next. His eyes involuntarily returned to the motionless figure on the path ahead.

He went up and leaned over the body to get a closer look. The man's face was covered in blood. The bullet had obviously hit him right between the eyes. He went back to Valya and touched her shoulder.

'Come on, I'll take you home.'

'They'll find me,' she whispered through her tears. 'Oh, why did I go with you? I asked you not to wear your uniform!'

'It's all right, don't worry.' Igor squatted down beside her and started stroking her wet hair and her shoulders. 'Come on, let's go. We'll think of something. Do you know who it was that ran off?'

'Fima,' she sighed. 'Fima Chagin . . . He wanted me, but I said no . . . I told him that I love my husband . . . What now? What's going to happen now?'

'Don't worry,' said Igor, more confidently. 'I'll definitely think of something.'

He took her home, but she wouldn't let him past the gate. She'd stopped crying by the time they reached her house; only her eyes betrayed her fear. Igor put his arms round her.

'I forgot to tell you something important,' she whispered into his ear.

'What?' whispered Igor.

'You left your gobies on the counter. I'll give you some next time, if I have any.'

He managed to kiss her cheek before she gently pushed him away and hurried into her yard.

23

Left alone by the gate, Igor looked around. He took in the unfamiliar street, the sudden stillness of the cool air, the silence and the dark sky that rose up from the barely discernible outlines of trees, roofs and telegraph poles. The house that Valya went into hadn't reacted in any way to her arrival, neither creaking as she opened the front door nor lighting any windows to welcome her home.

The insides of Igor's boots were wet with the water running out of his breeches. The only thing that wasn't wet was the cloth bag containing the Soviet roubles.

The water felt as out of place in his boots as Igor himself felt standing in an obscure backstreet in this town, which was becoming increasingly familiar to him. Everything that had happened had lowered Igor's body temperature by at least two degrees. He stood there, constrained by his wet clothing, by inertia, by a strange fear, which felt alternately incredibly real and ludicrously childish. A sharp knife had flown past his head – close enough for him to see the predatory gleam of steel. But in reality he hadn't even been born yet. The knife had flown past his head on an autumn evening in 1957, which meant that it couldn't have killed him. Or could it?

Igor ran his left hand over his tunic. It felt cold and wet. The water was definitely real, there was no doubt about that, otherwise he would be feeling a lot more comfortable. So the knife must have been real too.

Igor looked along the fence outside Valya's house. Noticing a small bench outside her neighbour's gate, he went over and sat down on it. He pulled his boots off and shook the water out of them, then put them back on again.

The town was fast asleep. Igor's thoughts became clearer and clearer, as though someone were typing them out inside his head in large capital letters. He remembered how Valya had crouched down in fear. He'd been frightened, but her fear had been different – as though she'd known exactly what to be afraid of and was afraid with all her might. At that point her fear had intensified his own. Fear was what had pulled the trigger of the gun, but it wasn't supposed to fire! If it hadn't fired, though, then . . . Igor couldn't bear to imagine what those two would have done with them. The fact remained that a shot had been fired, and one of the men – the one who'd thrown the knife – was still back there on the path.

He recalled Vanya Samokhin's comment about Fima Chagin having an affair with Valya. If there was something between them, that would certainly explain both her fear and Chagin's fury. It also meant that the fear and the fury would stay with them for a long time, until the fear killed the fury or the fury killed the fear . . . Either way, there would be no happy ending. That much was clear.

Igor sighed. He looked around again. Suddenly he got the feeling that Fima was hiding nearby, knife in hand. Waiting for Igor to get up and walk away, leaving Valya's house unprotected. This thought made him uneasy. Should he sit here all night, guarding Valya's house until the sun came up?

A soft rustle came from the fence on the other side of the road. Igor leaned forward, peering into the darkness. Two green cat's eyes stared back at him. A dog barked somewhere in the distance and the cat's eyes disappeared.

'No, I can't protect her,' Igor whispered to himself. He looked back at Valya's house. 'She's got a husband – it's his responsibility.'

Igor stood up, but he couldn't bring himself to leave so he sat down again.

I can't prevent or change anything here, he thought. I have nothing in common with this town and its people. They have their own lives, their own time, and I have mine.

This argument wasn't particularly convincing. Chagin had been very much alive in the memory of the inhabitants of Ochakov quite recently, when Igor and Stepan had come here and broken into his house. Time is a flexible concept. The present is woven from the recent past, after all, and as long as people remember the past it will remain alive, somewhere nearby, watching you and telling you what to do.

I have to stop Chagin, Igor resolved. His fear had retreated. I'll give him some money and explain that Valya and I . . .

His thoughts trailed off into a series of questions. What

exactly would he explain to Chagin? Was anything going on between him and Valya? If so, what?

I have to stop Chagin! The same thought kept coming back to him, and this time it demanded action.

Igor stood up more decisively. He grabbed the cloth bag and touched the cold, dry handle of the gun in its holster. Then he started walking.

He didn't know the way, but either his feet or his boots did. They led him first to the market then to Kostya Khetagurov Street.

Igor stopped in the same place as before, on the side of the street opposite Fima's gate, so that he had a good view of the three steps up to the front porch.

There didn't appear to be any lights on in the house, but Igor took a few steps to the right and saw a glow coming from a little side window, so faint that it was barely visible from the street.

Igor checked again to make sure the holster was open. His fingers brushed the cold metal of the gun, and this calmed his nerves. Feeling bolder, he crossed the street and went through the gate, then hunched over and crept towards the right side of the house. He stopped beneath the little window and listened. Silence. He crouched down and pressed his back to the brick wall, holding his breath. The cold from the wall passed straight through his wet tunic.

What should he do now? Burst into the house waving his gun? Knock on the window? Igor's thoughts buzzed about like agitated wasps. No, he shouldn't burst in. He had to try and talk to him. Calmly, man to man.

The silence was starting to irritate Igor. He didn't

know what time it was because he hadn't brought the gold watch with him. He didn't know when it would start getting light. He had no idea what he was going to do.

Then suddenly, like a lifeline, he heard the sound of footsteps and men's voices in the darkness. The footsteps drew nearer, then the gate banged shut.

'We should tell his mother,' said a familiar dry, wheezing voice.

'No need. She'll understand,' replied Fima's voice. 'Are you coming in?'

'No. Here, take the spade.'

There was the sound of metal striking the stone doorstep. The door creaked as it opened, and the gate banged again.

So, Chagin had gone into the house alone. Igor was pleased. It would be easier to talk one to one, without having to keep an eye out for anyone else.

From somewhere above his head, on the other side of the window, came the sound of a bottle being placed on a table, then the sound of liquid being poured.

Perfect timing, thought Igor.

Surprising himself with the vigour of his movements, he stood up straight, took the roubles out of the bag and stuffed them into the pockets of his breeches, leaving the empty bag on the ground below the window. Then he crept round the corner of the house, went up the steps and carefully pulled the front door towards him. He expected it to swing open, but when the door had opened a little way it stopped. Igor stuck his hand into the gap and felt a long metal hook. He lifted it out of its catch, opened the door and went inside, to be met by the sound of rapidly approaching footsteps. Igor turned and shut the door behind him. The light bulb hanging from the ceiling in the hall was switched on, and Igor was temporarily blinded. Then he saw Fima, who was standing just a few paces away, with a less than welcoming expression frozen on his face and an empty shot glass in his right hand. Powerful fumes were emanating from his mouth from the vodka he'd just drunk. His eyes came to rest on Igor's open holster and his expression suddenly brightened.

'We need to talk,' said Igor.

'About what?' asked Fima.

'What?'

'What do you want to talk about? Sanka, the man you killed?'

'No.' Igor shook his head.

Fima's slow reactions gave Igor the chance to get his thoughts straight.

'About Valya. Look, there's nothing going on between us . . . I'm just helping her out. I want you to leave her alone.'

'You're *helping* her?' repeated Fima, as though he genuinely didn't understand the meaning of the word.

'She's really sick. I got her some medicine.'

'Did you indeed? A police officer with contacts in the pharmaceutical trade, eh?' Fima's eyes widened in mock surprise. He held his empty glass up in his right hand and looked around. His eyes fell on a chair in the corner. Taking a step towards it, he put his glass down on the worn brown seat.

'I'm not a police officer,' said Igor, as convincingly as he could manage.

Fima looked Igor up and down with a drunken sneer. Their eyes met again.

'If you're not a police officer, does that mean you can drink with a thief?' asked Fima. A strange, involuntary smile crept over his face.

'Yes,' Igor nodded. 'We can talk over a drink.'

Fima opened a door behind him.

'After you!' he declared with a flourish.

Igor knew Fima was being facetious, but he managed to hide his anxiety and walk past his host apparently unperturbed.

Igor heard the sound of the metal hook behind him as the front door was locked from inside. Fima stumbled after him and Igor quickened his pace, stopping only when he reached the window in the living room. He turned and looked around him. A half-empty half-litre bottle of vodka stood on the oval table, along with a plate of salted cucumbers, an earthenware salt cellar and hunks of black bread on an open newspaper. There was an oak dresser against the opposite wall, with cut-glass panels in the wooden doors. Igor watched as Fima took out a couple of glasses. He placed one in front of Igor and the other in front of himself, then pulled up a chair and sat down across the table from his guest. He picked up the bottle and emptied it into his own glass.

'Oh!' he said, pretending to be surprised. 'It's run out! I'll have to open another one!'

He got up and left the room.

While he was gone, Igor took another good look around the room. His eyes settled on a little car made of tin cans, evidently a home-made child's toy. It stood in the corner by the dresser, as though it had been abandoned there by its young owner.

Fima returned with another half-litre bottle, which had already been opened. He filled Igor's glass, then sat down again.

'Please, take a seat!' he said, peering at Igor through narrowed eyes.

Igor sat down.

'So, shall we drink to getting to know each other?' asked Fima.

'Let's talk first,' said Igor, his voice mild and amiable.

'Are you on about Valya again?'

'Yes,' nodded Igor. 'You swore that you'd kill her . . . Now she's terrified.'

'Me? Kill her? How can you say such a thing?' Fima clasped his hands together theatrically. 'Well, it might have come out of here,' he said, prodding his mouth with his forefinger. 'In the heat of the moment. Maybe, but . . . they were the words of a desperate man!'

'So you're not going to touch her?'

'Not going to touch her? I never said that. I can't wait to get my hands on that bitch!'

'Listen,' said Igor again, trying to sound firm and conciliatory at the same time. 'I won't come here again. If you promise you won't touch her, then I promise this is the last time you'll ever see me. OK?'

As Fima contemplated Igor's offer, a perplexed but otherwise inscrutable smile played on his lips.

'I still don't get it,' he said, shaking his head. 'But we need to drink! Come on,' he raised his glass. 'To getting to know each other!'

They drank at the same time – Fima in one gulp, Igor in

three. Igor felt a burning sensation in his mouth and throat, and the vodka left an unpleasant aftertaste.

'Eat something.' Fima nodded at the bread. 'You weren't expecting branded vodka, were you?'

Igor chased the home-made vodka with some bread, then a piece of salted cucumber. The fire was extinguished but the unpleasant taste remained.

'So how else are you going to make it worth my while?' Fima placed his elbows on the table and leaned forward, resting his sharp chin on the back of his folded hands.

'I can pay you,' said Igor.

'How much?'

Igor quickly estimated how many hundred-rouble notes he had in his pockets.

'Ten thousand.'

Fima flinched in astonishment.

'You're bluffing,' he said menacingly.

Igor took the unopened bundle of roubles from his left-hand pocket and placed it on the table.

'Well, well, well . . .' murmured Fima, standing up and walking round to Igor's side of the table. He leaned over the bundle of banknotes and peered closely at it, almost inhaling it, but he didn't touch it. Instead he took the bottle from the table and poured some more home-made vodka into Igor's glass. 'Oh dear, it's run out again!' he smiled. 'I'll get another one!'

He left the room a second time, returning with another full bottle. He filled his own glass and sat down.

'I think we can come to some arrangement,' he said, baring his crooked teeth. 'Let's drink!'

They both drank. This time, the fire burned all the way down Igor's throat to his feet. His whole body felt warm, and he was no longer aware of his wet clothes.

'All right,' continued Fima, chewing a piece of bread. 'I give you my word that I won't touch the bitch – thief's honour! Happy now?'

Igor nodded. His unsteady gaze fell on the little car made out of tin cans.

'Did you make that for your little boy?' he asked, pointing to the corner of the room.

Fima followed the direction of his guest's gaze, and another strange smile crept over his face.

'Yeah,' he nodded. 'Well, someone else's. I haven't got any kids.'

'This little boy . . . he wouldn't happen to be called Stepan, would he?'

Fima instantly stopped smiling. He shuddered as though he'd just been given an electric shock.

'If you're not a police officer, why are you asking me so many questions?' Fima leapt to his feet and grabbed the bottle, but he let go of it straight away and sat down again. 'I don't know what's the matter with me,' he said apologetically. 'What a day I've had! My neighbour's son was murdered in cold blood, for no apparent reason . . . I saw that bitch Valya sitting on the beach with a police officer . . . Oh, I'm sorry! I didn't mean . . .'

Fima's voice was full of menace. Igor could hear it, but he was preoccupied with his own body, which no longer seemed to be obeying him. His arms were like lead weights, and he couldn't move his legs or even feel his toes. There was an unpleasant warmth in the pit of his stomach, which soon turned into a burning sensation and began to rise upwards, towards his mouth. Igor started greedily gulping air.

Fima was no longer grimacing or smiling, and his face suddenly looked completely normal. 'This is it, time to say goodbye. You promised I'd never see you again . . . Well, now nobody else will either!'

Fima stood up and walked slowly round the table. When he reached Igor, he put his right hand on his shoulder and gave him a hard shove. Igor crashed to the wooden floor and lay there without moving. His body was no longer paying any attention to him, although his eyes were still working and his ears were full of noise, both real and imaginary.

'Never mind,' said Fima, standing over him. 'You'll suffer for a couple of hours, then it'll all be over! You're not afraid of death, are you? You've got a gun!'

Laughing, Fima left the room. Igor heard the metallic sound of the hook as the front door opened and then closed again. The burning had reached his mouth. It hurt to breathe. Igor lay on his side on the wooden floor. He could see the table above him and the light bulb hanging from the ceiling. It was growing darker by the minute, as though some unknown force were raising the ceiling higher and higher into the sky until the last remaining speck of light dissolved in the darkness that enveloped him. Now it no longer mattered whether he opened or closed his eyes.

The life that had previously reigned throughout Igor's body took refuge in a secret little corner, where nobody else could possibly find it. His body was still. His eyes were closed.

Half an hour later the door of the house opened again and

two men came in. They stopped in the living room and looked down at the body in the police uniform.

'He's not a police officer, he's from the KGB!' said Fima. 'And you were the one who brought him here! Why the hell did I take you on? Eh?'

'What makes you think it's my fault?' his accomplice wheezed in surprise.

'Iosip, he was asking about your Stepan! How would a regular police officer know anything about your son? Eh?'

'So you bumped him off?' Iosip barked gruffly. 'That's a bit . . . Well, what's done is done. I'm glad I sent Stepan to Odessa – just in time, too. I knew something like this was going to happen. We'll have to go on the run!'

'Run? From my own home? I don't think so! I'm used to things going my way, and they will this time, too! Let's dump him by the bird with balls. Yeah, imagine the cops finding a dead KGB agent, his breath reeking of moonshine!'

'Maybe we should just stick him under the floorboards, like the other one?'

'Iosip, Iosip . . . you never know when to stop, do you? You're just a peasant! I don't have to listen to you. I didn't in Ust-Ilim, where the thieves helped you, and I don't here. Do you think I want to spend my life living above a cemetery, sleeping on top of dead men, drinking on top of dead men? No, one's enough! We need to get rid of him. It's the middle of the night, no one'll see us. The nights in Ochakov belong to us, not them. They might be in charge during the day, but at night we take over.'

'How are we going to get him there?' asked Iosip.

'I've got an army greatcoat. We can wrap him up in that.'

The life that was hiding in the depths of Igor's motionless body felt this body being rolled over, lifted up, lowered again and carried off somewhere, rocking and swaying.

That night Ochakov was still and quiet, deserted and devoid of stars.

24

The life that was sheltering deep in Igor's motionless body suddenly heard a dull thud, which echoed and reverberated throughout his entire frame.

Two pairs of feet in coarse, heavy boots came to a standstill nearby.

'Maybe I should take his gun out and shoot him in the head,' suggested Fima, his voice hesitant and weary. 'They'll think he got drunk and shot himself . . . Or shall I just take the gun?'

'No, it's not worth it,' murmured Iosip. 'Why shoot a man who's already dead? And if the gun goes missing you'll have the cops all over you, given your reputation.'

'All right,' agreed Fima. 'Let's get the coat out from under him, though. I can use it again.'

Quick as lightning, Fima leaned over the body and, with one smooth motion, struck it in the side. Then his fingers closed firmly over the edge of the greatcoat.

Jerked roughly as the greatcoat was yanked out from under him, Igor now lay on his back, his head almost touching the base of the 'bird with balls' – a pyramid of cannonballs surmounted by an eagle, commemorating Suvorov's victory over the Turks in the siege of Ochakov.

The footsteps of both pairs of boots faded into the darkness. A baby hedgehog shuffled out from a patch of grass nearby and stopped, lifting its pointed nose to the sky.

It began to rain. At first large drops drummed onto the ground, rustling the grass. Soon they were coming down in torrents, and the whole town was plunged into a nocturnal downpour. The earth, the grass, the memorial, everything glistened. Igor's tunic was soon wet through, for the second time that night. The water running over his face seemed to give some kind of signal to the life that was hiding within him. Or perhaps it was the rain streaming into Igor's half-open mouth, but whatever the trigger something happened inside him, something shifted, some kind of mechanism was released and began to press, weakly at first, on other mechanisms that controlled the body's internal and external movements. Igor's eyelids twitched and opened, and his mouth suddenly filled with the sweet taste of water he'd been longing for. He sensed the possibility of salvation – he didn't understand it, he felt it instinctively, as though he were a wild animal rather than a human being.

Summoning all of his strength, Igor turned his face towards the earth, towards the puddle spreading out beside him. He felt the sweet, cold water on his lips. He swallowed and leaned further into the water, sticking his tongue out and lapping it up like a dog, the only difference being that his tongue was thicker and considerably less agile than any dog's. He stuck his tongue out as far as it would go, probing the depths of the puddle and licking the firm, rough ground beneath it.

'Water,' he whispered, the word trembling on his lips as he pressed himself into the puddle once more.

The life that had been hiding deep within him grew bolder, running through his blood and bones, amazed to feel his body coming alive and growing warmer by the minute.

Meanwhile, the downpour continued in full force. Ochakov was no longer shrouded in nocturnal silence. Water flowed noisily in every direction, even where there was no obvious channel, gathering strength and furrowing deeper into the earth.

After resting for a while, Igor drank more rainwater. He became aware of his fingers and moved them slightly. Then, pressing his palms flat against the ground, he raised himself up. He could still feel a burning sensation in his stomach but the fire was weaker now, more subdued.

'Am I alive?' he whispered in astonishment, looking all around. 'I'm alive!'

Greedily inhaling air, he struggled to his feet and staggered towards the nearest house. There was a street lamp next to it, illuminating the house number and the name of the road. He made it to the gate, pushed it open and stared at the dark windows of the house. Then he stepped back and let the gate swing shut. Swaying and holding his hand to his right side, which was hurting now more than his stomach, Igor shuffled on further down the street.

It was still raining, but Igor couldn't feel it. Nor could he feel that his clothes, hair and face were already soaking wet.

Every now and then he forced himself to look up, to try and get his bearings. Unfamiliar houses and fences were gradually replaced by ones he recognised. Igor stopped when he came to Vanya Samokhin's gate. Feeling desperately thirsty all of a sudden, he staggered to the side window of the house. He just about managed to raise his arm, which seemed incredibly heavy, and knocked on the glass.

Vanya let Igor into the hallway. He was wearing nothing but a pair of purple underpants.

'Oh! What's happened to you?' he exclaimed, aghast.

Shivering and trembling with exhaustion, Igor staggered forwards and collapsed, scattering droplets of water over Vanya's bare legs. Aleksandra Marinovna hurried over in her long nightdress.

'Good heavens!' she clasped her hands together. 'He's gone blue!'

Igor turned his head and looked up at the faces above him, his eyes fading as he spoke.

'Poison,' he whispered. 'I've been poisoned . . . with vodka . . .'

'Get him under a blanket!' Vanya's mother instructed her son. 'Quickly!'

She ran into the kitchen, lit the paraffin stove and placed a pail of water over the burner. Taking a linen bag full of dried herbs from the cupboard, she opened it and inhaled before adding two handfuls to the water.

'Whatever is the world coming to?' she murmured as she stared at the water in the pail, willing it to hurry up and boil.

As soon as the herbal decoction had brewed to her satisfaction, Aleksandra Marinovna took the pail into the living room where Igor was lying on the sofa, covered up with a blanket. He was barely conscious. She placed the pail on the little table next to the sofa.

'Go and get the big basin,' she instructed her son.

Vanya did as he was told. Then he was sent to fetch the tin funnel that they used for decanting wine.

'He's so cold!' said Aleksandra Marinovna anxiously, placing her hand on Igor's forehead. 'Now, put that funnel into his mouth.'

Vanya looked doubtfully at the pail, which had steam rising from it.

'But it's boiling water,' he said. 'Shouldn't we add some cold water first?'

'No,' his mother cut him off. 'It has to be hot or it won't work! Go on, put it in!'

Vanya tried to stick the narrow neck of the funnel between Igor's teeth, but they were clamped shut.

'Use your fingers! Quickly!' urged his mother, who had picked up the pail and was standing at the ready.

Vanya forced Igor's mouth open, inserted the funnel and turned to his mother. Aleksandra Marinovna tipped the contents of the pail into the funnel. A rasping noise escaped from Igor's throat, like the sound of a thin piece of paper being ripped. His right arm twitched, as though he were trying to lift it. Vanya's mother leaned forward and held it down, her heavy bosom suspended just above Igor's head.

The entire decoction disappeared down the funnel into Igor's throat. His body twitched and convulsed. Aleksandra Marinovna jumped back from the sofa.

'Hold him over the basin!' she cried.

Vanya grabbed Igor and pulled him onto his side, moving

his head to the edge of the sofa and positioning the basin underneath it. Igor's throat emitted another rasping sound, which was followed by an emetic squelch. Another convulsion racked his body. Igor drew up his legs, and dark liquid spewed violently from his mouth.

'Hold him there like that. I'll go and brew up the next lot,' said Vanya's mother. Meanwhile, Vanya removed Igor's clothes.

Neither Vanya nor his mother got any more sleep that night. After the third irrigation Igor's forehead finally started to warm up. Aleksandra Marinovna warmed an old flat iron on the paraffin stove and started drying his police uniform with it, but when she found the bundle of roubles in the pocket of his breeches she panicked. She put the money on the table and stared at it for several minutes without blinking. Her alarm gradually gave way to a pleasant feeling of composure. That must be why they tried to kill him, she decided. She ironed the uniform until it was dry, then folded it neatly and left it on a stool next to the pale, sleeping figure of Igor. She placed the bundle of roubles, his boots and the belt with the holster on the floor nearby, but took the dry socks to her room. Switching on the light, she stretched one sock over a light bulb and began to darn the hole in its heel.

Vanya glanced at the grandfather clock on the wall and decided to spend the final hour before dawn looking through *The Wine-Maker's Handbook*, which calmed his nerves.

Igor was woken, or rather brought to his senses, by a sharp pain in his right side. He tried to sit up, but a new wave of pain washed over him and he collapsed back onto his pillow. He lay there, staring at the green lampshade on the ceiling, then brought his right hand to his side and froze as his fingers felt something warm and sticky.

Igor suddenly felt very thirsty, and the cramps in his stomach reminded him of the night before.

'Ma!' he shouted. His voice was so weak he could barely hear it himself. He lay still for a few minutes, trying to breathe evenly and rhythmically. Then he shouted again.

The door opened slightly.

'Is that you?' His mother's eyes were wide with surprise. 'Where on earth have you been? Your mobile was ringing all day yesterday. It didn't stop until gone one o'clock in the morning! Where have you –'

His mother suddenly fell silent and approached his bed.

'What's the matter with your face? You've gone blue!'

She placed her hand on Igor's forehead.

'You're burning up!'

'I was poisoned,' sighed Igor.

'With home-made vodka?' asked his mother, frowning in disapproval.

Igor nodded and grimaced.

'I've got a pain in my side. Can you have a look?' he asked, glancing down at his right side.

Elena Andreevna lifted the blanket and gasped. She looked horrified.

'You're bleeding! I'm going to call the doctor! I –' She broke off, scanning the room frantically as though she were looking for help. 'I'll fetch Stepan!'

Igor's mother ran out of the room and he heard the front door slam. He made another attempt to sit up but collapsed again, and this time he passed out. He had no idea how long he had been unconscious, but he gradually became aware of voices in the darkness that surrounded him.

Somebody was doing something to his body, and whatever they were doing was resonating painfully in his ribs.

'I've never seen anything like it,' a man's voice said quietly. 'I shall have to report it to the police. I'm afraid I've got no choice, it's standard procedure.'

'Is that so?' breathed Stepan's voice.

'He's very lucky, you know. Just look at that! It's a wonder he's still alive.'

'Are you taking him to hospital?' His mother's voice interrupted the men's hushed conversation. 'He needs urgent medical attention!'

Igor desperately wanted to break free of the darkness. He felt capable of doing so – after all, his ears were working all right, weren't they? He opened his eyes and waited until the blurred images turned into the ceiling and the green lampshade.

'Don't,' breathed Igor.

'Don't what?' asked the doctor, looking into his patient's eyes.

'Don't take me to hospital!'

'I wasn't going to,' the doctor replied with a shrug. Igor could see him now – a short, feeble-looking man, his thin nose underlined by a moustache. 'I've already treated your wound, and there aren't any beds free anyway. If his temperature goes above forty, call me. But for the time being I'll dress the wound, and we'll leave it at that.'

'What do you mean, "we'll leave it at that"?'

Igor detected the threat of an argument in his mother's voice. He raised his hand and looked at her.

'I don't want to go to hospital,' he said.

'Why don't I come back this evening? I'll change the dressing and see how he is. There's a discount for repeat visits.'

Igor's mother was silent. Her face showed that she was wrestling with her doubts.

'I'll pay,' said Igor. He looked up at Stepan, who was standing to his left.

Stepan nodded to indicate his support. Meanwhile, the doctor was rolling up the piece of oilcloth he'd laid out on the floor, having already sterilised his instruments and put them back in his bag.

He turned to Igor's mother. 'I'll pick that up later,' he said, referring to a shallow enamel bowl containing the knife blade that he'd removed from Igor's stomach. It was just a blade, no handle. 'The police will take the knife,' he added.

'You don't need to get the police involved, do you?' asked Igor.

The doctor shook his head. 'Don't ask me not to,' he said. 'I've got no choice! It's like the Hippocratic oath. Whenever we treat bullet wounds, stab wounds or other injuries sustained as a result of crime we have a duty to inform the police. Even when the injuries are inflicted by a member of the same family!'

The doctor left. Igor's mother wiped the tears from her eyes.

'Who did this to you?' she asked, leaning over her son.

'I didn't see,' said Igor. He lowered his head and glanced

at the bedside table, then froze. The police uniform wasn't there.

'Where is it?' he asked his mother.

'What?'

'The uniform, the belt . . .'

'I put it away,' said Stepan. He stepped forward and pointed at the wardrobe. 'I put everything in there.'

'Thank you,' breathed Igor.

'Elena Andreevna, could I have a word with Igor in private?' asked Stepan.

Igor's mother nodded and left the room.

'Who did this to you?' asked Stepan, leaning in towards Igor and lowering his voice to a whisper. 'Tell me! We can deal with it together!'

Igor shook his head.

'This is serious.' Stepan's voice was steeped in fatherly concern. 'It wasn't just a random attack, I can tell . . . See, the blade's been filed right down, to make sure the handle would break off.'

'What are you talking about?' asked Igor.

'Someone planned this, and they intended to leave the blade inside your body so that it would be almost impossible to get it out. The person who stabbed you knew exactly what he was doing . . . and if he finds out you're still alive, he'll do it again.'

A motorbike stopped outside. Stepan went over and looked out of the window.

'It's the police,' he sighed. 'I'd better go.'

Stepan glanced into the kitchen and told Elena Andreevna that the police had arrived. The front doorbell rang. Elena Andreevna let the police officer in and took him to Igor's room. Stepan waited until Igor's door closed, then he left the house.

The police officer examined the blade in the enamel bowl. 'Well, now,' he said, nodding his head. His eyes were burning with an almost ecstatic curiosity. 'I've only ever read about things like this in detective novels! Right, first things first. We have to follow the correct procedures . . .'

The police officer, a junior lieutenant, was so young that if he hadn't been wearing a uniform Igor would have assumed he was interviewing him for a homework assignment. The fact that he was wearing a uniform didn't make Igor any more respectful or cooperative. The police officer's carefully worded questions met with evasive responses: 'I didn't see,' 'I didn't notice,' 'I don't know.'

'Look, people who have no enemies and never argue with anyone don't just get stabbed in the stomach for no reason!' exclaimed the police officer, whose patience was wearing rather thin.

'Well, they obviously do,' replied Igor, calmly contradicting him. 'Maybe they thought I was somebody else? It was quite dark, you know.'

'Yes, we are aware that there's a problem with the street lamps,' nodded the police officer. 'All right, I'll take the blade. We'll keep it with the case file as evidence.'

The police officer left, promising to call again. Igor shut his eyes, but he was unable to ignore the pain in his side. A car drove past, with Ukrainian rock music blaring from the radio, and Igor finally dropped off to the sound of the singer's gravelly voice drifting through the little top window into his bedroom.

25

Igor and Elena Andreeva were woken at 6 a.m. the following morning by the doctor, who apologised for not coming the previous evening, although he offered no explanation. He immediately set about changing Igor's dressing, then smiled in anticipation of payment. As soon as he'd been paid he picked up the enamel bowl and left, promising to return that evening.

Igor thought he felt better once his dressing had been changed. He tried to sit up in bed but instantly realised that he'd overestimated his capabilities.

He felt thirsty. He asked his mother to pass him his mobile phone, so he could check the missed calls. Most were from Kolyan, but there were also two from a number he didn't recognise.

He called his friend back. He expected the nurse to answer, but Kolyan himself picked up.

'Did you call?' asked Igor.

'Yeah,' murmured Kolyan. He sounded half asleep.

'Are you still in hospital?'

'I'm going home today.'

'Aren't you nervous?'

'No, it's all sorted. I had a chat with him . . . I'll tell you about it later. How are you?'

'Terrible,' said Igor. 'I got attacked just after you did!'

'Were you beaten up?'

'Worse. Stabbed and poisoned.'

'You're kidding! Shall I come and see you?'

'Well, I'm not going anywhere.'

'OK, I'll call you as soon as I get home,' promised Kolyan.

Igor's mother brought him a cup of tea and a fried egg. She put the plate on the stool and moved the stool closer to his bed, to make it easier for him to eat.

'I'm going round to Olga's,' she said as she left the room, carefully closing the door behind her.

Igor rolled over onto his right side, picked up the fork in his left hand and carelessly chopped up the egg. Wincing in pain as he ate, he thought about moving the plate and pillow so he could eat lying on his left side but then decided that he couldn't be bothered. When he'd finished eating, he rolled over onto his back again for a rest. The doorbell rang.

I wonder who that is, thought Igor, lifting his head from the pillow.

It rang several times, then fell silent. Igor noticed something moving outside the window. He twisted round and saw someone's head peering through the white lace curtain.

'Who's there?' he asked.

'It's the police! Let me in!'

'I can't stand up,' said Igor. 'Just push the door hard, it's not locked.'

He heard the sound of footsteps in the hallway.

'Which room are you in again?' called the young police officer.

'Second door on the right.'

The officer came in and looked at Igor suspiciously. Then he looked around the room, and his eyes fell on the stool at Igor's bedside. He sat down next to him.

'So, have you remembered who stabbed you yet?'

'No.' Igor shook his head. 'It was dark, and they got me from behind.'

'I was up half the night reading,' said the police officer. He sounded annoyed, but that might just have been sleep deprivation. 'I learned a lot about stab wounds. For example, you couldn't possibly have been stabbed from behind – the blade would have gone in at a different angle. You were stabbed in a horizontal position, when you were already lying down or after you'd fallen.'

'I don't remember,' said Igor, sounding less sure of himself. 'I was drunk. Completely out of it.'

'Do you seriously expect me to find the person who stabbed you, with nothing but a broken blade to go on?' the police officer asked indignantly.

'No, I don't expect you to. I don't even want you to!' exclaimed Igor. Then his voice softened and he said, almost apologetically, 'Just forget about it.'

'How can I forget about it?' The officer's eyes widened. 'The doctor and I both signed the report!'

'You could always "lose" the report,' suggested Igor. 'Then you wouldn't have to worry about it.'

The police officer thought about it. He shook his head and frowned. Then he opened his satchel and took out a piece of paper and a pen. Resting the paper on the satchel, he placed it on the mattress in front of Igor and handed him the pen.

'Start writing!' he said.

'What do you want me to write?'

'A declaration. I, so-and-so, living at . . . whatever your address is, stabbed myself with a kitchen knife while suffering from acute alcohol intoxication. Junior Lieutenant V.I. Ignatenko has cautioned me regarding the health risks of alcohol abuse. I do not wish to press charges. Date. Signature.'

Igor wrote it all down, then looked up at the police officer.

'Can I have the blade back?' he asked.

'What do you want it for?'

'A souvenir.'

'Well, I was hoping to keep it,' admitted the officer, with childish disappointment. 'This is my first case!'

'Please,' said Igor. 'There is no case! I've just written a declaration explaining everything.'

'All right,' the police officer reluctantly agreed. 'I'll bring it back later.'

After a while Igor made another attempt to sit up, this time successfully. His wound still hurt, but either the pain had lessened or Igor had grown used to it. He sat up in bed for about five minutes, then lay back down again. He repeated this exercise several times.

His mother returned bearing an old jam jar that Olga had given her, which contained some kind of suspiciously yellow, greasy substance. She placed it on Igor's bedside table.

'Tell the doctor to put some of that on the wound,' she said. 'It's a mixture of herbs and goose fat.'

'What is it – some sort of folk remedy?' sneered Igor.

Elena Andreevna didn't answer. She just glared at her son and left the room.

That evening, when the doctor came, she reappeared in

Igor's bedroom to make sure he applied the grease as directed. The doctor sniffed it and nodded, as though he recognised the smell. He asked no further questions.

After the doctor left Igor had another visit from the police officer, who returned the blade. When he left, Igor suddenly burst out laughing.

'What's the matter?' asked Elena Andreevna, putting her head round the door.

'Nothing,' said her son. 'I just feel like a celebrity! Everyone keeps coming to see me, bringing me things, dressing my wound . . . It's like some kind of circus!'

'You'll have even more guests at your funeral,' his mother observed wryly. 'You've already been a victim of knife crime, thanks to this lifestyle you've chosen.'

'What do you mean, "this lifestyle"?' Igor replied indignantly. 'I'm not an alcoholic, a drug addict or a thief, am I?'

Igor's mother waved her hand at him, indicating that she had no wish to continue the conversation. Just then Stepan appeared, holding a bag.

'Oh,' said Igor, looking at him cheerfully. 'Another visitor!'

'I'm not stopping,' said the gardener. 'You're stuck in here with nothing to do, and that's unhealthy. Not to mention boring. So I've brought you something to read. Here.'

'What is it, *The Three Musketeers*?'

Ignoring Igor's remark, Stepan took a large book out of the bag. Igor thought it looked familiar.

'It's the volume my father wrote, *The Book of Food*. It was in one of those suitcases from Ochakov. His handwriting's neat enough, you shouldn't have any trouble understanding it.' The gardener held the book out to Igor. 'Read it – you might learn something.'

The bedroom door creaked. His mother had obviously been listening in, but now she'd gone.

'I wanted to ask you a couple of questions,' said Stepan, suddenly lowering his voice to a whisper. 'First of all, there's a bullet missing from the gun. And the barrel smells of gunpowder.'

He narrowed his eyes, and they bored into Igor.

'Yeah, we were mucking about at the barbecue, shooting bottles in the forest.'

'There's only one bullet missing,' said Stepan, with barely concealed scepticism in his voice. He clearly didn't believe Igor's version of events.

'Yes, we only shot one.'

The gardener reached out and took the broken knife blade from the bedside table, where the police officer had left it. He turned it over thoughtfully in his hands.

'So you're determined to sort this business out yourself, without any help?' he asked calmly.

'Yes, I'll take care of it.'

Still holding the blade, Stepan made several sharp movements with his hand, watching the metal slice through the air. Then he held it up to his face and inspected it closely.

'You see, just two millimetres left, it's not completely filed through. Very risky! You'd have to be very sure of yourself to try a trick like that. You'd have to know exactly how much force to use.'

'Why is it risky?'

'If a knife like this hits a rib, the handle will break off too soon and the attacker will cut himself on the blade.' He ran the tip of his forefinger along the edge of the blade. 'And it's sharp!'

'So whoever stabbed me must have known he wouldn't hit a rib,' mused Igor.

'Exactly,' agreed Stepan. 'Which means he must have stabbed you when you were already lying on the ground. And one of their rules is that if you're attacked with a knife, you respond with a knife – you don't use a gun!' Stepan looked searchingly into Igor's eyes.

'Whose rules?' asked Igor.

'The rules of thieves.'

Igor recalled his last night in Ochakov.

'Seeing as you know so much about their rules,' he began, with something approaching respect in his voice, 'what does "thief's honour" mean?'

Stepan cleared his throat. 'Well,' he said, running his hand over his clean-shaven chin. 'It's stronger than "scout's honour", but it only works among thieves.'

'So if a thief promised something on "thief's honour" to someone who wasn't a thief, then he wouldn't have to keep his word?'

'A thief wouldn't promise anything on "thief's honour" to someone who wasn't a thief,' declared Stepan seriously. 'That's against the rules.'

'Interesting,' murmured Igor. 'Do you know the best way to stab someone?'

'Yes,' nodded Stepan.

'Will you show me?'

'Yes, I'll show you, once you've made a full recovery. For now, you'd better get some rest.'

The gardener gave him a warm smile and left the room.

26

Outside it was raining for the third consecutive day. Igor was initially puzzled by *The Book of Food* Stepan had lent him, and then he began to find it amusing. The book consisted of a seemingly random collection of strange culinary inventions, which were rather like traditional folk remedies, interspersed with solemn declarations arguing that the fate of the nation depended on the food people ate. Some of the comments were worthy of attention, whereas others were more like the ravings of a madman. The pages were covered with neat, childlike handwriting, and one page had been divided into pencil-drawn rows and columns, forming a graph. Various alimentary products had been sorted into groups under the headings 'Enemy', 'Reactionary', 'Hostile', 'Benevolent', 'Natural' and 'Curative'. Igor noticed that meat products, pasta, seaweed, rice, citrus fruits and whale blubber were 'enemy' foods, whereas sour fruits, vinegar, herring, dried fish, halva and chocolate were considered 'hostile'. The 'natural' group included buckwheat, pearl barley, millet, corn, dried peas, chickpeas and goat's cheese.

'Interesting chap, but clearly insane,' murmured Igor, closing the manuscript.

He got out of bed and walked slowly and carefully over to the window. Accelerated by the inclement weather, twilight was taking over the world outside.

He thought back to Kolyan's visit the previous day. Although his lips were still swollen and sore, his friend had smiled and cheerfully boasted that there was no longer any danger of him being 'finished off', because he'd been offered a deal, and fortunately for Kolyan the task could not have been easier. All he had to do was to hack into someone's computer and copy all files and email correspondence containing any password information.

'What are you going to get out of it?' asked Igor.

'His forgiveness!' answered Kolyan.

They relaxed over a bottle of brandy that Kolyan had brought from the city, chasing it with apples that Stepan had picked from the garden.

Stepan looked in a couple of times and peered closely at Kolyan. When the time came for Kolyan to leave, he happily agreed to take the five undeveloped films and drop them off at the photography studio on Proreznaya Street.

After Kolyan left, the gardener knocked on Igor's door.

'Was that the banker you were telling me about?' he asked.

'He's not a banker, he's an IT specialist. He just works in a bank.'

'Seems about the right age for my daughter,' said Stepan, half questioningly, as though he were seeking Igor's approval.

'He's not exactly marriage material,' said Igor, looking into the gardener's eyes with genuine concern. 'He works as a hacker on the side, and that can be a dangerous business.'

Stepan looked puzzled. 'What's a hacker?' he asked.

'Someone who steals information from other people's computers.'

'You mean he's a thief?' asked Stepan, surprised.

'No, he's a hacker.'

Stepan suddenly looked suspicious. 'Is he the one who made a promise on "thief's honour"?'

Igor burst out laughing.

Before leaving, Stepan asked Igor what he'd thought about the manuscript.

'Interesting, very interesting,' nodded Igor, not wishing their conversation to end on an argument.

A faint smile appeared on Stepan's face.

'There are some serious messages in that book,' he said. 'You should read it more carefully.'

Igor's recollections were interrupted by a lorry driving past noisily outside. He lay down again. Being confined to his bedroom, albeit temporarily, had made him desperate for company. He'd enjoyed seeing Kolyan the previous day, and talking to the gardener, but this evening seemed dull and interminable. His mother was watching television. The emergency doctor had already been and gone, noting with approval that Igor's wound was healing remarkably quickly.

Igor was about to resign himself to switching the light off and going to sleep when Stepan knocked on the door and peeped into his room. He was wearing his new suit.

'Igor, can I borrow your umbrella?' he asked.

'Where are you off to in this weather?'

'I found a nice cafe the other day . . . I'm just going there for a bit.'

'It's in the hallway, on the coat stand,' said Igor.

'You mean the red one? That's a woman's umbrella! I've seen you with a black one.'

'In there,' he said, pointing at the wardrobe. 'At the top.'

The gardener found the umbrella, thanked him and left.

Igor switched the light off, but he couldn't sleep. His thoughts were in turmoil, flitting between Fima Chagin, the blade that had been left in his side as a souvenir of Ochakov, Stepan's father Iosip and his *Book of Food*, and Valya and her fear. All of a sudden he could feel his mouth burning, either as a distant aftertaste or as a memory – it was the same feeling he'd had after drinking home-made vodka at Fima's house.

Igor reluctantly got up, went into the kitchen and poured himself a glass of brandy, without bothering to switch the light on. He sat down at the table by the window to drink it.

It occurred to him that this was the time of night he usually drank brandy before putting on the police uniform and going out to walk along the road to the past, the road to Ochakov in 1957. A path that only he knew. Igor shivered with either cold or fear. He didn't know which, until he realised that he'd come into the kitchen wearing nothing but his underpants. The little top window was wide open, and a cold, slanting rain was lashing down outside.

He finished his brandy, returned to his bedroom and got under the blanket. His thoughts returned to Red Valya. He was really worried about her.

'May God keep her safe,' Igor whispered with his eyes closed. 'If anything happens to her, I'll never forgive Him!'

As he spoke, the anger and determination in his own

voice seemed unfamiliar. He sounded more like an actor in a gangster film.

The following morning, the house was unusually noisy. Igor could hear the sound of clattering dishes and of doors being slammed. His mother burst into his bedroom with a bucket of water and started mopping the floor. Igor watched her from the bed for several minutes. She didn't once look in his direction, let alone speak to him.

'What are you doing?' he asked her eventually.

'The house needs a good clean,' said Elena Andreevna. 'We've got guests coming today!'

'Who?'

'Stepan's daughter from Lviv. He's already gone to meet her at the station.'

Igor got up and put on his tracksuit bottoms. He touched the dressing over his wound. It hardly hurt at all, which surprised him.

'You can get your own breakfast,' said his mother, looking up from her mop.

The kitchen floor was still wet. Igor fried himself an egg and sat down at the little table. His eyes were immediately drawn to the window, whose transparency had been thoroughly restored. It was dry outside, and the clouds seemed thinner. It looked like it was going to be a lovely day.

Is Stepan's daughter going to be staying in the house with us? Igor thought suddenly. While her father sleeps in our shed? That'll be an interesting arrangement.

Igor's mother suddenly appeared in the doorway. 'You've got a woman, haven't you?' she asked.

'What are you talking about?'

'An older woman,' said Elena Andreevna.

If Igor had still been eating his egg at this point, he would almost certainly have choked on it.

'What's the matter with you?' He started laughing. 'You've been watching too many soap operas.'

By way of a response, his mother walked over to the table and put a pair of Igor's socks down next to his dirty plate.

'Do you think I can't recognise the signs?' she asked indignantly, prodding the darned heel of one of the socks. 'You ought to find yourself a young girl and get married. Maybe then you'll start behaving sensibly and people will stop attacking you with knives!'

'I just –' began Igor, and then he broke off and looked at his socks. 'She's just a friend. She noticed that they had holes in.'

Elena Andreevna gave a sarcastic smile. 'You should be ashamed of yourself, visiting a woman with holes in your socks!' she exclaimed. 'It's disgraceful!'

The door closed behind her as she left the kitchen. Stunned, Igor stared at the socks for a moment, then brushed them to the floor and kicked them under the radiator.

'Whatver,' he muttered irritably. Then he went back to his bedroom.

'And wear something smart!' said Elena Andreevna, appearing at the door.

'Where's she going to sleep?' Igor stared at his mother.

'I thought we could put her in here,' she replied, looking at her son's neatly made bed.

'Right, so you want me to sleep in the shed with Stepan? So he can teach me how to be a tramp?'

'Stepan's not a tramp,' said Elena Andreevna, leaping to the gardener's defence. 'He's buying a house! You can sleep on the folding bed in my room for a couple of nights.'

'A house?' Igor was having trouble processing all of the morning's news, as though he'd only just woken up from a deep sleep. 'What kind of house?'

He remembered the conversation he'd had with Stepan recently, when the gardener had asked him to find out whether there were two neighbouring houses for sale in Irpen.

'A big house. Olga and I have already been to see it. Actually it's one big house, and another smaller one.'

Igor suddenly noticed that his mother, who had been mopping the floors in a purple flannel robe just a little while ago, was now wearing her best dress. Not only that, but she had accessorised it with an amber necklace.

'Are you feeling better?' she asked solicitously.

Igor touched the dressing over his wound, as he had already several times that morning. It still hurt a bit, but it was more of a dull ache than a shooting pain.

'I guess so,' he said with a shrug.

'In that case, please wear something smart,' she said again. 'Your graduation suit is still in that wardrobe. You've hardly worn it.'

'Why do I have to get dressed up?' cried Igor. 'I already feel like a man, I don't need a suit and tie to prove it!'

Something suddenly stopped him mid-rant. It could have been the way his mother lowered her eyes, hurt by his insinuation, or because he knew in his heart that he'd gone too far. He looked back at the wardrobe.

'Just tell me why it's so important that I wear a suit. I met her in Lviv, and she's perfectly normal. She wears jumpers and jeans! She won't care what I'm wearing.'

'It's not about her!' Elena Andreevna waved her hand airily. 'Today is a very important day for both of them. Oh, you're too young to understand. They're going to buy two houses, and they want us to go with them . . . Olga's coming too.'

Igor marvelled at his mother. She'd become so provincial since they'd moved from Kiev. They've got so much in common, her and Stepan. Who'd have thought it?

'And don't forget to shave,' she added.

The door closed behind her as she went out. Igor opened the wardrobe and took out his suit, which he must have worn on no more than three previous occasions. He laid it on the bed, then returned to the wardrobe and rummaged around until he found the old police uniform. His hands sought out the bundles of money and the gun in the holster. He found the gold watch and chain too, which were wrapped up in an old scarf of his mother's.

This is ridiculous, thought Igor. What if I put the police uniform on instead of the suit? He smiled. She'd take me straight to a psychiatrist! The same way she dragged me round to all those doctors after the incident with the carousel.

His thoughts jumped to Ochakov. A vision of Valya's frightened face swam before his eyes.

'Everything's ridiculous,' sighed Igor, closing the wardrobe door.

Half an hour later, the sun emerged from behind the clouds. Almost at the same time an old brown Mercedes pulled up outside the gate. Igor recognised it from the bus station, where it usually stood waiting for passengers.

Igor was already wearing his suit and a white shirt and tie, which, like Stepan, he'd been unable to tie without his mother's help. It was like a noose around his neck. He felt constrained by his breathing, his body and his thoughts.

Stepan and his daughter got out of the car. Stepan handed some money through the driver's window. His daughter was holding a small sports bag, which looked like it was quite full.

She's here for a couple of days then, Igor thought.

As she entered the house, Alyona Sadovnikova shyly introduced herself and shook Elena Andreevna's hand. Still holding her bag, she followed Igor's mother to his bedroom.

'Make yourself comfortable,' said Elena Andreevna.

Igor smiled at her and went out into the hallway, where Stepan was waiting in his suit. His neck was also constrained by a tie, although it didn't seem to be bothering him in the slightest. He glanced at his watch, then looked at Igor.

'Oh,' he said, pleasantly surprised. 'Very smart! You look like a banker. Are you coming with us?'

'Are we going shopping?' Igor asked with a smile.

'No, I've already found two houses and a plot of land. I'm going to sign the purchase deeds in an hour and I have to pay straight away. As far as I'm concerned, the more people there, the better.'

Igor paused. 'All right,' he said with a nod. Then he thought for a moment. 'Shall I take the gun? Just in case?'

The gardener shook his head. 'Don't take the knife either,' he added, his tone brusque and serious. 'Anything could happen, of course . . . But it's best not to take it.'

'Why didn't you talk to me about the houses?' asked Igor, sounding slightly aggrieved.

'Either you weren't around at the time, or you were in bed. Anyway, I can see what you think of me . . . I've clearly outstayed my welcome, but I'll be out of your way soon!'

'But,' protested Igor, spreading his hands, 'I thought we were getting on all right . . . I even went to Ochakov with you!'

'Yes,' nodded Stepan. 'You did indeed. Look, everything's fine, we can talk about it later. Right now all I can think about is signing the purchase deeds and getting the keys. Then we'll really have something to talk about!'

Half an hour later a strange procession began making its way down the street in the direction of the bus station. First came two men in suits, the elder of whom was carrying an old canvas rucksack, which was clearly half empty, over his shoulder; then a young woman wearing a dark green imitation leather raincoat and jeans, which were tucked into her low-heeled boots, and two elegantly attired elderly women. Olga was also wearing a necklace, and she'd pinned a brooch in the shape of a lizard to her cardigan. Igor looked round a couple of times as they walked, and Stepan's rucksack kept catching his eye.

Well, he thought, no one would ever guess that there's enough money in there to buy a couple of houses. People usually carry that kind of money in briefcases and without an entourage of OAPs dressed in their Sunday best!

When they got to the bus station, Stepan looked at his watch and stopped.

'We're a bit early. Let's have a coffee,' he suggested, pointing at the kiosk.

They all went over to the kiosk. Stepan ordered five instant coffees and handed the disposable plastic cups of coffee to each of them in turn. They stood outside the kiosk and drank their coffees in silence. Stepan kept checking his watch.

'Right then,' he said, throwing his empty cup into the bin. 'Time to go. The real-estate agency isn't far from here.'

The agency in question was situated in a private house. On the gate next to the house number, which had been painted on it in white, was a sign featuring an image of a fierce-looking dog.

Stepan reached the gate first and opened it. He looked over his shoulder and nodded to indicate that the others should follow him. Igor hung back, on the off chance that a ferocious dog might run out and start barking at him, but no dog appeared. Stepan went up to the front door and rang the bell.

The door was opened by a young man wearing a neatly pressed grey suit, a pink shirt and a red tie, who looked like he ought to have been at school. He was wearing a pair of leather shoes with very pointed toes. As soon as he saw Stepan, he held his hand out respectfully. Igor noticed several pairs of slippers neatly lined up in the hallway.

'Come in, Stepan Iosipovich, the vendors are already here.' The estate agent's voice sounded thin and reedy, as though it hadn't yet broken.

As soon as they were all inside, the young man fastened both locks on the front door and led them to where his visitors were waiting in a large room.

Igor couldn't help but smile as he took in the incongruous mix of office and domestic furniture in the room. Photographs of houses, buildings and plots of land lined the walls, which were covered with green wallpaper. It was impossible to ignore the conspicuous ticking of the cuckoo clock. The vendors – an elderly couple with dazed, anxious faces – were sitting on a sofa on the opposite side of the room. They were both about seventy years old.

'The contract is ready to sign,' said the young man in the grey suit. He pointed at a file that lay open on the table. 'The notary's here too. He's drinking coffee in the kitchen. I'll fetch him as soon as the funds have been transferred.'

The gardener suddenly turned to his daughter, with a nervous look in his eyes.

'You didn't forget your passport, did you?'

'Don't worry, I've got it,' nodded Alyona. She touched his hand, seeking to reassure him.

Stepan looked at the vendors. 'So, was it five hundred thousand?'

They nodded meekly.

Stepan dropped the canvas rucksack onto the table, then opened it and started taking out bundles of 200-hryvna notes. He stacked them up on the table, next to the file.

Igor looked at the young estate agent. He was standing motionless, about two metres from the table, unable to tear his eyes away from the growing pile of banknotes. He licked his lips greedily, his mouth clearly dry with excitement.

The empty rucksack fell to the floor. Stepan straightened up the pile of money and looked at the vendors.

'It's all there. Count it.'

Igor saw alarm in the eyes of the elderly couple. They both stood up and shuffled towards the table. The man was wearing a suit too, although his was black. His wife was wearing a long black skirt and a dark blue blouse.

'Could you help us?' the man asked the young estate agent. 'My hands are shaking . . . I might make a mistake.'

Igor suddenly felt overwhelmed with exhaustion. He sat on the sofa vacated by the vendors. Elena Andreevna sat down next to him and wiped the perspiration from her forehead with a handkerchief. She looked at her son for support. Igor placed his damp hand over hers.

Igor closed his eyes and listened to the rustling of banknotes, which seemed as though it would last for ever. Suddenly the young man in the grey suit announced, 'This is Sergei Ivanych Kuptsyn, the notary. He will witness the signing of the contract.'

Igor opened his eyes to see a grey-haired, middle-aged man taking a seat at the table. He put on a pair of glasses with gold frames, picked up the contract and started reading it to himself, silently moving his lips.

'Passports, please,' he said, looking up at them.

Stepan glanced at Alyona. She took her passport out of her pocket and put it on the table. The vendors held out their passports.

'So, buyer – Alyona Stepanovna Sadovnikova,' the notary read ceremoniously from the contract. 'Vendors – Pyotr Leonidovich Ostashko and Lidiya Alekseevna Ostashko. Sign here, please.'

Igor noticed that the money had disappeared from the table. He looked around the room.

'That's it,' said the notary. 'All signed and sealed. Now you can shake hands!'

Stepan shook the vendors' hands. The elderly couple still looked anxious. The man in the black suit took an envelope from his pocket and held it out to Stepan.

'Here are two keys for the new house and the key for the padlock on the old one,' he said.

'Would anyone like a glass of champagne?' asked the young estate agent, rather nervously.

They all declined. The vendors asked the estate agent to call them a taxi. Igor looked at the elderly couple and felt a stab of pity at the thought of the two of them getting into a taxi with that amount of money. If it were him, he would have made sure he had some friends with him. He would have asked one of them to drive, too – there's no way he would have gone in a taxi! On the other hand, they were so ancient, what was the likelihood of them having any friends who owned cars? Igor's thoughts started to depress him.

The estate agent told Stepan and Alyona how to register the houses with the local real-estate inventory office. Olga was standing by the door that led to the hallway, shuffling her feet impatiently. Finally the estate agent, clearly also the occupant of the house, unbolted the two locks and released them all into the sunshine. There was already a taxi waiting at the gate. Igor studied the driver – he had a trustworthy look about him, and Igor felt reassured.

Stepan's face bore a gentle, weary smile. His daughter walked along next to him, thinking her own thoughts. Olga and Elena Andreevna were chatting together, about ten paces behind them.

'You go on, I'll catch you up,' Stepan said suddenly when they reached a grocery shop. 'I'll buy something for dinner. We have to celebrate!'

'I'll give you a hand,' volunteered Igor. Stepan did not object.

Inside the shop, Igor looked directly into the gardener's eyes.

'Did you really put both houses in your daughter's name?' he asked quietly.

'We used her passport, so yes, they're hers,' said Stepan. 'I haven't had a passport for ten years. I lost it. But I'll get a new one. I know what to do . . . I just need to fill in a loss report and hand it in to the police. I haven't got a criminal record or anything.'

Igor nodded. Stepan turned away and peered closely at the selection of salami and ham under the glass counter. Then he looked up and called out to the sales assistant, 'Excuse me, miss, I'm ready to order.'

27

Olga, Elena Andreevna and Alyona spent a long time preparing the celebratory meal. Six hands and three voices, all fully engaged. Igor glanced into the kitchen and immediately withdrew, his desire for a sandwich remaining unfulfilled.

'Open up the table in the living room,' said his mother, looking up from the frying pan on the hob. 'And tell Stepan that we'll be ready to eat in half an hour.'

Igor did as she requested then went out to the front gate. As he stood there looking down the street, he decided that he'd been stuck at home convalescing for long enough. Now he'd been for a walk, he wanted to go again. Preferably without the suit and the noose round his neck.

Igor loosened his tie, surprised at himself for not changing into something more comfortable. Nevertheless, he kept his suit on until dinner. The others also came to the table in the same outfits they'd worn to the signing that morning – except Alyona, who had changed into a light blue sweater. Her cheeks were flushed and she was holding an envelope, which she put first on the table in front of her and then on her knees.

'Open the champagne, son!' said Elena Andreevna.

Igor opened the bottle, then stood up and poured a glass for everyone but Stepan.

Elena Andreevna pushed her chair back and stood up. 'So, Stepan Iosipovich,' she began, 'here's to your new houses – may they be full of happiness, may you enjoy good health and may all your dreams come true! I hope you will remember us in your new life!'

Igor sipped his champagne. Unable to ignore his hunger any longer, he helped himself to two pork rissoles, some mashed potato, a spoonful of mimosa salad and a couple of sprats.

Elena Andreevna caught Igor's eye as he was about to tuck in and pointed at the bottle of champagne. He topped up everyone's glass and glanced at Stepan, whose expression was perfectly serene.

'May I?' said Alyona.

She stood up, holding her glass in her left hand.

'Papa,' she began, 'I . . . Maybe I haven't . . . thought very highly of you in the past. I hope you can forgive me . . . I've got a present for you. I've had it for a few years.'

She took the envelope from the table and handed it to Stepan.

'It's a certificate confirming the rehabilitation of my grandfather . . . your father.'

Stepan's lips trembled as he took the envelope from his daughter. He opened it and took out a document with an official stamp on it, which he scanned briefly.

'At last,' he said quietly. 'Now I really can make a fresh start.'

He looked up at his daughter gratefully.

'Thank you, Alyona.' He looked round at the others. 'You should all drink to his memory. Today is proof that my life has turned out well . . . His didn't, but I think he'd be happy if he knew about my plans!'

The pork rissoles were meltingly tender. As Igor chewed his food, he wondered what plans Stepan had in mind.

'I'd like you all to come with me tomorrow,' said Stepan, towards the end of the meal. 'So I can show you round my new home. Yes, the time has come for me to move on.' He looked at Elena Andreevna. 'I'm sure you'll be glad to have your shed back!'

'Don't be silly,' she said, waving him away. 'I haven't even paid you the hundred hryvnas I owe you for this month!'

'A hundred hryvnas,' repeated Stepan, smiling at his own thoughts. 'So, tonight will be my last night here . . . I've enjoyed getting to know you.'

Everyone left the table shortly after this, as though they sensed that the meal was over. The three women took the dishes into the kitchen and Olga started washing up.

Igor followed Stepan out onto the doorstep.

'Congratulations,' he said to the gardener. 'And I'm sorry if, you know . . . if I've offended you in any way. I didn't mean to.'

Stepan nodded. He was still holding the certificate of rehabilitation.

'Can I see it?' asked Igor.

Stepan handed him the document.

Maybe I should tell him about Iosip and Chagin? thought Igor, after reading the certificate, but he immediately shook his head. No, he won't believe me. He'll think I'm winding him up again.

'Do you know much about him?' asked Igor.

'I know more now than I did. At least I know why they put him in prison.'

'Why?'

'For slandering the Soviet system.'

'You mean he was a dissident?' Igor was surprised. He couldn't reconcile this piece of information with his observations of Iosip in Ochakov.

'No,' said Stepan. 'You obviously didn't read *The Book of Food* properly! He was arrested for slandering Soviet food. He claimed that workers' canteens prepared "enemy food" and that "enemy food" was enslaving the people, making them weak-willed and passive. He criticised the food in the labour camp too, so he spent all his time there in solitary confinement. They thought he'd incite the other prisoners to an uprising, but they all agreed with him anyway. Then they sent him to a psychiatric institution, and he was only released after Stalin died. His fellow inmates helped him once he got out.'

Stepan fell silent and gave a heavy sigh.

'Could I borrow the book again?' asked Igor.

'Let's go and get it,' said Stepan, and he started walking towards the shed.

He switched the shed light on, found the manuscript and handed it to Igor. There was another book on the makeshift bed, and Igor was sure he'd seen it before. He read the title: *Restaurant Marketing*.

'Well, goodnight,' said Igor, and he went out into the yard.

The gate creaked as he was going up the steps to the porch, and he turned round and saw their neighbour Olga disappearing down the street. The light was still on in the kitchen window, but when Igor went in carrying the manuscript he found his mother just about to switch it off.

'I think I'm going to read in here for a bit,' he said, sitting down at the table.

He opened the home-made book and flicked through it, scanning the recipes. He stopped at one of the pages.

Enemy food enslaves the people. Take the fisherman, for example – he lures his fish before catching it, so that it becomes accustomed to the place where death awaits. Enemies of the people lure them in the same way, getting them used to food on which they will become dependent, like the fish before it is caught. Then the man who has been lured by this food can be made to do three shifts instead of one! First the enemies of the free man came up with the idea of replacing money with food, as payment for labour. These food payments were measured in units known as workdays. This was just the start of an extensive experiment, the ultimate aim of which was to control the people by means of food . . .

'Wow, he really was a dissident!' whispered Igor, astonished. He bent his head over the manuscript and continued reading.

Igor spent half the night engrossed in the painstakingly recorded thoughts and reflections of the late Iosip. He eventually closed the book and went to bed just before 4 a.m., when his head began to ache, but even then sleep did not come to his weary body immediately.

Was he crazy, or not? Igor lay on the folding bed in the darkness, listening to his mother's peaceful breathing and thinking about everything he had just read. His thoughts kept jumping to Stepan, and he asked himself the same question: Is he crazy, or not? He remembered the book that he'd seen lying on the bench in the shed. 'I wonder if he even knows what the word "marketing" means,' smirked Igor. Seconds later, the smile fell from his face as he suddenly made the connection between *Restaurant Marketing* and *The Book of Food*.

'That's it!' whispered Igor, staggered by his discovery. 'So he's not crazy, and the plans he mentioned over dinner . . . I think I know what he's up to.'

Stepan came to the house the following morning in his suit again, having managed to tie his tie himself this time without Elena Andreevna's help. He stood in the living room and his presence alone lent a sense of urgency to proceedings, encouraging the others to hurry up and get ready if they wished to see his two houses.

They spent a further ten minutes standing outside Olga's gate. Finally, when all members of the previous day's delegation were present, they set off towards the bus station. On the way Olga and Elena Andreevna called into a grocery shop and bought two round loaves of bread.

'You should never visit a new house for the first time without taking a loaf of bread,' explained Elena Andreevna, in response to Igor's quizzical look.

They turned into Teligi Street and continued walking for several minutes until Stepan stopped by an old wooden fence that ran in front of two adjacent houses: a new, two-storey brick house and an old wooden bungalow with a new slate roof. Though undeniably more modest than its neighbour, the second house was still a respectable size.

'Well, here we are,' announced Stepan, looking round at them all with pride. Jingling the keys in his hand, he was the first to walk through the gate, turning immediately onto the path that led to the new house.

Inside, the house smelt of paint. The spacious rooms were unfurnished but for a selection of mismatched chairs. There were also a number of trestle tables dotted about, along with tins of paint and paper sacks full of powdered plaster.

'May this house be blessed with happiness,' Olga declared solemnly, as though she were in church. She placed the loaf of bread in its cellophane wrapper on the windowsill.

They went up to the first floor. Several narrow doors led off the landing, all of them closed.

'That's a bathroom with a toilet,' said Stepan, gesturing like a tour guide. 'And those three are bedrooms.'

'It's not a house, it's a palace!' exclaimed Elena Andreevna, unable to hide her amazement. 'You could get lost in here!'

'We won't get lost.' Stepan smiled.

Igor found the little wooden house next door far cosier, probably because it was warm and furnished and already felt like a home. There were curtains at the little windows, and the old-fashioned furniture left by the previous occupants seemed to suit the house perfectly. The living room was dominated by a handsome oak dresser, with glazed cabinets. Igor was sure he'd seen one just like it somewhere before. He closed his eyes, trying to remember where . . . Yes, that was it! At Fima Chagin's house in Ochakov. Fima had taken the shot glasses from it before he'd attempted to poison him. There had been something oppressive and sinister about that dresser, though, whereas this one exuded warmth, nostalgic charm, well-being and prosperity.

'May there be happiness here too!' said Elena Andreevna.

She walked over to the dresser and placed the second loaf of bread in the recess beneath the cabinets. Stepan joined her by the dresser. Opening the left-hand cupboard door, he took out a bottle of brandy and several old-fashioned glasses.

'I won't have one myself, but the occasion definitely calls for a drink,' he said.

He opened the brandy, poured it into the glasses and took a step back.

There was a round table in the room, covered with a maroon velvet tablecloth, but they all drank their brandy standing near the dresser. Stepan put the bottle back, without offering anyone a refill.

Igor's mobile phone rang in his pocket. He saw that it was the photographer calling and went outside to answer it.

'Hello,' he said. 'Did my friend bring the films?'

'Yes, I've already processed them, and the prints are ready for you to collect . . . I have to say, they've come out exceptionally well,' gushed the photographer. 'What incredible photographs! I've never seen anything like it!'

'I've been a bit under the weather lately,' said Igor. 'I'll try and drop by in a couple of days.'

'I was wondering if we could have another chat,' said the photographer, and Igor heard him sigh. 'It's such an amazing collection of photographs . . . simply outstanding! They would make a fantastic exhibition, and I'm sure that all the photography magazines would be interested in running a feature on it. I wish you'd agree . . . I would be willing to print the photographs in large format, completely free of charge . . . And I could organise the advertising, and the catalogue . . . What do you say?'

Igor looked all around him. He gazed at both houses and the trees in the old garden. Then his eyes were drawn upwards, to the blue sky and its scattered wisps of clouds.

'All right,' he said, and he sensed the photographer's face light up with a smile.

'Thank you so much! I'll start work on the prints today, and I'll be in touch again soon. Goodbye!'

Igor slipped his phone back into his jacket pocket and smiled. He turned back towards the old house. The front door had just opened, and Alyona was the first to come out. Like Igor, she looked all around her. He had the impression that her eyes were also drawn to the sky.

Stepan and his daughter stayed at the old house; Olga, Elena Andreevna and Igor went home, after they'd all agreed to hold a housewarming party in a few days' time.

About twenty paces from Igor's front gate, his mobile phone rang again.

'It's me,' said the photographer, sounding flustered. 'I forgot to ask your full name! We need it for the catalogue and the poster.'

Igor stopped and thought about it. His mother, who had gone into the yard ahead of him, turned round and looked at him expectantly. He waved his hand to indicate that she should go on into the house without him.

'Are you there?' the photographer asked impatiently.

'Yes, sorry,' said Igor. 'I'm just thinking.'

'Are you concerned about using your real name? Would you prefer a pseudonym?'

Igor jumped at the idea. 'Yes, a pseudonym would be better.'

'Shall I call back later? Give you some time to think about it?'

'No,' Igor said more decisively. 'Put Vanya Samokhin.'

'Ivan Samokhin?'

'No, Vanya. Vanya Samokhin.'

'OK, I've made a note of that,' said the photographer. His voice sounded calmer now. 'I'll take your promotional portrait from one of the photographs, to use in the poster and the catalogue. There's a good one of you looking straight at the camera.'

'Fine,' agreed Igor.

28

Later that afternoon, Igor went out for a walk. His initial plan was to walk to the bus station and back, but he changed his mind on the way. He was curious to know exactly how far away Stepan would be living and decided to time the journey to his new house. Before Igor had even reached the familiar turning, Stepan himself appeared. He'd changed out of his suit into a pair of black trousers, a jumper and a red shirt, the collar of which was just visible.

'Are you going to our house?' Igor asked him.

'Eventually,' nodded the gardener.

They continued on their separate ways. When Igor reached the corner he glanced over his shoulder to see whether Stepan was watching him, but he had already disappeared.

Igor walked past Stepan's houses and on to the end of the street. On the way back, he slowed down again and scrutinised the gardener's new properties in the gathering twilight. Igor was still having trouble making sense of everything that had happened over the last month. An old man, who was not exactly a tramp but a bit of a vagrant, met a young man who helped him to decipher an old tattoo on his shoulder. This tattoo led them to Ochakov, where they discovered suitcases full of surprises, gifts from the past. Now the man had bought two houses for himself and his daughter, whereas the young man who had helped him was still stuck in a rut, drifting aimlessly through life. All he had to show for it was a knife wound in his side and an unhealthy obsession with the fate of a fish seller from old Ochakov. So what if he knew the path to the past like the back of his hand? Igor's 'achievements' did not even come close to Stepan's!

Igor found himself near the brightly lit kiosk at the bus station, although he had no idea how he'd got there. He bought a cup of instant coffee and drank it outside the kiosk.

On the way home he bumped into his mother's friend Olga. She was hurrying towards him in a state of considerable excitement.

'What's the matter?' he called out.

She stopped to catch her breath. 'I'm just going to the shop,' she said.

Igor could tell by the look on her face that she wanted to say more. She obviously had some news that she was bursting to share.

'Guess what,' she said, pausing for dramatic effect. 'Stepan has just made me a proposal!'

'Lucky you,' smiled Igor.

Unimpressed by his reaction, Olga waved her hand dismissively and went on her way.

When Igor got home, the house was unusually quiet. The atmosphere had changed somehow since Stepan had left. It had been nice having his daughter to stay too, even though it had only been for a couple of days. Now, as he walked down the hallway, Igor couldn't even hear the television.

He found his mother in the kitchen. She was sitting quietly

at the table with a glass of home-made wine, looking pensive but calm.

'Can I join you?' asked Igor.

'If you like,' nodded Elena Andreevna. 'Sitting here by myself isn't helping . . . It's just going round and round in my head.'

'What is?' asked Igor, pouring himself a glass of wine.

'Stepan proposed to me,' she said, looking closely at her son.

Igor's mouth fell open.

'It took me by surprise too,' admitted Elena Andreevna. 'Of course, he's a respectable man –'

'You think so?' asked Igor, glancing at the scales on the windowsill. 'He proposed to your friend Olga too, you know. I've just seen her on the way to the grocery shop, quite beside herself with joy!'

He regretted his words as soon as he saw the effect they had on his mother. Her face fell, she turned pale and her hands started shaking. She stood up and went into the hallway, and Igor heard her putting her coat on. The front door slammed behind her.

It's all going to kick off now! he thought, imagining his mother storming round to Olga's and the two of them having an almighty row.

Igor picked up his glass of wine and took a sip. He didn't particularly feel like sitting there waiting for his mother to get back, so he took Iosip's book from the windowsill and went to his own room. He moved the reading lamp to his bedside table and settled down on his bed with the book. He was soon absorbed in the eccentric ramblings of Iosip Sadovnikov, avowed enemy of Soviet canteen food. Igor found himself noting with regularity how easily the handwritten text overcame his scepticism, making him look at certain culinary issues in a new, more serious way.

He found the chapter about salt and sugar completely fascinating, for example – so much so that he didn't even hear his mother come back. He didn't hear her throw her coat angrily at the coat stand, or the way the coat slipped off and fell to the floor.

His mother glanced into the kitchen, then opened the door to Igor's bedroom. She marched over to his bed and raised her hand as though she were about to slap his face, but she managed to restrain herself. Only her eyes, aflame with anger, fell on her son's face.

'You stupid fool!' she exclaimed. 'You almost gave me a heart attack!'

'I didn't do anything!' protested Igor. 'I only told you what I'd heard!'

'What did you hear, exactly?' cried his mother. 'He didn't "propose" to her, he "made her a proposal". Don't you get it?'

'What's the difference?' asked Igor, recalling that Olga had indeed told him that Stepan had 'made her a proposal'.

'When you "make someone a proposal", it means a business proposal. He asked her to be the manager of his cafe. But he proposed to me in the other sense of the word . . . He asked me to marry him!'

'I wonder if he'd consider making me a proposal too,' remarked Igor, his lips curling into a smile.

His mother turned round and left without another word, slamming the door. Igor moved the reading lamp to the edge of his bedside table and opened the manuscript again at page 48, which bore the heading 'Man and Food'.

People can be divided into two categories, according to the way they naturally relate to the world around them: gardeners and foresters. Gardeners essentially see the world as a garden, in which it is their responsibility to behave appropriately, to fix whatever is broken, to decorate whatever is built and to keep order. Foresters, on the other hand, prefer an uncultivated environment. They are more inclined to break things and live in disorder than to build, renovate or repair. Foresters are more ruthless, but they are also physically stronger and more robust. They believe that it is impossible to change the world, whereas gardeners are always trying to improve it. Most men are foresters, and most women are gardeners. Male gardeners are able-bodied but often lack tenacity in their undertakings and the courage of their convictions. Foresters and gardeners differ also in their approach to food. This does not mean that foresters prefer simple food, merely that they tend to lose their natural ability to distinguish and evaluate refined tastes. They are more interested in the size of their portion – when everyone at the table is served an identical meal, the first thing they do is check to see who has been given the most. Gardeners do not usually lose their ability to distinguish refined tastes. In fact, sometimes their perception of taste is developed to such an extent that they are capable of detecting nuances that are not really there.

Igor looked up from the manuscript, deep in thought. The words he had just read made perfect sense. He automatically thought about Stepan. Was he a gardener or a forester? A gardener, it would appear. Igor thought about himself, about his own culinary preferences and, if truth be told, about his growing indifference to food and to the world around him.

'I don't seem to be either a gardener or a forester,' he concluded sadly. 'Neither fish nor fowl . . . But I used to build such beautiful sandcastles on the beach in Yevpatoriya when I was little! So, I could have become a gardener.'

Igor smiled at his memories, then shook his head.

I'm taking it all far too seriously, he decided. It's not a psychology textbook, it was written by an ordinary man of the people . . . He might not even have finished school!

But Igor wasn't convinced by his attempts to dismiss the book's significance. It sounded unnatural and insincere, like a second-rate actor whose gestures do not correspond to the spirit and sentiment of his lines. He turned his attention back to the page he had been reading.

> The world has so far been spared from devastation because foresters and gardeners frequently enter into marriage, thereby creating unnatural but stable unions. When a male forester marries a female gardener, the husband enjoys the complaisance and timidity of his wife. But when a male gardener takes a female forester for his wife, then her spontaneity will curb his idealism and restrict his endeavours.

'That's like Valya and me!' Igor was struck by the revelation. 'So I must be a gardener after all! At least, more of a gardener than a forester.'

Igor was too nervous to read the rest of the page. As he flicked forward through the manuscript he saw a chapter entitled 'Reducing Natural Products – Dish of Buckwheat and Barley Flour'. He cleared his throat and flicked forward another couple of pages. Then turned back – page 72 featured two recipes: 'Foresters' Stew' and 'Gardeners' Stew'.

Igor carefully closed the manuscript and placed it on the stool by his bed. He switched off the reading lamp and lay there for another half an hour, looking at the ceiling and thinking about gardeners and foresters.

He spent the whole of the following morning with his nose buried in *The Book of Food*. When he got to page 150, he realised he was hungry. He went into the kitchen and prepared himself a bowl of buckwheat. While he was eating it and marvelling at his new-found enjoyment of such a simple dish, his mother looked into the kitchen.

'What are you doing?' she asked, surprised. 'I was going to make borshch.'

'Good idea,' said Igor, looking up at her. 'Borshch is a natural dish. Don't put too much salt in, but be generous with the pepper. I'm sorry about yesterday, by the way.'

'Don't worry about it,' she said with a shrug. 'So, what shall I tell him?'

'It's up to you,' said Igor. 'Gardeners are basically good people . . . You just need to control them.'

'In what way?' His mother was surprised again. 'He doesn't drink or play cards!'

'I meant in general. It doesn't matter.'

Elena Andreevna gave a deep sigh and went out.

Igor finished reading Iosip's handwritten book at about 6 p.m. and took it straight back to Stepan. Returning the book was a perfectly valid reason to visit, but Igor was also hoping to see Alyona. He wanted to see if he could work out whether she was a 'gardener' or a 'forester'.

Igor rang the doorbell of the old house first, but there was no answer. Turning towards the new house, Igor noticed that the lights were on in the ground-floor windows and the front door was wide open. There were big plastic sacks full of rubble and other building debris piled up outside.

'Hey, Stepan, are you there?' Igor called into the house.

'Hang on!' answered Stepan's voice. 'Don't come in, it's really dusty!'

A dust mask hung around Stepan's neck, and his old tracksuit bottoms and striped sailor's undershirt had turned an unappealing shade of grey. As he came outside, he brushed his vest down vigorously and a dusty cloud rose up around him in the evening air. He brushed his tracksuit bottoms with equal vigour, and they were soon restored to their original dark blue.

'Here you go, I've finished it,' said Igor, holding the book out to Stepan. 'I thought it was really interesting. Especially the bit about gardeners and foresters.'

Igor felt that Stepan was now looking at him with greater respect.

'How's the wound?' asked the gardener.

'I can hardly feel it.'

'Are you still having trouble remembering who stabbed you?' There was the trace of a smile on Stepan's lips.

'No, I've remembered,' Igor said quietly. 'It was a "forester". You promised to show me the right way to stab someone. Can you show me now?'

'There's not much to it,' Stepan said with a shrug. 'If you're facing your adversary you have to strike upwards, or directly from your stomach to his stomach. If you're coming at him from behind, then you have to strike downwards, and get him in the back or the neck . . . But that's not really advisable.'

Igor raised his hand to his stomach and then, gripping an imaginary knife in his hand, thrust it forward sharply, stopped just to the left of Stepan.

'Like that?' he asked.

'Like that,' said Stepan.

'Where's Alyona?' Igor looked behind the gardener, towards the brightly lit doorway.

'She's gone to an Internet cafe, to check her emails,' said Stepan. He made a vague gesture with his right hand as he spoke, apparently indicating the direction in which she had gone.

'Do you need any help?' asked Igor, nodding at the plastic sacks.

'Come back tomorrow,' said Stepan. He took the dust mask off over his head and looked at it. 'We're fine for today!'

29

Images of foresters and gardeners continued to occupy Igor's mind, even while he slept. In his dream they were clearly preparing to go into battle, having taken up position on opposite sides of a stretch of land that separated a dense forest and an old garden. Igor sensed that the outcome was predetermined, as the foresters greatly outnumbered their opponents. He tossed and turned, growing anxious in his sleep. Rolling onto his right side, he felt his wound begin to ache again – tentatively, almost apologetically. He lay on his stomach and pressed his face into the pillow, but this made it difficult to breathe so he turned his head to the right, towards the window. Igor's dream, which had begun to recede, now returned to play out on the screen of his imagination. Only this time the sound had disappeared. There hadn't been much sound in the dream to begin with – just the rustling of the trees and the howling of the wind – but now there was a sterile silence, and this made it more disturbing.

From somewhere outside his dream came a tapping sound. At first it was dull and muffled, as though someone were knocking on wood, then it grew louder and more resonant, like a stick hitting glass.

'Igor!' His mother's voice was accompanied by the creaking of the door. 'There's someone walking around outside the house! I'm frightened!'

Igor opened his eyes. It took him several seconds to separate the inertia of sleep from reality. His mother was standing next to his bed in her long nightdress, barefoot. He reluctantly hauled himself out of bed, went over to the window and listened. The tapping sound continued at random intervals. As Igor's eyes grew accustomed to the darkness, he noticed something lying on the path between the porch and the gate.

Suddenly the doorbell rang. The tapping had stopped.

'Go and see who it is,' urged his mother in a half-whisper. 'Just don't open the door! Tell them we're calling the police!'

Igor's mother's anxiety inevitably communicated itself to her son. He also felt cold, standing there in his underpants and a T-shirt with the little top window open.

Igor tiptoed into the hallway, then crept into the kitchen and pressed his face against the window. It was quiet again. Igor stood on a stool, opened the little top window and stuck his head out of it. From this angle the dark object on the path looked like a bag full of shopping.

'Who's there?' Igor called in a low voice. He listened for a reply.

A snapping sound came from the corner of the house, from the direction of the shed, as though someone had stepped on a dry twig.

'Who's there?' called Igor, raising his voice a little. He could feel his mother's warm breath on the small of his back. She had followed him into the kitchen, terrified, and was now peering out of the window from behind him.

They heard hurried footsteps. Igor stiffened. He pulled his head in from the little top window and stared at the corner of the house. As they watched, a figure stealthily emerged. It was Kolyan. He scanned the dark windows of the front of the house.

'Hey, what are you doing here?' called Igor.

Kolyan couldn't tell where the voice was coming from at first. He moved towards the house and eventually spotted his friend.

'Open up, quickly!' he hissed. His voice was shaking, as though he were shivering from the cold.

'Go to the front door,' said Igor. He climbed down from the stool without taking his eyes off his friend.

As soon as Kolyan was inside the house, he threw his bag to the floor and locked the door behind him.

'Has something happened?' Igor asked him.

Kolyan nodded. He noticed Igor's mother in the depths of the hallway.

'I'm sorry to come so late,' he said hurriedly.

'I'm going back to bed,' said Igor's mother.

'Bring some chairs or stools out here,' whispered Kolyan. 'We need to talk.'

'Let's go and sit in the kitchen,' suggested Igor.

Kolyan shook his head. 'I'd rather not be near any windows.'

Igor didn't move. He was staring in astonishment at his friend, who was dressed strangely and too warmly for autumn. Kolyan was wearing winter boots with ski trousers tucked into them, a warm padded jacket zipped up to the chin and a black ski hat.

'Hey,' said Kolyan, 'did you hear me?'

Igor nodded. He brought two stools. Kolyan sat down heavily on one of them.

'Why don't you take your things off?' suggested Igor. 'And I'll go and put some on. It's a bit chilly out here!'

He went into his bedroom and put on a tracksuit, then went back out to the hallway. Kolyan was sitting on the stool exactly where he'd left him, except the ski hat was now lying on his lap. He was looking up at the overhead light.

'Switch it off,' he said.

Igor flicked the switch and sat down opposite his friend, blinded by the sudden darkness.

'So,' he muttered, 'are we going to talk like this?'

'Yeah,' whispered Kolyan, 'I'm afraid so. I'm scared . . . You're not going to believe it . . . I was nearly killed!'

'Who was it this time?' asked Igor.

'The same guys,' said Kolyan, unzipping his jacket. It made a sinister sound in the silence, like the hissing of a snake. 'You know how I told you that guy was going to let me off, in exchange for a load of files and email correspondence . . .'

'I remember.'

'Well, I did everything he wanted but then he went back on his word . . . He handed me over to the enemy! Turns out it was all just a game.'

'Businessmen don't kill people,' said Igor, who suddenly felt cold, in spite of the tracksuit he'd put on.

'Depends what kind of business they're in . . . A sniper tried to shoot me when I was sitting in the kitchen. Can you imagine? I'd just leaned back so I could reach the kettle without standing up, and suddenly there was a hole in the window and a bullet whizzing right past my ear like a metal bee, bzzz! I felt the heat of it.'

Kolyan touched his left ear. 'Go on, feel it,' he whispered.

'Why?' asked Igor, surprised. 'So what are you going to do now?'

'I don't know,' said Kolyan. He sounded desperate. 'I can't go back to Kiev. I can't go home . . . I can't go anywhere! They won't leave me alone. I had a look at the files before I handed them over, you know, and it was all about money, big money . . . That banker, the one whose computer I hacked into, had done a runner with his bank's money. Overseas . . . Do you get it? I'm dead!'

'Well, you can stay here for a bit.'

'Thanks,' said Kolyan bitterly. 'But if they start intimidating people to find out where I might be hiding, anyone who knows me would immediately give your name.'

'Not immediately, I hope,' said Igor.

'On top of everything else, I've got a splitting headache,' said Kolyan, rubbing his right temple.

'We'd better think of something,' whispered Igor. 'We've got to sort this out.'

'Please do! I'm your problem now,' said Kolyan, in the voice of a doomed man.

'Let's go into my room,' suggested Igor.

Kolyan stayed where he was and said nothing.

'Do you want some brandy?'

Kolyan liked this idea, so Igor went into the kitchen and fetched a bottle of Koktebel brandy and two glasses.

They drank in silence. Igor could tell that Kolyan was on a mission to get drunk, and he was so focused on topping up his friend's glass that he barely sipped from his own.

Finally, Kolyan relaxed enough to agree to go into Igor's bedroom. Leaving his jacket and boots in the hallway, he insisted that they sit on the floor of the bedroom, as far as possible from the window.

'Have you got anything else to drink?' he asked.

'We're out of brandy, but there's some of Ma's home-made wormwood liqueur.'

'Let's have some of that!'

Again they drank in silence. Or rather Kolyan did, because he was the only one drinking, but no matter how much he drank he couldn't get drunk.

'What am I going to do?' he asked, his voice faltering

slightly. 'You've got no idea . . . Life has just been one long headache since I ended up in that hospital.'

'Since you got beaten up, you mean,' said Igor. 'It's not the hospital's fault. They were just looking after you.'

Kolyan ignored him.

'If only I could get away from it all, go abroad somewhere . . . But how, and where? They'd still find me. Oh, I'm so sick of all this!'

'You need to go somewhere they'll never be able to reach you,' mused Igor.

'South America?' whispered Kolyan. 'I'd die of boredom. Or tequila.'

Igor shook his head. 'No, not South America . . .'

The two friends sat in silence. The little top window was open, and they could hear the distant drone of an aeroplane high in the sky.

'Say something!' whispered Kolyan, his lips trembling. 'Think of something! You haven't got very long . . . Maybe a day, at most. That sniper's obviously been paid to do the job, and he'll keep on trying until he gets me!'

'Come on, let me make you up a bed in here, on the floor,' suggested Igor. 'You can have a sleep, and I'll have a think.'

Kolyan nodded his assent. He lay down on the thin mattress from the folding bed and fell asleep immediately, without taking off his ski outfit. Igor brought Kolyan's bag into his bedroom. He lay down on his own bed and stared at the ceiling, listening to the agitated breathing of his sleeping friend.

Maybe I should ask Stepan if Kolyan could stay at the new house for a while? thought Igor. He could give them a hand with the building work at the same time.

He imagined Kolyan carrying a sack of building debris out of the house, while Stepan and Alyona were painting inside . . . Suddenly, a black jeep pulled up by the fence, with the men who were looking for Kolyan inside. How did they know he was here, at Stepan's house?

The more Igor thought about it, the more complicated the problem seemed to be. The combination of stress and fatigue was making his head ache. He rubbed his right temple with his fingers, and as he did so he remembered Kolyan complaining of a headache in the hallway and rubbing his temple in the same way.

'What's the answer? What's the answer? Come on, brain, think!' muttered Igor. He was yawning, on the point of surrendering to sleep but still trying to keep his eyes open.

'A distant border,' he whispered, his voice already fading.

As Igor's eyes began to close, he saw an image of Red Valya – her beautiful face terrified by Chagin, her large eyes full of despair. Igor rarely saw fear in people's faces or heard fear in their voices, but recently there had been a lot of it about.

His eyelids snapped open as an idea occurred to him.

I have to send him back to Ochakov in 1957, thought Igor. The rush of adrenalin that accompanied this idea made him break out into a cold sweat. Yes! He can put the uniform on, I'll tell him everything!

Igor raised himself up on his elbows. He looked at Kolyan, asleep on the thin mattress, then he sat up and put his feet on the wooden floor.

He doesn't believe any of it, thought Igor, hesitating briefly as the shadow of a doubt surfaced in his mind. But what's the alternative? Igor grinned, chasing the doubt away. This is our only hope!

He walked over to Kolyan and squatted down by his head.

'Get up,' he whispered.

But Kolyan was out for the count, his sleep strengthened by brandy and home-made wormwood liqueur. Igor shook him by the shoulder. Kolyan mumbled something and turned his head away.

'Get up, or I'll switch the light on,' Igor said firmly and confidently.

Kolyan raised his head and looked round.

'What?' he whispered.

'Get up, I've had an idea.'

Kolyan sat up on the mattress with his mouth open. His head dropped towards his shoulder, and his eyes looked as though they were about to close again.

'Listen to me . . . You need to go to Ochakov! You'll be able to start a new life there.'

'Not that old nonsense again.' Kolyan sighed heavily. 'Seriously, you woke me up just to tell me that?'

'You need to look at it a different way,' urged Igor. His voice was enthusiastic and persuasive. 'Let's assume that you're already dead . . . It'll be like going to a world beyond the grave. They're all dead too, from the present-day point of view at least. But back there, they're still alive!'

'OK,' nodded Kolyan, suddenly more receptive.

'So you can go and join them and live . . . well, the rest of your life. You won't meet anyone from here, and if you do, then you won't even know about it.'

Kolyan nodded again. 'Tell me more,' he said.

'Do you really want to know?' asked Igor doubtfully.

'Yes. If it's the only option, then yes . . . I'll go, I'll go back to the past . . . I'll be dead soon anyway, so what difference does it make? No, seriously, I do want to know.' He looked up at Igor.

'You'll believe it when you get there,' said Igor, with conviction. 'I'll give you some photos . . . you'll be able to recognise people from them. Someone'll meet you, help you settle in. Get your things ready.'

'What for?' asked Kolyan in alarm.

'The first commuter train to Kiev is in an hour. That photographer has developed some photos for me. I haven't seen them yet. I'll be able to show you the town and the people . . . I'm in some of the photos too. You still don't believe me, do you?'

'I do,' Kolyan said weakly, almost helplessly. 'At least, I'm starting to believe you . . . But what if I get killed there?'

'In Ochakov?'

'No, in Kiev.'

'Killers don't get up this early. We'll get a taxi straight back here. I'll call the photographer right now. He'll be fine with it, I'm sure he will.'

Igor listened to the outgoing ringtone on his mobile phone for about five minutes. Several times the phone cut itself off, and each time Igor redialled. Eventually the photographer answered

'Who is it?' he asked sleepily.

'It's Igor, about the exhibition.'

'What time is it?'

'I'm sorry, I know it's early, but I need to ask you something . . . Have you printed the photographs yet?'

'The large-format prints? Yes. They're drying.'

'Do you live near the studio?'

'Yes, on the next street.'

'I've got a friend with me, and I need to show him the photographs urgently. Can we come and see them in a couple of hours?'

'Well,' the photographer began hesitantly. He was obviously still not fully awake. 'I suppose so, it's just that –'

'We'll give you a call when we get there,' said Igor.

'Fine,' was all the photographer managed to say before Igor hung up.

30

Getting Kolyan out of the house in his morose, drunken state was no easy task. Igor tried persuading him gently, then talking to him sternly. Eventually he fetched Kolyan's padded winter coat from the hallway and forced him to put it on. He made him pull the warm hood with its fake fur trim over his head and pull the drawstring around it taut, leaving just a small gap for his eyes. Then Igor took a vial of bright green antiseptic ointment from the medical kit and painted the visible part of his friend's face green. Kolyan decided to cooperate. Either that or he could no longer be bothered to resist.

'They'll think you're a drunk and that you've been beaten up,' said Igor, helping his friend to stand up so he could look at himself in the mirror. 'Honestly, I wouldn't recognise you!'

He looked at Kolyan's reflection – a pair of eyes, apparently bruised, staring vacantly out of the 'burrow' formed by the tightly pulled drawstring of the hood.

'Yeah,' sighed Kolyan. His voice sounded lost and helpless. Igor knew that he had to seize the moment and drag his friend out into the yard before he gathered the strength to stand his ground or to panic in the face of his destiny.

'What about my bag? It's got my laptop in it,' protested Kolyan, looking back at the front door as Igor pushed him towards the gate.

'Don't worry, we'll be back here in a couple of hours.'

Kolyan didn't speak for the rest of the journey. To begin with, he walked quite energetically. Only the closely drawn hood betrayed his fear. After a little while, clearly over-heating, he released the drawstring and greedily inhaled the cool, moist air.

The first commuter train was almost empty. They had the whole carriage to themselves. Kolyan sat on one of the wooden benches and tightened his hood again. Thanks to Igor's newly discovered artistic talent, Kolyan's face was genuinely unrecog-nisable – he looked like a typical alcoholic, on the well-trodden path to becoming a tramp and thereafter to the eternity of winter, to a blizzard and a snowdrift from which there is no return. The brandy and home-made liqueur he'd consumed helpfully reinforced this impression. Igor smiled as he admired his own handiwork and the effects of the antiseptic ointment.

'You don't look like yourself at all,' Igor whispered to his friend.

'I'm never going to look like myself again,' Kolyan muttered gloomily.

He seemed to be starting to sober up, but the return to sobriety is a lengthy process and not even the walk from the station to Proreznaya Street was enough to turn Kolyan back into a normal, fully functional human being.

As they passed the Opera, Igor called the photographer and told him that they would be there in ten minutes.

When they arrived, the photographer was already waiting for them in the courtyard. He was yawning, and his eyes were still adjusting to the light of the breaking day. He looked alarmed at the sight of Kolyan, but his expression softened when he saw Igor and he visibly relaxed.

'Everything's nearly ready,' said the photographer, opening the door. 'Would you like a coffee, perhaps?'

'I think we could all do with a coffee,' nodded Igor.

Igor-the-photographer hung his all-weather hunting jacket on a hook near the door and disappeared into the kitchen.

Igor beckoned Kolyan into the living room and reached his hand out to the wall. There was a click, and light flooded the room. In front of them, a number of photographs had been attached to makeshift washing lines with plastic pegs and were moving gently, as though they were swaying in a breeze.

'What are those?' murmured Kolyan.

'All in good time! Just wait a minute. Let's sit down,' said Igor, quickly scanning the photographs. The order in which they were hanging was not particularly conducive to a virtual tour of Ochakov. Igor lowered himself onto the sofa next to Kolyan.

'All in good time,' he repeated, feeling the weight of exhaustion beginning to press down on his shoulders. 'Let's have our coffee first. The photographer will go through them all with us.'

This necessary pause gave Igor a chance to concentrate and work out what he actually wanted from the viewing. Revived by the smell and subsequently the taste of his coffee, the photographer already had a clearer idea than his two guests did.

'I'd like you to show them to us in sequence,' said Igor. 'The complete series, I mean, like they're going to be on display at the exhibition.'

The photographer drank his coffee and nodded decisively, then started walking among the suspended photographs.

'We need to start from the beginning,' he said. 'I've got the first prints ready.'

He rustled about behind the screen for a few minutes, then came out and placed a pile of large black-and-white photographs on the coffee table in front of Igor and Kolyan.

'Look at those ones first. I've already gone through and put them in order,' he said. 'While you're doing that, I'll take the others down – they're dry now.'

'Look at them closely and try to remember everything,' Igor whispered to Kolyan, relieved that the photographer was out of earshot. 'There, you see, that's Ochakov. That's the street where Vanya Samokhin lives with his mother. There they are, the two of them, and that's Vanya and me. That's Chagin's house, and that's Iosip and Fima on the doorstep . . . Don't worry about those two. If you see them, cross the street . . . Ah, look! That's the market. And there's Valya! You can't tell from the photo, but she's got red hair. She really is beautiful . . . There's something completely wild about her,' he went on, shaking his head with a sigh.

Igor saw that Kolyan was peering at the image of Valya standing behind her display of Black Sea flounder and gobies.

'I would go anywhere for a woman like her,' added Igor, glad that the photograph had aroused his friend's interest. 'Into the past, or into the future!'

He heard footsteps behind him, and another pile of large prints was placed on the table.

'There, that's the rest of them,' said the photographer, settling down in one of the armchairs.

As he reached for the next photograph, Igor froze. It was another close-up of Red Valya, but what unnerved him was that Fima Chagin was standing right in front of her. He was staring at her with a look of undisguised menace, and it was obvious that she was genuinely terrified.

'What's going on between those two?' asked Kolyan, although he didn't sound particularly interested. 'Are they lovers, or what?'

'She's married. Her husband's a fisherman, and she sells his catch. I don't think they're lovers.'

Kolyan looked strangely at Igor, out of the corner of his eye. He started to raise the hood of his padded jacket.

'Just tell me,' said Igor, his tone completely serious. 'Can you see how real it all is?'

Kolyan nodded and glanced at the photographer, who was listening to their conversation.

'It's real all right,' whispered the photographer, looking straight back at Kolyan. Then he nodded at Igor. 'Only he won't tell me how he does it!'

'I'll tell you one day,' promised Igor, with the hint of a mischievous smile.

'I hope so,' said the photographer. 'It would revolutionise photography. I mean, it already has, but –'

'Have you got any small prints from the latest films?' interrupted Igor.

'Yes, I made some test prints. Do you want to take them with you?'

'Yes!'

They walked back down to the station at a brisk pace. It was clear that Kolyan had completely sobered up. His hood was up over his head, and the gap left by the drawstring revealed only his eyes, his nose and a bit of green skin. There was hardly anyone about, and to add to their good fortune it began to rain heavily, which helped to slow the start of the new day.

When they got to the station, the driver of an old Zhiguli agreed to take them to Irpen for a hundred hryvnas.

The windscreen wipers on the Zhiguli squeaked noisily, scattering drops of rainwater from the windscreen. Igor sat next to the driver. Kolyan, with his hood still up, fell asleep on the back seat.

'So, have you two had a good time?' asked the driver, a working-class man of around sixty.

'Yes,' answered Igor. He nodded at his sleeping friend. 'He's going to be out of it for a while!'

'In a good way, or a bad way?' asked the driver.

'In a good way,' said Igor pensively.

As the elderly driver contemplated Igor's response, his thoughts turned to the vicissitudes of his own fate.

31

When they got back to the house Igor's mother was already bustling about in the kitchen, preparing breakfast. Kolyan took his boots and jacket off in the hallway. He went into the bathroom and spent a long time washing the green antiseptic ointment from his face. Then he went into Igor's bedroom and sat down on the mattress where he'd slept, though not for long enough.

'Here, look at these. Try to memorise them,' said Igor, handing his friend the stack of photos that the photographer had given him.

'Can't I take them with me?'

Igor thought about it. 'I'll give you a few,' he answered. 'You won't need all of them, will you?'

Kolyan started looking through the photographs again, screwing up his eyes and peering closely at them. Igor pulled the bedside table over to where he was sitting. He angled the reading lamp so it was pointing directly at Kolyan's hands.

'Breakfast's ready,' said Elena Andreevna, looking into the room. 'Come and eat!'

'Let's go,' said Igor.

Kolyan frowned. 'I'm not sitting anywhere near a window,' he said stubbornly.

'Fine, I'll bring it in here.'

Kolyan devoured his fried egg and sausage sitting cross-legged on the floor. He drank his tea in the same position.

'So, when are you sending me?' he asked, nodding at the photos that lay nearby on the floor.

'Wait a minute,' said Igor. He thought about it. 'We need to think about the logistics. It's like going abroad. We could do with a few documents. If only we could get you some official Soviet identity papers . . . then nobody would suspect a thing.'

'Documents?' repeated Kolyan. 'Are you kidding? We're living in the Information Age! A diplomatic passport, a certificate stating that you're a descendant of the Romanovs, whatever . . . you just order it online, and it arrives the next day.'

'Yes, but we need old Soviet documents. I've got an old police lieutenant's ID pass – have a look at that if you think it'll help.'

'I don't need to,' shrugged Kolyan. He pulled his bag towards him and took out his laptop. 'Right then, let's see what we can find.'

'While you're doing that, I've got a few jobs to do,' said Igor. 'I promised to help a friend.'

'How long are you going to be?'

'I'll be back before dinner.'

Igor left Kolyan in his bedroom. He told his mother that he was suffering from depression and asked her not to disturb him. Meanwhile, Igor himself went to Stepan's new house, where he was immediately given a dust mask and some protective gloves. They even found a pair of overalls for him to wear. The builders had left some steel girders and planks of wood on the first floor of the new house, and there were also a number of radiators that needed to be removed.

Working together, Igor and Stepan carried everything downstairs. They worked until Alyona called them for lunch, which she had set out in the old wooden house, in the same room where they had modestly celebrated the signing of the purchase deeds. After the meal, as he was drinking tea, Igor started to worry about Kolyan. He apologised for not being able to help any more that day and ran home.

He found his friend exactly where he'd left him, sitting on the mattress in the corner of his room. Except for some reason Igor's passport was now lying open on the floor next to him.

'What are you doing with that?' Igor asked nervously.

'It's all sorted,' said Kolyan, raising his hand in a gesture of reassurance. 'I couldn't order documents in my own name, could I? So I ordered them in yours. I sent my own photo, though.'

'So what have you ordered?' asked Igor.

'A passport from 1957, a business trip certificate for a police lieutenant and a few other documents as well. They knew what I needed. The company I ordered from is affiliated with the state archives. As well as all the samples, they can provide blank documents too. For a price, of course!'

'How much does it all cost?'

'Five hundred dollars. I've already paid.' Kolyan waved his credit card at Igor. 'Look after this for me, OK? Maybe I'll be back this time next year!' A slightly crazed smile played on Kolyan's lips.

'When are you going to get them?'

'Tonight, believe it or not, by courier!'

'Congratulations,' said Igor, glancing from Kolyan's open laptop to his own passport. 'Now you're me, and I . . . I'm not quite me . . . Well, I'm still me, but I'm also Vanya Samokhin.'

'What interesting lives we lead,' Kolyan said with a grin.

'We live in an interesting country, these are interesting times . . . we can't help being interesting ourselves,' said Igor, smiling back at his friend. 'I'm afraid you're going to have to stay here for a little while longer. Just a day or two.'

'Why?' Kolyan's smile dropped.

'I'm going to Ochakov, to arrange for someone to meet you . . . And to say my goodbyes,' said Igor. His voice was uncharacteristically firm.

A scooter pulled up outside the gate, and the doorbell rang a few moments later. Igor's mother answered it.

'Who is it?' she asked.

'A courier. I've got a delivery for Igor Vozny.'

'It's for you, son,' called Elena Andreevna.

Igor took the package from the courier and returned to his bedroom. He held the package out to his friend. Kolyan ripped it open immediately and took out a plastic folder containing his documents.

'Do you want a drink?' asked Igor. 'This feels like a fairly momentous occasion.'

'I don't need an excuse these days,' nodded Kolyan, looking up. 'I'll have whatever's on offer.'

By 11 p.m. they were coming to the end of one of the bottles of brandy Igor had bought on the way home from Stepan's house. They were both drinking this time, at the same pace.

'So you're just going to go there and come straight back?' asked Kolyan, glancing nervously at Igor.

'Yes, I'll be as quick as I can. Do you want me to leave you something to read while I'm gone? To stop you getting bored? I can recommend a great book about food, written by a man of the people. Actually, maybe it's getting a bit late –'

'No, I can't read . . . I'm too scared to concentrate. I'll just wait. I'd rather you left me something to drink.'

'I will,' Igor assured him.

He went to the kitchen and came back with the second bottle of brandy and two bottles of wormwood liqueur.

'Will that be enough?' he asked.

'Yes,' said Kolyan. 'Enough to get drunk and sleep it off three times over.'

Igor changed into the police uniform in silence. He fastened the belt and holster around his waist, pulled on the boots and put on the peaked cap. Then he put his waterproof jacket on over the top of the tunic. Kolyan watched Igor's transformation in stunned fascination. He didn't say a word.

'Right, I'm ready. Stay here,' said Igor. He gave Kolyan a farewell glance and left the room.

A cold wind was blowing outside. It wasn't particularly strong, but it was blowing right into Igor's face, as though it were coming directly from the past.

The darkness was growing thicker. The houses and fences on both sides of the street receded from view. A little light trembled in the distance up ahead. Igor felt a few raindrops. He automatically tried to pull up his hood but the peaked cap was in the way, so he took it off and carried it.

Igor's feet led him to the square in front of the wine factory. The rain had stopped, leaving the air damp and heavy.

The factory gates opened slightly. Vanya peeped out of them, then emerged with a sack of wine over his shoulder.

'Hi,' Igor called to him.

Vanya stopped, looking around guardedly. Igor walked out into the part of the square that was illuminated.

'It's me,' he said.

'Yes, I recognised your voice,' nodded Vanya. 'We haven't seen you for a while . . . Something happened while you were away.'

They turned into the road that led to Vanya's house.

'What happened?' Igor asked as they walked.

'Valya's husband was stabbed.'

'Is he in hospital?' asked Igor.

'No, he's in the cemetery. She doesn't go to the market any more. She just sits at home, wearing her mourning scarf and crying.'

Igor gave a heavy sigh. 'Did they find whoever did it?' he asked despondently.

'No,' said Vanya, shaking his head. He stopped and adjusted the sack of wine on his shoulder. 'He was stabbed so that the handle of the knife broke off, and the blade stayed between his ribs.'

They walked the rest of the way to Vanya's house in silence. When they got there, they went and sat in the kitchen and Vanya poured them both a glass of wine. He smiled at his own thoughts.

'The newspaper bought one of my photographs,' he said proudly. 'I've started taking my own! A friend developed and printed it for me.'

'Which newspaper?' Igor asked absently.

'Our local paper, the *Ochakovan*,' said Vanya. He paused to sip his wine. 'They said they'd pay me twenty roubles for it. I love taking photographs. I've even read a book about it – *Photography for Beginners.*'

'Yes,' said Igor, sipping his own wine. 'You're good at it.'

'I wish I could develop and print them myself too, but you need to buy special trays for the chemicals. And an enlarger.'

Igor took several hundred-rouble notes from the pocket of his breeches. He pushed the money across the table towards Vanya.

'There you go. Buy whatever you need.'

'Oh, thank you! You . . . I don't know what to say,' stammered Vanya, overwhelmed with gratitude.

'Then don't say anything,' said Igor.

'What kind of coat is that? Is it fashionable?'

'It's a waterproof jacket. You can have it, if you like.'

'Really?'

Igor took his jacket off and gave it to Vanya. Then he nodded at the cupboard in the corner of the kitchen.

'Is that where you keep your knives and forks?' he asked.

'Yes.'

Igor got up and pulled the top drawer towards him. His eyes fell on a kitchen knife with a solid wooden handle. He picked it up and turned to Vanya.

'Have you got a sharp file?' he asked.

'We've got all kinds of files.'

'Can I borrow one?'

Vanya left the kitchen and returned with a wooden box, which he put on the table. He opened it and took out a bundle of imitation leather.

'There you go,' he said, unrolling it onto the table. It was a storage pouch with lots of little pockets, containing files of different shapes and sizes.

Vanya was watching his guest intently. Igor began to feel irritated by his curiosity, so he stuck the kitchen knife into one of the little pockets and rolled up the pouch.

'You know, next time a different . . . police officer will come, instead of me. His name is Nikolai. I want you to help him, show him the town, tell him everything.'

'What about you?' Vanya's face fell. 'I've got used to you coming.'

'Then you'd better get used to me not coming,' Igor said coldly. 'I . . . I'm leaving. It's to do with work . . . I'm leaving the police force.'

'Because it's so dangerous?'

'Yes.'

Igor had no desire to prolong this conversation. He finished his wine, then went into the room with the old sofa, switched the light on and sat down on a chair. Selecting one of the files from the pouch, he began sawing into the blade of the knife at the point where it met the wooden handle.

It was hard work. Igor persevered until his hand was sore, although the notch he'd managed to file into the blade was still no more than a couple of millimetres deep. He put the knife on his knees and paused for breath, flexing his fingers. Then he picked up the file and tried again. Through sheer effort and determination he managed to file a further millimetre and a half, by which point his fingers had started to hurt too, so he took another rest. He found a sharper file, and thereafter his progress improved.

When the blade was sawn through almost completely, with

only a couple of millimetres still connecting it to the handle, Igor stopped work. He looked at his hand. There were two broken blisters – testimony to the urgency with which he had applied himself to the unfamiliar task.

He thought about Stepan, about his 'words of wisdom' on stabbing techniques. It was strange that a gardener should know so much about it – paradoxical, even. A gardener is supposed to know how to use a fork and spade, how to nurture flowers and trees, how to enhance the beauty of the surrounding world . . . You can't make the world a better place by stabbing someone.

Or can you? he suddenly thought. One stabbing ruins lives and makes the world a terrible place, but another, even with the same blade, might make the world and life itself more beautiful.

Igor thought back to the spring, when his mother had asked him to fetch a bag of carrots up from the cellar and sort them out. He had topped and tailed them, cutting off the bits that had started to rot and leaving the edible parts of the fat red rhizomes. His mother had made them into spicy Korean carrot salad, which he loved.

Weird . . . Why was he thinking about those carrots all of a sudden? Because of the knife?

Igor shrugged. Standing up, he turned to face the high, wooden back of the sofa and looked at his reflection in the old mirror. He bared his teeth, as though he wanted to see how ferocious he could make himself look. He thought about Fima Chagin's face in the darkness on the cliff path, then in the light, in his own home. He seemed to be physiognomically predisposed to malevolence and menace. It was impossible to imagine a genuine smile on his face . . . it would never reach his eyes. Then again, why should it? Fima Chagin's role in life did not involve smiling. He was both a source and a conduit of aggression and evil. This evil was also a kind of energy, like electricity. And like electricity, it could be fatal.

But what about me? thought Igor. Stepan's a gardener, Chagin's a forester . . . but who am I?

The doubt that had interrupted Igor's thoughts made him shrink inside. He felt sorry for himself, as though he were a small child lost in a forest. He even imagined a child of about five years old, wearing shorts and a T-shirt, wide-eyed with terror as he looked around at the endless pine trees towering above him.

'The forest,' said Igor. 'No,' he murmured, eyes smiling, as though he were suddenly laughing at himself for thinking such thoughts. 'Everything's fine. I'm at a crossroads, but I know which way to go. I'm going to spend a couple more hours in this forest, and then I'm going back to the garden. A couple more hours of pretending that I'm a forester, and then that's it – I'll never set foot in the forest again!'

A bold, almost arrogant smile had begun to play on Igor's lips. He adjusted his belt, checking the holster to make sure it was fastened. Then he put on the peaked cap, grasped the handle of the knife and crept out of the room.

The rest of the house was quiet. As he left, Igor pulled the front door towards him as far as he could without actually closing it.

Ochakov had a decidedly autumnal feel about it that night. The fallen leaves were no longer crisp and dry but squelched underfoot, saturated with the moisture from the air. There was no light in the windows of the houses, no sound from the trees. Not even the slightest trace of an echo.

Igor walked slowly, barely looking at the road. His boots knew where he wanted to go. They led him straight to Fima's house. Igor stopped by a tree across the road, and he looked at the house. The darkness to the right of it was thinner, somehow lighter. The living room, where he'd almost been poisoned, was on that side of the house.

Igor crossed the road, trying to make as little noise as possible. The gate opened and closed without creaking. He glanced around the right side of the house and saw a faint light coming from the window.

'He must still be up,' whispered Igor. 'Perfect! I won't have to wake him.'

Returning to the porch, he walked up the steps to the front door. He held the knife in his right hand and looked at it with respect. Then he knocked on the door twice with his left hand.

He heard a noise, then footsteps.

'Who's there?' snarled Fima's voice from behind the door.

'Iosip,' wheezed Igor, trying to imitate the voice he'd heard several times before.

The internal bolt slid open with a metallic clang. The hook jingled as it was lifted from its catch. The door swung open and Igor burst in, forcing the astonished Fima to take a step backwards. It was dark in the hallway, and Fima didn't immediately realise who was standing before him. Even if he had, it's unlikely that it would have changed his destiny.

Igor thrust the knife he was holding up under Fima's ribs. It went in smoothly and quickly, without meeting the slightest resistance. For a brief moment Igor panicked that his hand would also disappear into this strange hollow cavity, but the handle stopped when it came up against Fima's body, which suddenly seemed heavy and unpredictable. Fima was still standing in front of Igor, opening and closing his mouth, either gulping air or mouthing words he could no longer speak. Igor held firmly onto the handle of the knife as he felt it grow heavier and heavier. Fima's legs buckled under him. He leaned towards Igor, who pushed him away and let go of the knife. Fima's body crashed to the floor. The thud reverberated up the walls of the house and through the air.

Igor bolted the door and switched on the light. Fima was lying on his back, his arms spread wide. His stomach was rising and falling, which meant that the handle of the knife was rising and falling too. Igor stared at the wooden handle, willing it to stop. Fima raised his head slightly then dropped it back again. Igor squatted down next to him. Fima's eyes were open and he was staring straight ahead. Igor raised his hand, which was still sore from the blisters, to Fima's open mouth. He was no longer breathing.

Igor took the handle of the knife and pulled it towards him, hoping that it would break off, leaving the blade inside Fima's body, but it didn't. It was holding too tightly onto the blade.

Igor stood up. He looked at the open double doors to the living room, where the light was on. He went in and saw what Fima had been doing before he'd arrived. On the oval table lay eight bundles of hundred-rouble notes, fastened together with strips of paper. Alongside the money lay a white linen bag, a saucer of water and the stub of a pencil. The pencil had already been used to scrawl on the bag 'I.S.S. To collect in 1961. Himself or his s . . .'

'"Himself or his s" . . .' Igor read aloud, trying to guess what Fima had been writing. Suddenly he realised. 'Himself or his s-s-son!' Igor was very pleased with himself for working it out. 'His son . . . Iosip or his son. That's why Iosip tattooed Stepan! It's like the slowest ever postal service, or the slowest ever bank transfer . . . the criminal version of Western Union!'

Igor put the money into the white bag and looked around. The room was so familiar, he felt almost at home. Over there, opposite the little window, in the top cupboard of the dresser behind the cut-glass panels – that's where the glasses were kept. It probably wouldn't take him long to find the bottles, if he wanted to. But Igor didn't feel like drinking at that particular moment.

What had she said, that old woman in Ochakov who'd put him and Stepan up that night? That they'd found Fima stabbed, with two bundles of money nearby and a note that read: 'For a proper send-off'.

Igor picked up the pencil. He walked over to the dresser and pulled the top drawer towards him. Among the assorted odds and ends, postcards and sets of fishing hooks, he saw three police station attendance forms.

'Interesting,' murmured Igor.

He picked up one of the forms and turned it over. The back of it was completely blank. He placed it on the table, bent over it and wrote painstakingly in pencil, 'For a proper send-off'.

Igor walked over to Fima's body. He took two bundles of roubles out of the bag and put them next to his head, then placed the note on his chest.

'Now there's one less forester in the world,' he whispered,

looking at Chagin's body as impassively as if it were a patch of grass or a stone.

It had grown colder outside by the time he left. On his way back to Vanya's house Igor kept stopping, thinking that he'd forgotten something, that there was something he should be carrying. Then he remembered that he was no longer holding the knife and he felt calmer, knowing that he would never need it again. He couldn't help feeling a little disappointed that the handle hadn't broken off, like it was supposed to, but he was consoled by the idea that it was because he'd stabbed Chagin like a 'gardener', not like a 'forester'.

There will be no more knives in my life, thought Igor. Filed down or not. From now on, everything in my life is going to be beautiful.

The word 'beautiful' made him think about Red Valya. He wanted to see her, even in her mourning outfit. He wanted to comfort her, because she was no longer able to pity her husband and her pity had been stronger than love. She was probably at home right now, all alone. Sleeping or crying . . . No, he would never see her again! He would never come back to this time or this place. But there was nothing to stop him writing her a note, or even leaving her some money . . . Yes, he would ask Kolyan to go and see her, to introduce himself. Maybe Kolyan would fall in love with her and replace her husband, her fisherman, who enabled her to do what she loved best – selling fish at the market. Maybe she would feel as sorry for Kolyan as she had for her murdered husband, and Kolyan would benefit from the strength of her pity a hundred times more than he would from her love.

Igor pushed the front door open, then walked through to

the room with the old sofa. He took his boots off, undressed and lay down, covering himself carefully with the blanket he'd left on the stool earlier.

Even on the brink of sleep he continued to think about Valya and Kolyan's future together, as though his imaginary scenarios would inevitably lead to a wedding in real life. Once he'd finished deciding their destiny, his thoughts turned to Alyona, the gardener's daughter. He fell asleep thinking about her.

32

Igor was woken by a loud cough nearby. He opened his eyes and reached out a hand to the reading lamp on his bedside table.

The dim light was gentle enough not to startle him. It just nudged the pre-dawn greyness back out of the window. Igor was lying in his own bedroom. Kolyan was sleeping on the mattress in the corner. He was no longer coughing but lay still, wheezing almost with every breath. At the head of the mattress on the floor stood a glass containing some of Elena Andreevna's liqueur. A little further away, by the wall, stood two empty bottles and one that was half full.

Igor sat up in bed. His head was buzzing, but as soon as his eyes came to rest on Kolyan the noise receded. It was replaced by a number of vague, unformed thoughts and a distinct sense of pity. Igor felt sorry for Kolyan, but only mildly.

Kolyan clearly deserved more pity, and more sympathy. His hacking skills had backfired somewhat, leaving him with a closed-head injury and in fear of his life. As a result he was having to get used to the idea of entering into a different reality that wasn't really any more humane than the one he knew. There would still be threats and dangers, just of a different kind. At the same time Igor felt slightly envious of his friend. It was only a niggling feeling, but he couldn't ignore it. Say the happy future Igor had imagined for Kolyan and Valya really did involve a wedding, and say they asked Vanya Samokhin to be their wedding photographer . . . Then their happiness could turn out to be considerably greater than Igor's own vague, imagined happiness. It was a lot easier to imagine Kolyan and Valya's good fortune and, equally, to believe in the reality of it. Igor hadn't yet allowed himself to fantasise about his own future in such detail. Maybe now would be a good time to start.

He forced himself to file away his virtual portrait of Valya, with her bold, ardent eyes, and summoned up a mental snapshot of Alyona instead. Alyona's image was calm and gentle. She had no wish to compete with an outspoken market seller. Alyona was a 'gardener' – hard-working, quiet and modest. Valya, on the other hand, was a 'forester'. This distinction helped Igor to balance the two worlds in his mind, and by extension he naturally came to think of them as the 'world of gardeners' and the 'world of foresters'. His envy of Kolyan evaporated, as did the pity he had previously felt for him. Kolyan was a 'forester', and he would almost certainly be at home in the 'world of foresters' – as much as he was here, if not more so.

As though he sensed someone thinking about him, Kolyan turned over onto his side, facing Igor. He raised his head slightly and reached out for the glass, then brought it to his lips and drank. When he put the glass back down, he noticed Igor in the light of the reading lamp.

'Are you back already?' he croaked.

'Yes,' nodded Igor.

'So when am I going?'

'Tonight.'

Later that morning, after a breakfast of sausages and buckwheat on the floor with Kolyan, Igor went off to help Stepan again. Stepan was in a good mood, singing what sounded like military marches to himself while he worked. After lunch, made by Alyona, they carried on working on the first floor of the new building.

'What are all these going to be?' asked Igor, referring to the rooms they had just finished emptying of rubbish and the remains of building materials.

Just at that moment, Alyona went into one of the rooms with a bucket and floorcloth and started wiping down the new parquet, which was covered in building dust.

'Bedrooms,' answered Stepan. 'There's going to be a cafe downstairs, and the owners are going to live upstairs.'

'Four bedrooms?' Igor couldn't contain his surprise. 'Plus the ones in the old house . . .'

'The old house is for the old owner, for me,' smiled Stepan. 'And the new one is for the new owner and her family. Incidentally, I've got a proposal for you.'

Igor froze, remembering how he'd almost received a slap

from his mother for his inability to distinguish between the two types of proposal. This was obviously the business kind.

'You want me to be the assistant manager of the cafe?' asked Igor, with a hint of irony, although he succeeded in keeping a perfectly straight face.

'No,' Stepan answered calmly, 'I want you to help in the kitchen.'

'And who will I be helping?' Igor couldn't help his lip twisting in a supercilious smile, as he imagined their neighbour Olga standing over the hob and himself next to her in a chef's hat.

'Alyona, my daughter. She's going to be the chef.'

Igor's mood suddenly changed.

'Will you take my employment record book?' he asked.

'Yes, it'll all be above board.'

'What are you going to write in it? Sous-chef?'

'What would you prefer? I can write "kitchen manager", if you like.' Stepan smiled.

'No, I'd prefer "gardener".' Igor smiled back at him.

'Kitchen gardener?'

'Just "gardener",' said Igor, his face serious again.

'All right, let's shake on it,' said Stepan, nodding solemnly and pressing his lips together.

Just then Alyona came out of the bedroom. The freshly washed parquet floor gleamed behind her. She couldn't hide her surprise when she saw her father and Igor firmly shaking hands.

'What's going on?'

'We're shaking on a deal,' answered Stepan. 'Now we just have to sign it.'

'What's the cafe going to be called?' Igor asked suddenly.

'Cafe Ochakov,' answered Stepan.

'So in my employment record book, it's going to say "gardener" and "Ochakov"? I'm going to be the gardener from Ochakov!' Igor smiled happily at the thought.

'It would appear so.'

'Excellent! By the way, I've got some old photographs of Ochakov, blown up in large format . . . Maybe we could hang them on the walls?'

'Why not? The recipes will be from Ochakov too, from my father's book. All our food will be healthy and beneficial!'

Igor's mind began to wander as he imagined the photographs on the wall of the cafe, showing Valya, Vanya, Aleksandra Marinovna, Stepan's father Iosip and Igor himself. An amusing thought struck him: what if Stepan were looking at them one day and noticed Igor? He would ask him what he was doing in old Ochakov, and Igor would tell him everything. He would tell him about everyone in the photographs, including Iosip.

'Did your mother tell you that I'd asked her to marry me?' Stepan asked suddenly.

'She did,' nodded Igor.

'Do you have any objections?'

Igor shook his head.

'Your mother will move in with me,' continued Stepan. 'And she'll leave the house to you.'

'The house with the scales?' mused Igor.

'No,' said Stepan. 'She's bringing the scales with her. What do you want them for?'

'Never mind,' said Igor, waving his hand dismissively.

He bought a bottle of brandy on the way home. Elena Andreevna looked out into the hallway when she heard him come in.

'Is your friend going to be sitting on your bedroom floor for much longer?' she asked in a half-whisper.

'No,' said Igor. 'He's leaving this evening.'

'There's a leftover cutlet and some potatoes in there,' said his mother, nodding at the kitchen door.

'Thanks. You know, Ma, Stepan made me a proposal too,' said Igor, with a sly smile on his face. 'Of the business variety.'

'What did he say?' asked his mother, her eyes burning with curiosity.

'I'm going to be a sous-chef at the cafe.'

His mother's response to the news was less than enthusiastic.

'Who's the chef?' she asked indifferently.

'Alyona.'

Elena Andreevna's face lit up with surprise, followed by contemplative approval.

'Well, then,' she murmured, 'maybe you'll learn something useful. It's a good profession, and at least you'll never go hungry.'

Igor and Kolyan began their last supper at 9.30 p.m. Igor's mother was watching the end of one of her soap operas. Outside, darkness reigned. Kolyan's fork shook in his hand but he ate hungrily, as though he were storing up for the future. He seemed thirsty too.

'I think I believe you now,' muttered Kolyan, holding out his empty glass so that Igor could fill it again with brandy. 'I didn't believe all your fairy tales before, but I do now.'

'Amazing the difference a closed-head injury can make! You

used to be thick-skulled, like most people in this country. But now you're in the minority, like me.'

'Why, have you had a closed-head injury too?' asked Kolyan, looking suspiciously at his friend.

'Yes, when I was little. My father wasn't looking after me properly and I ran into a spinning carousel. Now listen, I'm going to give you some money to take with you. A lot of money. I want you to take two bundles of cash and a note to Valya. Remember? I pointed her out in the photos.'

'Ah, yes.' Kolyan shot him a knowing look. 'She's not the kind you forget!'

The faintest trace of a smile crossed Igor's face.

'Just don't flash it about. They don't appreciate that sort of thing.'

Kolyan nodded obediently.

At around 11 p.m. Igor helped his friend to put on the police uniform. When Kolyan pulled the boots on, he winced in discomfort.

'They're a bit tight,' he grumbled.

'Walk around the room for a bit,' suggested Igor.

In the darkness Kolyan walked across the room and back several times, then sat down again.

'That's weird,' he said. 'Now they fit . . .'

'The uniform and the boots represent the past, and the past changes its shape and size to fit whoever tries it on.'

'Whatever!' Kolyan shook his head and took the belt and holster from Igor. He opened the holster and looked at the gun.

'Shame it doesn't work,' he murmured.

'It does when you're there,' said Igor, nodding earnestly.

He waited while Kolyan fastened the belt around his waist, then handed him a dark cloth bag in which he'd placed the bundles of Soviet banknotes and an envelope containing a note for Valya.

What if Kolyan reads the note? Igor suddenly panicked. Well, it doesn't say much anyway . . . It's just a request for her to pity him as much as she can.

'Here, take this too,' said Igor, handing his friend the gold watch.

'That's an expensive gift,' whispered Kolyan.

'Let's call it an exchange. Your laptop in return for my watch. It'll work there too, by the way, and it'll show the right time.'

They left the house at around midnight – Kolyan in the old police uniform, holding the cloth bag, and Igor in a tracksuit and a leather jacket.

'Come on, best foot forward and all that!' Igor said cheerfully, trying in vain to impart some enthusiasm to his friend. Kolyan couldn't have looked less enthusiastic if he'd tried.

Houses stretched along both sides of the street. There were no lights in their windows. Igor peered at them as though he were seeing them for the first time, which perhaps he was . . . After all, on previous occasions he had only ever looked straight ahead, seeking out the little lights in front of the gates of the wine factory. Fences and houses had been relegated to his peripheral vision. But this time he felt an exhilarating sense of freedom – he could look wherever he wanted! Kolyan was the one looking straight ahead as he walked, as though he'd been hypnotised.

At some point Igor noticed that the darkness had grown thicker and the houses had disappeared. He stopped.

‘I’m not going any further,’ he said to his friend. ‘You’re on your own now.’

Kolyan stopped too, a little way ahead.

‘On my own?’ he repeated.

‘Well, not completely. Someone will meet you soon. His name’s Vanya Samokhin. Tell him I said hello. Oh, and this is really important – don’t ever take the uniform off. Treat it like a second skin. Without it, you’ll disappear.’

‘What do you mean, disappear?’

‘You’ll come straight back here.’

‘Back to the present, you mean?’

Igor nodded.

‘That’s good to know. If it’s worse there than it is here, at least now I know there’s a way out. So we don’t need to say goodbye!’

Without another word, Kolyan turned away from Igor and continued walking along the road. The darkness swallowed him a few moments later.

Igor stood there for a while, looking and listening, then he turned round and walked quickly back along the road. His steps were surprisingly light, which might have been something to do with the imported Chinese trainers he was wearing. They weighed next to nothing.

Houses appeared again along both sides of the street. There were still no lights in their windows.

Kolyan stopped when he reached the illuminated square in front of the green gates of the Ochakov Wine Factory, unsure what to do next. He looked around.

The gates suddenly creaked open and Kolyan took a step

back. An old lorry rolled noisily out of the gates and turned onto the road, which was visible only in the glow from its headlights. It drove away from him, soon disappearing from view. The gates closed and all was quiet. Kolyan's sense of hearing was more alert than usual, and after just a few minutes he detected the creak of the gate hinges again. A young lad appeared in the gap, carrying something over his shoulder. The gates were bolted behind him. The sack was obviously heavy, and as the lad lowered it to his feet it seemed to squirm as though it contained a live piglet.

Kolyan peered closely at the young lad and the sack.

'Are you Vanya?' he called out of the darkness.

'Yes.'

Kolyan walked over to him.

'Igor says hello!' he said.

'Thank you.'

Kolyan sighed heavily. He had to say something, to break the ice somehow.

'Is that heavy?' he asked, pointing at the sack.

Vanya nodded.

'Let me give you a hand.'

Kolyan bent down towards the sack of wine, and Vanya gladly helped him to hoist it onto his right shoulder. They began walking along the dark road, following the route taken by the lorry.

'I've got a note for Valya,' Kolyan said quietly. 'Will you introduce me to her?'

'Tomorrow morning,' promised Vanya Samokhin. 'She's having a difficult time at the moment, but she's got a soft spot for men in uniform. We're going back to our house now.

Mother said she'd fry some gobies. You can stay with us for a while . . . The wine will help you sleep.'

'What wine?' asked Kolyan, confused.

'This wine!' Vanya slapped the sack and it wobbled on Kolyan's shoulder. 'It's a dry white . . . Your friend loved it. You can drink it on its own, without food, and the dreams it gives you . . . well, they're better than any film!'